FLAMING DEATH

A dozen main battle tanks rumbled up, hatches closed. Ben Raines used the outside phone on the lead tank. "You flame-equipped?"

"That's a ten-four, sir."

"Spearhead us." He hung up and turned to Cooper. "Let's go!"

His team spread out behind the tanks and followed them in. The bodyguards assigned to protect Ben could do nothing to stop him. How do you tell the commanding general he can't do something? They fell in with him and surged forward.

The rattle of machine gun fire came from a building with a faded sign, SPORTING GOODS, painted on the front of the bricks. The slugs howled off the armor of the MBT as the tank clanked around, lowering its canon. The muzzle spewed liquid fire, engulfing those inside in flames. The screaming of the torched lasted only a moment.

"Mop up!" Ben shouted, and a team lanced the smoking interior of the old building with automatic-weapons fire.

BOOK YOUR PLACE ON OUR WEBSITE AND MAKE THE READING CONNECTION!

We've created a customized website just for our very special readers, where you can get the inside scoop on everything that's going on with Zebra, Pinnacle and Kensington books.

When you come online, you'll have the exciting opportunity to:

- View covers of upcoming books
- Read sample chapters
- Learn about our future publishing schedule (listed by publication month *and author*)
- Find out when your favorite authors will be visiting a city near you
- Search for and order backlist books from our online catalog
- Check out author bios and background information
- Send e-mail to your favorite authors
- Meet the Kensington staff online
- Join us in weekly chats with authors, readers and other guests
- Get writing guidelines
- AND MUCH MORE!

Visit our website at
http://www.pinnaclebooks.com

FURY IN THE ASHES

WILLIAM W. JOHNSTONE

Pinnacle Books
Kensington Publishing Corp.

http://www.williamjohnstone.com

PINNACLE BOOKS are published by

Kensington Publishing Corp.
850 Third Avenue
New York, NY 10022

First Zebra Printing: 1991

First Pinnacle Printing: March, 1999
10 9 8 7 6 5 4 3

Printed in the United States of America

Dedicated to J. K. Sparks

Book One

The first requisite of a good citizen in this Republic of ours is that he shall be able and willing to pull his own weight.

Theodore Roosevelt

Oh, goddamnit, we forgot the silent prayer!
Dwight D. Eisenhower—at a Cabinet meeting

Chapter One

Ben was leaning slightly out of the Jeep, admiring the denim-covered derriere of a very attractive lady. A lady that he had not seen before.

"You're going to fall out of that damn Jeep if you're not careful." The voice came from behind him.

Smiling, Ben straightened up and turned his head, looking at his longtime friend. The previous view was not easy to turn away from, and Ben vowed he would check it out. "Good to see you, Ike. Any trouble in your sector coming down here?"

"Nothing we couldn't handle. In case you're interested, and it's obvious that you are, her name is Linda Parsons. She's a survivor from over Nevada way. She's thirty-five years old. Lost her husband and kids a few years back during an outlaw raid."

Ben got out of the Jeep and stretched his six-feet-plus frame. "How in the hell do you know so much about her, old married man?"

" 'Cause I got here yesterday and inquiring minds want to know!"

Both men laughed at the references to the old TV commercial that many in the Rebel ranks would be too young to have anything but a vague memory of.

Linda turned her head at the laughter and looked at the men. She had been introduced to General Ike, and the tall man with him had to be General Ben Raines. He was handsome, not in a pretty-boy way, but in a rugged, interesting way. Looked to be about fifty, she guessed.

Ben lifted his eyes to hers and for an instant, they stared at each other. Someone called to her and she walked away.

Ike cleared his throat and said, "Big job ahead of us, Ben."

"Yeah. Let's get to it."

Ben Raines and his Rebel Army, including the forces of the Russian, Georgi Striganov, had started this campaign on the banks of the Mississippi, at St. Louis. Now they were all but finished in the lower forty-eight, the campaign taking them cross-country to the Northwest. They were now preparing for the final leg, the assault on Los Angeles, with its thousands of street punks and Night People.

Once on the West Coast, the Rebels had discovered that all the talk of nuclear destruction—which they had all believed for years—had been a gigantic hoax. The West Coast was clean all the way down into Mexico and beyond. Ben had been hearing radio chatter for months about the Mexican people reforming their army and cleaning out the nest of creepies and outlaws. So far as he could tell, the Mexican people were slowly gaining the upper hand.

In the United States, so far as the Rebels now knew, only the Washington, D.C./Baltimore area and Kansas City had actually taken nuclear strikes during the Great War. Most of the other cities had taken chemical strikes.

What Ben did not know was that Lan Villar,

Khamsin, Ashley, Kenny Parr, and the outlaw bikers had pulled together what remained of their shattered forces after butting head-to-head with the Rebels in the Northwest, and were heading for Alaska, a spot that Ben had decided to investigate after cleaning out southern California. Alaska had been code-named Northstar.

Ben's Husky pup, Smoot, rolled over on her back in the back seat of the Jeep and started snoring, deep in contented sleep.

"What's the word on the flyovers?" Ike asked.

"Not good. From what our pilots have been able to observe, Los Angeles is pretty well carved up by various gangs, but the Scouts have taken a few prisoners, and under interrogation, they admit that all the gangs will pull together and work as one if attacked by a large enough force."

"What are we facing?"

"Just about anything you'd care to name," Ben said, disgust in his voice. "Offshoots of those punk gangs of the eighties make up a lot of the enemy. Dickheads with gang names like the Boogies make up a lot of the enemy. The Boogies and the Skulls and assorted punk crap like that. The Night People have their own section of L.A., and the gangs respect it. At least the Believers haven't renamed themselves the Purple Twats or something equally stupid."

Ike laughed at Ben. "Oregon is clean, Ben. The rest of the teams will be pulling in here over the next couple of days."

"We won't have much time to rest and reorganize. I won't kid you, Ike. Taking California is not going to be easy. The gangs here have had years to arm and train; they've known for a long time that someday they'd have to face us. And they'll probably be

11

ready, at least mentally geared up for it. If any of our people are thinking easy, tell them to hang it up."

"Still no word from Khamsin, Kenny Parr, Lan Villar, or any of the rest?"

"Not a peep. I know we knocked the props out from under them, but I don't believe we killed them all. They're in deep hiding somewhere. They'll show up. Bet on that."

The Rebels were now almost certain that there had been a massive cover-up on the part of America's politicians after the Great War. From what they had been able to piece together, many members of Congress had been secretly supporting the movement of the Believers, the Night People—creepies to the Rebels—a bizarre religion that embraced cannibalism. Why they'd supported a movement that horrible was something that Ben realized he would probably never know.

Ike wandered off to rejoin his command and Ben walked through the milling crowds of the Rebel army, or at least a part of it.

The Rebels had concluded their sweep of the Northwest, and Washington and Oregon had been declared ninety-five-percent clean. The Rebel outposts they had established would settle up with that remaining five percent of creepies, warlords, thugs, punks, and other malcontents. And they would do it the Rebel way: with a bullet or a rope. The Rebels did not believe in lengthy trials. Plea-bargaining was a term that had been stricken from the English language. Fuck up bad and the penalty was death.

Cecil Jefferys and his command were making ready to push south out of Medford, Oregon. They had taken the town without having to destroy it—as was usually the Rebel way with larger cities—and were using the airport to resupply. The Russian, Striganov, and the mercenary, West, had pushed down to the small town of Lakeview and supplies were being trucked to them. Five and Six Battalions of the Rebel army had been shifted over to the east side of the state and they were in position to start the push south. For the time being, they were under the command of Georgi Striganov.

Ben was leaning up against a fender, studying a map. He waved for a runner to join him, and also for his radio operator. "You find Ike and tell him to pull out as soon as possible. Corrie, bump Cecil and tell him to link up with Ike; they'll take the coastline highway all the way down to San Francisco. There is no point in putting this off. We'll take Interstate 5 south. Georgi and West will push south on 395. All units will be rolling in two days."

"Right, sir." She waited, knowing that more was coming.

"Tina and her Scouts will join Georgi and West, for the time being. Buddy will join Ike and Cec. Everyone else will remain with us."

"Yes, sir."

"Tell Leadfoot and the Wolfpack to get ready to move out. I want them to penetrate as far south as Yreka and halt there. They are to radio back with their assessment."

"Right, sir."

Leadfoot and his Wolfpack had, at one time, been outlaw bikers. Ben, seeing more than a spark of decency in the bikers, had given them a choice of lifestyles. They had accepted it. Leadfoot, Beerbelly, Hoss, and Wanda and her bunch had joined the Rebels. They had proved to be fierce fighters and totally loyal to Ben and the Rebel movement.

"General, what about the new bunch?" Corrie asked innocently.

"What new bunch?"

"The group that came in from Nevada. The one Linda Parsons was with."

"Incorporate them into our units. Spread them out. Send the noncombatants to Base Camp One. You know all that, Corrie. What's going on here?"

"Yes, sir. Right, sir. Linda was trained as an RN."

"Wonderful. So what?"

"Ah . . . I gather that Doctor Chase has not yet informed you of his decision."

"I haven't seen the old goat in several days. Where is he? What decision?"

"He's assigned Linda to our team."

Ben looked at her. "I love the way people make decisions without consulting me."

"Yes, sir. Doctor Chase said it was for your own good."

"That's very interesting. Get her over here, will you?"

Beth, another member of Ben's personal team, had walked up, listening to the exchange. "Doctor Chase said that since you refuse to behave like a commander is supposed to behave, that is, directing operations from behind the lines, he felt it best to assign a medical person to the team."

"Do remind me to thank him from the bottom of my heart," Ben said dryly.

"Yes, sir. I will certainly make a note of that."

"Have the mechanics finished with our vehicle?"

"Be ready in the morning," Beth told him.

Ben's vehicle was a big, nine-passenger Chevy wagon, with armor plate and bullet-proof glass. Ben's driver was Cooper. His self-appointed bodyguard was the cute and diminutive Jersey.

"Where is Jersey?" Ben asked.

"Probably harassing Cooper," Beth said.

"Thermopolis and Emil?"

"In a deep philosophical discussion over by the river."

"That should be a conversation to be recorded for the ages."

Thermopolis and his band of 21st-century hippies had thrown their lot in with Ben, considering him to be the lesser of the evils that faced their way of life. Emil Hite was a little con artist who usually had some religious scam going—the last one had been the Great God Blomm. But both Therm and Emil and their followers had proven themselves in battle many times and Ben was glad to have them on the Rebel side.

Corrie brought Linda Parsons over to meet the general.

The woman had a very pretty, heart-shaped face that reminded Ben of a movie actress . . . he couldn't think of her name. Linda, Ben guessed, would stand about five-five and was very nicely proportioned. Light brown hair, worn short. Green eyes that were studying him as closely as he was studying her.

"You understand the Rebel philosophy, Mrs. Parsons?" Ben asked her.

"I understand it."

"Do you agree with it?"

She nodded her head. "I agree with enough of it to live with it."

Ben could accept that. A lot of Rebels felt the same way. The Rebel way was harsh and usually uncompromising. There were no niceties of law. If you fought the Rebels, you died. If you chose not to ac-

15

cept the Rebel doctrine but remained non-hostile, the Rebels would not harm you. But in most cases neither would they help you. Ike had once said that a man couldn't get much plowin' done with both mules wanting to pull in opposite directions. The Rebels knew it was a hard and terrible time, worldwide, and they understood that there was no room for fence-straddlers. Let's get the nation back together again, and then we'll debate the fine points of law.

"The bunch you came in with," Ben said, "how many of you?"

"About fifty adults. There are eighteen children. I understand that you are sending the children down to your base camp in Louisiana."

"That's correct. And any of the adults who wish a noncombatant role."

"Then that will knock it down to about forty who will remain here."

"Whatever, Mrs. Parsons."

"Please, just Linda."

"Fine. Beth, go with her and get her into uniform. Draw supplies and equipment and then both of you rejoin me at my CP." Ben looked around him. "Wherever the damn thing is."

"I get the impression that the general doesn't like me," Linda said, as she and Beth walked toward the supply area.

"Don't make any snap conclusions," Beth warned her. "The general is sometimes hard to read." She grinned. "Besides, I think you're wrong. He was sizing you up a few minutes before you joined us. I was watching him."

"I heard he was a womanizer."

16

"He likes the ladies, for sure."

"How old is he?"

" 'Bout fifty."

"That's what I guessed. You been with him long?"

"Pretty good while. We've been in some scraps, I'll tell you that for sure."

"He married?"

"No. I think he was, a long time ago; or else they were just living together. She was killed during the battle for the Tri-States. Tina is his adopted daughter. Buddy is his blood son. By a woman that now hates both Ben and Buddy."

"Sister Voleta?"

"That's right. News gets around."

"General Raines is an . . . interesting-looking man," Linda said. "He can be very . . . well, intense when he looks at you."

"He is also one of the most dangerous people you'll ever meet. And he likes to take chances. It can get interesting staying around him too. He'll usually find some way to get right in the middle of a fight."

"I thought generals were supposed to direct operations from far behind the lines, in some safe bunker?"

Beth laughed. "Not in the Rebel army, honey. And for sure, not Ben Raines. You'll see."

Linda looked around her at the crush of Rebels, drawing supplies, checking in malfunctioning equipment, and receiving other equipment. Many were lined up at MASH tents for medical or dental work. She did not see a single person just loafing.

Beth seemed to read her thoughts as she followed the woman's eyes. "There's a war on in the lower forty-eight. And the sooner we win it down here, the sooner we'll head for Alaska and kick butt up there."

"And then?"

"Europe."

"*Europe!* Isn't that a rather ambitious undertaking?"

Beth shrugged. "Not really. We've kicked ass all over the United States, haven't we?"

"Maybe they don't want the Rebel way over there." It was not put as a question.

"And maybe they do. We won't know until we get there, will we? Here we are. Louise?" She grinned at the woman behind a long table filled with clothing. "This is Linda. Load her up with gear. She's been assigned to the general's team."

Linda looked at her. "Does that make me somebody special?"

"Some might say so. It's good duty. You'll get to see lots of action up close."

"Yeah," Louise said, smiling. "And you get the absolutely mind-boggling conversation of Cooper thrown in for free."

"And all about what happened in the olden days from the general," Beth added.

Linda laughed. "Careful now. I'm closer to the general's age than to yours."

"That's right," Beth said, a twinkle in her eyes. "And don't think the general hasn't noticed too."

Linda noticed that Ben Raines seemed to be constantly on the prowl, popping up at the most unexpected times and places. And always with Jersey and her M-16 right beside or behind him. Usually, the entire team was with him. And he seemed to know everybody. There was a free-spirited stream of chatter—often laced with vulgar jokes and profanity—going on between the general and the Rebels.

General Ike McGowan had pulled out the previous

18

afternoon, heading for the west side of the state to link up with the black general, Cecil Jefferys. The entire Rebel force was to begin their jump-off at dawn the next day.

"Nervous?" The voice came from her right.

Linda looked up into the face of Ben Raines. She had not heard him approach her. And how did he know what she had been thinking? Maybe the rumors about him were true. A lot of people believed that Ben Raines was some sort of god; or if not that, at least possessed with some sort of supernatural ability. Linda didn't believe in ghosts and hobgoblins and psychic powers and all that. But she didn't know how she felt about Ben Raines. Except that he was very impressive. Tall, with brown hair peppered with gray. A rangy sort of man, but possessed of some strength, she felt. Unreadable eyes.

"A little, I'll admit it," she answered.

He sat down beside her on the ground. "I read your dossier. You haven't seen much combat, have you?"

"Not much. After the Great War, even during the few years of so-called peace under President Logan, we stayed in our little valley there in Nevada and no one ever bothered us. I worked as an RN in our clinic. Then everything fell apart a couple of years ago. I've been on the run since then."

"It must have been a very isolated little valley."

"Oh, yes. It was. But the outlaws found us."

"Were there so many coming at you that you couldn't fight them?"

She smiled at him. "We weren't warriors, General. We were teachers and technicians and nurses and medical doctors and scientists. And I suppose, looking back, very naive in our thinking that we would

19

be left alone in our little paradise."

"Even paradise must be defended, Linda. I've been told that even the gates of Heaven are guarded. The Rebel army has not cleared the United States of punks and thugs and crud by extending the olive branch of peace to them. They'd have snatched it out of our hands and stuck it up our ass."

She shook her head and tried to hide a smile. "Is it true that you shoot criminals, General?"

"That depends on the crime, Linda. Understand this now. We take very few prisoners. Anyone who fights us is our mortal enemy and we will destroy them. It's a brutal time we live in, Linda. Always has been, for that matter. It's just a little worse now. Or better, depending on your point of view."

"Better?"

"We've got a chance to start over. And we're doing it. Every sweep the Rebels make means we clear the crud and leave the good. There are people not fifty yards from us who were once criminals. They were the smart ones. They saw the writing on the wall and realized that the only thing that faced them was a bullet or a noose. We gave them a chance to redeem themselves, and they took it. But those days are over, Linda. There are too many outposts where people could surrender. Few do. What we are now facing is the hard-core criminal element. Those punks south of us know we're coming. They could surrender, and we'd accept it. But only for the next few days. After that, no."

"It seems so brutal."

"It's practical." He glanced at her. "I'm curious about something."

"Ask."

"With your almost total lack of combat experience,

why did you choose to be a part of a combat team?"

"Honestly?"

"That's the only way around here. You'll learn that."

"To try to understand you people. See what motivates you. Ever since the Great War, I've heard about the Rebels and Ben Raines. How you defied the government and carved out the Tri-States."

"We were looking for peace, Linda. For a place where we didn't have to lock our doors and live behind bars and chain locks and elaborate security systems. The United States wouldn't offer us a place—and they could have—so we built one of our own. It worked, and the government couldn't stand it. No one went hungry, no one was homeless, everybody had a job, no one was denied medical care, every child got a good education, and the life expectancy of thieves and punks and thugs and rapists and murderers was about fifteen minutes. The United States government couldn't stand our success. They destroyed the Tri-States, but they couldn't kill the dream. We just fought on."

"And you've been fighting ever since."

"That is correct. And we won't quit until we've won." He smiled at her. But his eyes were still unreadable.

Linda knew, somehow, at that moment that what Beth had told her was true. This was a very dangerous man. Dangerous not only because of his skill with weapons, but because thousands of men and women would follow him unhesitatingly through the gates of Hell in pursuit of their dream.

Was she one of them? She wasn't sure.

"Lamar Chase gives you high marks," said Ben. "He says you're a fine nurse."

"That's a crusty old man. But I like him. Isn't he a little old to be out in the field?"

"Lamar will die out in the field, Linda. I long ago ceased attempting to put him back in research at our base camp. Just as he has given up trying to tie me down to a desk or to make me stay behind the lines."

"You enjoy it, don't you, General?" she asked softly. "The fighting, the violence?"

Ben did not have to give that much thought. "I let myself get out of shape for a time, Linda. I was making lots of money and drinking too much. That was years back, when the world was more or less functioning; that is to say, when governments were still able to produce results, however small. I would sit and read the newspaper and watch the TV evening news and hear how grown men were able to kidnap small children, keep them prisoner for years, rape and sodomize them, and when caught, receive a five-year prison sentence. That's true, Linda. It happened more than once. How gangs of teenage punks could beat and rape and leave for dead in a ditch some unlucky person, and in many cases draw no prison time at all because some group of judges who sat on high had decreed that anyone under the age of seventeen was not responsible for his actions. But still he could get a driver's license. We had some strange laws, Linda. And I stress *had*. I would read or see how a family would come home from work and find their home vandalized, every precious memento they had gathered over the years destroyed, and when caught, the guilty parties would get a slap on the wrist and be turned loose. How perverted assholes could torture helpless animals and be guilty of no more than a misdemeanor. How people who dared stand up for their rights and use a gun to defend self, home, or

22

loved ones, would sometimes go to prison and the crud who broke into their homes or cars or attacked them on the streets could sue for damages. Did you ever stop and ponder that, Linda? That a criminal was allowed to sue his *victim* for damages? And in many cases *collect!*

"There were those of us who wrote letters to newspapers and national TV networks and news magazines. We said that in our opinion something was terribly wrong with our system of justice; it was warped, bent in favor of the criminal. Many of the media people would immediately brand us as bigots, or gun-nuts, or crazies. Therefore fewer and fewer of us chose to voice our opinions. Those who persisted were sometimes harassed by federal agents. I know that to be true, because I was one of those who were harassed.

"But because I had achieved some degree of fame as a writer, with a respectable, if not a massive following, I was not harassed nearly so relentlessly as others with no clout."

She noticed Ben's smile and wondered about that. He cleared it up.

"Of course, I had some years in the intelligence community too. That probably helped with the government, if not with the liberal media. An example, Linda. At one point in time, the federal government was turning loose murderers, rapists, and armed robbers, and sending agents out to arrest people who owned home-satellite systems capable of picking up signals from the *public* airways.

"Stupid? Sure, it was. But that didn't stop the government from doing it. Our government was spending millions of dollars enforcing the dumbest of laws while children were being beaten to death by abusive

23

parents. State governments were spending millions of dollars nationwide to subsidize high school sports, and our elderly were freezing to death in the winter, dying of the heat in the summer, or starving to death.

"Our welfare system was a disgrace, public housing was a profane joke, our highways and bridges were falling apart, the hands of the police were tied, the cops and schoolteachers were underpaid—the cops couldn't enforce the law because of judges, and teachers couldn't teach or maintain discipline for fear of lawsuits—drug dealers were peddling death on the street corners and killing innocent people who got in their way, and the government was sending out agents to *disarm* law-abiding citizens.

"Our wildlife was being killed off, entire species gone forever, because our forests were being raped by money-hungry developers and loggers and big farmers, our water supply threatened by the runoff of poisonous chemicals, and our elected officials were wringing their hands and stomping on their hankies saying that they couldn't do anything drastic to combat worldwide terrorism or international drug-trafficking because that might violate the criminals' constitutional rights.

"The whole damn world was going to hell in a handbasket. The Amazon rain forest, which at that time was producing about one third of the world's oxygen, was being destroyed by humankind, and very few of us even gave a damn. And those of us that did were told to shut up.

"When the Great War came, Linda, some of us seized the moment to break away, form our own society, and rebuild. And we did. I got back in shape and vowed I was going to put together an army and

24

kick the ass of every punk and thug and crud we found. So that's why we keep fighting, Linda. That's why we'll always keep fighting until we win. That's why the Rebels have got to win. We have to. We can't even think about defeat. We're the last known barrier against total, worldwide anarchy. If we fall, the whole damn world falls with us."

Chapter Two

Linda was rolled out of her sleeping bag in the middle of the night by Jersey. "Up and at 'em, Medic. Coffee's ready in the general's quarters."

"What *time* is it?"

"Three o'clock. Time's a-wastin', so let's go." She grinned down at the woman in the dim light provided by starlight. "You'll get used to it — believe me."

Linda sat up and groaned, fumbling for her boots. She was accustomed to wearing sandals most of the time, not heavy combat boots. "What's the rush? Is it breakfast yet?"

Jersey laughed softly. "Cold rations and hot coffee when we're pulling out, Linda. Don't worry, you won't be able to see what you're eating, so it'll taste all right. It's when you *can* see it that it gets rough."

After washing her face and brushing her teeth, Linda felt like she might make it, and the walk to Ben's quarters completed the wake-up process.

The entire team was assembled there, standing around the coffeepot. Beth grinned at her. "I risked life and limb saving you a cup, Linda. You'd better grab it before we're both attacked."

She gripped the camp mug and sipped at the

strong brew, lifting her eyes to Ben. Since she had first laid eyes on him, several days back, he'd never seemed to change, always looking calm and collected and ready to tackle any situation.

"Welcome aboard, Linda," Ben said.

"Thank you."

"Jersey, did you check her out with the M-16?"

"She . . . ah, did her best," Linda interjected, saving Jersey the explanation. "But I'm afraid I'm not very good."

"It'll come to you. Don't try to push it. When we bivouac this afternoon, I'll take you out and go through the steps with the weapon."

Jersey rolled her eyes and said a silent prayer for the general's safety.

"Uh . . . thank you," Linda said. "I'd like that."

"Now then," Ben said. "Leadfoot and the Wolfpack have found survivors in Yreka. Several hundred of them. We're going to stop there for a time today and set up another outpost. Then we'll move on. For you people who weren't with us some years back, this is the second time the Rebels have been in this area. We went down the state to just north of San Francisco. We did not enter the city at that time." He paused and sighed.

"I want to warn you all of a few things. There are mutants in the area just south of us. There are also tribes of people who call themselves the Woods Children, headed by two young men named Ro and Wade—if they're still alive. And a tribe called the Underground People. Both of those are to the east of Interstate 5. They will see us. It's doubtful that we will see them unless they want us to. Leave them alone. They are for the most part peaceful people.

27

They have fought alongside us and they believe in our ways. They live in the forests and are caretakers of it. Personally I wish we had more like them. They are not meat-eaters. They educate their young properly, and when they need medical treatment or advice, they seek out some Rebel patrol or outpost.

"The mutants? Well . . . leave them alone and they'll usually leave you alone. No one knows what caused them to be as they are. Perhaps they've always been here and they just avoided us. Perhaps the chemicals that poisoned the people had something to do with their growth. I don't know and neither does anyone else I've ever talked with."

He paused as Corrie announced a fresh pot of coffee was ready and they all poured and sugared and creamed. Ben said, "A question I've been asked is why didn't we encounter the warlords and creepies and street punks back then. For one thing, we didn't enter the cities and that's where they concentrate. And too, most of us were in mild shock because we'd been led to believe San Francisco and Los Angeles had taken nuclear hits and were gone. We just didn't have the time or the forces to move south."

Linda looked away. The others were listening, but she got the impression that this update was for her ears more than for anyone else.

"We're going to take our time on this sweep, people, and do it right. We're going to clear this state of crud and crap, establish as many outposts as possible, and then stand down for the winter in preparation for the exploration of Alaska. Ike says there is a good possibility that there are adequate ships still anchored in ports in Alaska that are suitable for our use. If we find that is the case, we'll load up and

28

head for Europe from Northstar. If not, it's back to the East Coast for us.

"All right, Coop, check out the wagon. Corrie, advise all commanders we shove off at 0500. Linda, get your gear together and Beth will show you how we pack the wagon. Let's go, people, we've got a war to fight."

From the blue waters of the Pacific east to the Nevada line, main battle tanks began roaring into life; M-42 Dusters as well, almost petite next to the big MBTs cranked up. Dozens of tanker trucks, carrying precious fuel, made ready to pull out. Rebels broke camp, packed up, and tossed their gear into the backs of deuce-and-a-halfs and climbed in. 155mm self-propelled howitzers coughed into life and lumbered into their positions in the lines. The RDF light tanks moved forward, most equipped with 75mm cannon, a few with 76mm cannon, which operate with about the same pressure as a 105mm.

"Scouts out?" Ben asked Corrie.

"Yes, sir. Colonel Gray sent his people out an hour ago. They're in position ranging three to five miles in front of the main columns."

"Load up and move to the front of the column," Ben told his team. "I'll meet you up the line." Ben walked from his quarters to the front of the long column, chatting with Rebels along the way, his M-14, affectionately referred to as a Thunder Lizard, slung on one shoulder.

"Come on, boys and girls!" Ben heard Sergeant Major Adamson roar. "Grandma moved faster than this."

"Here we go again, General!" a woman called from the cab of a truck.

"You bet, Jenny," Ben shouted back. "Time to kick ass and take names."

"What'd you do with the old sergeant major?" another Rebel shouted.

"I retired him to a desk back at Base Camp One. You all know and love Adamson."

Friendly boos and jeers greeted that, but Ben knew it meant nothing. Adamson was a former French Foreign Legionnaire who was all soldier and all Rebel. The men and women of the Rebel army liked and respected him.

Ben stopped by a light tank and looked up at the woman commander, her head sticking out of the open hatch. "You sure you know how to drive this thing, Susie?" He smiled with the verbal jab.

"Hell, no!" she fired back. "I just give the orders."

Ben laughed and patted the armor plate of the tank in reply and walked on.

The Rebels were made up of all races, all nationalities, all religions. The Rebel army knew no discrimination along racial, religious, or country-of-origin lines. It was not tolerated. Ben Raines had also taken the theory that women had no place in combat and tossed it on the junk pile.

The Rebels did discriminate against human trash of any color, usually just as long as it took to put a bullet in them. But there were no haters of people of another race in the Rebel ranks. Of any color. No pre-judging of a person based solely on race or religion. The Rebels took each person as an individual and reserved judgment—if any—until later. Among the Rebels, there were chaplains representing all religions, from Hindu to Seventh-Day Adventists. Whenever there was a break in the action, most Rebels went to some sort of worship service. It was not required that they do so. Religion and the worshiping of one's God was a personal matter and nobody else's business.

Not everyone could or would—as was usually the case—adapt to the Rebel way. The old Tri-States had been harshly criticized because Ben had admitted that perhaps no more than one person out of five—if that many—could or would live under and by the simple rules that the Rebels adopted. It was true that the Rebels took the best of people and culled the rest. The rules were simple. One did not steal anything, ever. One did not lie or cheat. You treated others fairly and with respect. You respected the land and the wild creatures that lived there. You respected the property of others. Loudmouths did not last long in the Rebel army. Bullies seldom made it through the first day. Those who were cruel to animals were not even considered. The Rebels were not perfect—far from it—but they tried. That was what Ben demanded of himself, and he could ask no more from those who followed him.

"Move, Smoot," Ben said, getting into the big armor-plated wagon. The Husky pup jumped into the back and landed in Beth's lap.

"You ready to go to war, Coop?" Ben asked the driver.

"Beats the hell out of a poke in the eye with a sharp stick, General."

"Give the orders, Corrie."

Hundreds of Rebels in tanks and trucks and Jeeps and Hummers and self-propelled artillery surged forward, moving across the Oregon line into Northern California.

In Cresent City, a warlord listened to radio transmissions from his forward observers. He paled.

"Holy shit!" he said, looking around him at those who had chosen to follow the outlaw way. "Ben Raines is on the move. The first bunch is about ten miles away and pushin' hard towards us. Let's get the hell out of here."

They grabbed whatever they could find that was readily at hand and got into their cars and trucks and roared south.

"This ain't legal!" one of the warlord's lieutenants said. "There ain't no justice in this. Ben Raines ain't got no right comin' in here and tellin' us what to do."

The warlord, who had called himself Larado for so many years he had difficulty remembering his Christian name, looked at the man, disgust in his eyes. "The Rebels don't pay no attention to that happy crap, man. All that legal jive is out the window. Ben Raines is gonna bring back law and order and he's gonna do it at the point of a gun. He'll roll right over anybody or anything that stands in his way."

"Where the hell we gonna go?" The question was frantically tossed out.

"We got no choice. We got to head south to L.A. and link up with them gangs down there."

"Why not Frisco?"

"All them cats in Frisco is gonna do is delay Raines. They'll buy us some time, but Frisco is gonna fall. Bet on it, man."

"There is another choice," another outlaw said.

"Oh, yeah? What?"

"Stop the car."

The rusty and battered old car slid to a halt. Laredo twisted in the seat. "What are you gonna do, man?"

"Find me a house, raise me a garden. Hunt some. And obey the laws that Ben Raines says to obey."

"You chicken-shit!" the driver sneered.

"Maybe," the man said, getting out and pulling his duffel out with him. "But I'll be alive and sittin' on the front porch with a woman and some kids long after your bones have been picked clean by the rats. See you boys." He walked into the timber by the side of the road.

"He's yeller!" a man sneered.

"Maybe," Laredo said. "And maybe he's smarter than all of us."

"Huh?"

"We gonna die, Slick. The days of the outlaw in the lower forty-eight is over. You all heard them radio transmissions from the Rebels the other day. They told us we either lay down our guns now and surrender, or we die. They wasn't kiddin,' boys. Make your minds up now."

"It's a big country, Laredo," he was reminded.

"It ain't big enough for us and Ben Raines. Let's go if we're goin'. We got to find us a spot and dig in."

Ike and Cecil's troops pushed down to Crescent City and found it deserted. The troops under the command of Striganov and West pushed down to Alturas and found the town in ruins; no signs of life. Ben and his contingent rolled into Yreka and stood

33

down while Ben met with the leader of the survivors in that area.

The town, once holding a population of six thousand, showed signs of many fierce battles, some of them quite recent. But it also had clean streets, neat homes, and many large, well-tended gardens. Neatness and cleanliness were almost always a sign of people who refused to knuckle under to any kind of disaster and who were not content to sit around and bitch and moan while waiting for somebody else to help pull them up.

The leader of the group, a middle-aged man named Chuck, showed Ben the small but well-furnished clinic, the school, and all the other improvements, including electricity, sewage treatment, and water.

"There were other survivors in this area, Chuck," Ben said, consulting a clipboard. "George Williams from Chico. Another George from Red Bluff. Harris from Redding. Pete Ho from Ukiah. John Dunnning from Santa Rosa."

Chuck shook his head. "Most of them are dead, General. At least as far as I know, they are. Only Pete Ho and his bunch and me and mine held out, and Pete had to move his people over to near the state line. Near the Plumas National Forest. We talk to each other every week on the radio."

"That explains why we haven't been able to make contact with anybody." Ben lined out the names on the clipboard. "What happened to the movement out here?"

"It just fell apart, General. I believe it was Harris who was the first to refuse to use the death penalty. The outlaws took him out first. Then one by one, the other groups were either destroyed or ran away. All except Pete's and this one."

It didn't surprise Ben. Only about half of the earlier outposts the Rebels had set up had survived. Their failure was due mostly to the breaking of the rules the Rebels had tried and tested over the years and found to work. Laws were not made to be broken. And people who broke them had to be punished. If not, the system — any system — simply would not work.

They were hard rules, and only the strongest-willed could follow them. But weak people do not rebuild a nation after that nation's collapse. Doers rebuild nations, and then they help the weak.

"You have a fine town here, Chuck. I congratulate you. Give the list of any supplies you need to Beth here, and she'll get them for you."

"Right now, General, we're desperately short of ammo and reloading equipment."

Ben nodded at Chuck and waved at a Rebel, telling the man to supply Chuck with whatever he needed. Ammo was something the Rebels were never short of. Back at Base Camp One, factories ran around the clock, seven days a week, to keep the field troops supplied.

"Corrie, bump Georgi and advise him that Pete Ho is alive and will probably need supplies. There is an airstrip at Susanville. We'll make that a drop-off point for that sector."

"Yes, sir."

"Chuck, what can you tell me about Redding?"

"A lot of gangs working out of there. It's outlaw headquarters for this part of the state."

"What's between here and there?"

"Nothing, General. And I mean *nothing.*"

"Do you have any idea what kind of shape the airport is in?"

"No, General, I'm sorry, but I don't. We're so small it takes all of us to defend this place. We used to send out patrols. They never came back."

"I get the impression that not much is working north of Sacramento."

"You mean like big gangs of outlaws?"

"Yes."

"You're right. But oh, boy, south of there is another story. You're going to hit a solid wall of resistance from there on down. Redding is about the only real bastion of crud working north of the old capital. But I have to warn you that there are dozens of smaller gangs working all over the place, like lice."

"The Interstate is clear from here on down?"

"It's still fairly clear of obstacles, but it is deteriorating badly."

"Bridges?"

"As far as we know, they're all right."

Ben shook hands with the man. "Stay healthy, Chuck."

"I intend to, General. We've got a nation to rebuild, right?"

"You damn right, Chuck!"

All Rebel contingents called it a day at 1600 that afternoon. When they were advancing in unknown or enemy territory, they broke off early in order to set up defensive perimeters. Few shots had been fired at them on their trek southward out of Oregon into California. But all had seen where a lot of people,

36

outlaws to judge by the trash they left behind them, had pulled out in one hell of a hurry, getting out of the path of the oncoming Rebels.

Ike and Cecil pulled over just north of Eureka, Ben and his people made camp at the deserted town of Lakehead, and Georgi and West bivouacked just west of Moon Lake on Highway 395.

Ben took Linda out to practice with the M-16.

"I'll pray for you," Jersey said.

She just couldn't hit anything with a rifle. Ben found her a shotgun to use and she seemed much happier with that. He warned the others that in the event of a combat situation they should make sure Linda had the barrel pointed in the right direction.

Over the first hot meal of that day, Ben said, "The crud and crap aren't going to stand and defend their turf, as I hoped they would. They seem to be pulling out, en masse, and heading south. Whether or not they're beefing up the gangs in San Francisco is something we have yet to learn. But if I had to take a guess, I'd say they're not. I'd bet they're heading for the L.A. area. San Francisco is a box that we're going to nail a lid on."

Leadfoot of the bikers said, "You want some of my people to roll south, General? We could get you some intelligence on where they're heading."

"It would be risky, Leadfoot. Maybe too risky. You'd be out of communication range in a few miles. If you carried anything that would reach us, that would immediately be a tip-off to any gang member with the sense of a warthog. We don't have repeater systems in this part of the country, yet."

"If we don't try, General," Wanda said, "we'll be going in blind."

"That's true. I won't make a decision until after Redding is taken tomorrow. We may get lucky and get our hands on prisoners who want to talk. Get a good night's sleep. Tomorrow is going to be a very busy day."

Ben walked back to his quarters and took down his M-14, cleaning it carefully. Smoot lay on her bed and watched him, waiting for a chance to sneak-attack him and give Ben a wet lick in the ear.

The old Thunder Lizard had taken a lot of criticism since its inception back in 1957 when it was introduced as the T44 and adopted by the military as the M-14. Critics decried the weapon as being too heavy (8.7 pounds, empty), and the sighting system as too complicated. The bipod was too heavy, they said. Ben had put his people to work on the weapon and they'd modified the rifle, coming up with a thirty-round staggered box magazine that worked and a bipod made of much lighter material. The 7.62x51mm bullet (.308) packed a much heavier wallop than the .223, and besides, Ben liked the weapon. He had carried a Thompson SMG for years, but finally had had to retire the weapon when he discovered the Rebels were holding it in as much awe as they did the general. The M-14 was a man's rifle, for on full auto the weapon could punish the shoulder of an inexperienced shooter. Ben did not fall into that catagory.

Ben turned his head and Smoot nailed him.

Ben was up long before dawn the next morning. He shaved and dressed while the coffee was boiling on his little camp stove. He heard a slight noise outside, and he dropped one hand to the butt of his .45 autoloader, which was carried cocked and locked.

"Permission to enter?" Dan Gray's question was softly offered.

"Come on in, Dan."

Colonel Dan Gray, a former British SAS officer and now in charge of Gray's Scouts, opened the door and stepped inside. He carried his own morning wake-up, a cup of tea. "My people are in place, General," he said, sitting down. "Early estimates are that about seven hundred outlaws inhabit the city. This should be no more than a walk-through."

"L.A. won't be," Ben said, pouring a mug of coffee and sitting down across from Dan at the battered old kitchen table.

"I'm afraid you're right. L.A. is going to be slow going, block by burning block. Even though it is a sprawling place, I think we can still use artillery to lessen our casualties."

Ben opened a worn map of California. Maps were getting harder and harder to find, and each one was used until it was falling apart. And due to the ever-changing conditions of highways—bridges out, overpasses collapsing, sinkholes in the roadbeds—maps were constantly having to be updated.

Ben studied the map, then opened a booklet, read for a moment, and tossed the booklet aside. "That thing says that Redding has numerous motels, fine restaurants, friendly people, and is a pleasant stop-over. Shit! What about county roads that would enable us to block off escape to the south, east, and west?"

Dan laughed at Ben's expression in the light from the portable lantern. "My people have found a way to link up with Highway 273; that will block west and south escape routes. East is up for grabs. There are all sorts of little roads leading in that direction."

"All right, Dan. Move the rest of your people out as soon as they've eaten. There is no way we can come up quietly. They'll be waiting for us. And we don't have the foggiest notion of how heavily they're armed."

"Or the number of children that might be in there," Dan added.

"Yes. I've been doing a lot of thinking about that. According to what I've learned, the Redding outlaws have been there for some time, so there probably will be families. That lets out standing back and blowing them to hell. Let's take the town, Dan."

Chapter Three

"Everyone in body armor," Ben ordered. "Berets stowed and into helmets."

They were a half mile from the Redding city limits. The long column of Rebel vehicles stretched out seemingly endlessly to the north on Interstate 5.

"Main battle tanks button up, first section group behind the tanks," Ben ordered.

Hatches were clanked shut and Rebels moved into position behind the steel and armor-plated monsters.

"Is Dan in position, Corrie?"

"Yes, sir. He reports sitting on go."

"Are you in communication with those in the city?"

"No, sir. They will not respond on any frequency."

"Order a main battle tank with loudspeaker capability up to tell the outlaws to surrender. Advise them that they are completely surrounded and they have no chance of survival if they choose to fight us."

The tank clanked into position and advised those in the small city to give it up.

The reply was small-arms fire and a rifle-fired grenade that missed the tank and exploded on the ground.

"The rocket was fired from that white house just

behind that old service station," the forward observer told Corrie, and she relayed that to Ben.

"Destroy it," Ben ordered.

The cannon on the tank lowered, the turret moved, and the cannon roared twice, fire and smoke leaping from the muzzle. The small house on the edge of town exploded as the first shell impacted. The second round was napalm and a burning body was hurled out of the house. The body bounced once off the ground and lay still, the odor of charred flesh drifting on the morning air.

"Tell the tank commander to repeat the surrender message once more," Ben ordered.

The message was repeated and once more the reply was unfriendly fire.

"Take the town," Ben said.

Four main battle tanks, turrets reversed, rammed through the barricades and drove straight into frame houses, totally demolishing them and crushing anyone inside. The tanks swiveled their turrets and cut loose with cannon, 7.62, and .50-caliber machine-gunfire.

Rebels quickly followed the tanks in, and one block of the town was taken.

The Rebels did not take any prisoners.

"Tell Dan to move in," Ben ordered. "Plug up all the escape holes he can."

If those in the town thought Ben Raines's initial attack was brutal, they quickly found that running up against Gray's Scouts was like swimming in a small pond filled with alligators. No matter where one turned, all they saw was hungry jaws filled with deadly teeth.

The leader of the thugs who occupied Redding got on the radio and called his counterpart thirty miles south in Red Bluff. "Get gone!" he shouted into the mike. "We've had it up here. Raines is not takin' no prisoners. Head for L.A. and link up with them down there. It's worser than we was told. Ben Raines and the Rebs don't got no mercy in them. They's out for blood and they don't give a damn for laws or courts or lawyers or nothin' like that. "He—"

The transmission ended abruptly as a Rebel-held rocket launcher burped and the house exploded in flames.

A squad of Rebels found what was once a lovely home that now contained about a dozen women and twice that many children, ranging in age from runny-nosed infants in filth-encrusted diapers to boys and girls nine or ten years old.

A Rebel looked at a woman, scarcely able to contain his anger and his contempt for her. "Get up," he said through clenched teeth.

"Don't take the babies from us!" one woman yelled. "They's good for trade."

"What?" a Rebel woman snapped at her. "Trade? Don't be stupid, you bitch. Trade?" Then it came to her who the women traded the babies to. "You goddamn slime!"

"You ain't got no rat to talk to me like 'at," the woman said. "Times has been hard."

"I wonder if these people have ever heard of soap," another Rebel said. "Jesus, it's rank in here."

The women and kids were escorted to the edge of town, where Ben's CP had been established. The children were taken from the women and turned over to Doctor Chase's medical people for exams and blood work.

"You cain't take my kid!" a woman screamed. "I done got me a trade set up."

She stopped wailing when she looked up into the very cold and unfriendly eyes of Ben Raines. She sensed instantly who he was, although she had never seen him before in her life. No Rebel wore insignia, and this one didn't have to.

"Shut up," Ben told her. "Did anyone hold a gun to your head and make you join outlaw gangs?"

The woman cringed and refused to answer.

"Answer me, goddamn you!"

"No. They didn't."

"Then why did you?"

"I got to eat!"

"Plant a garden. Join a group of survivors and live decently."

"Under rules? No way."

"You were going to trade your baby?"

"He's sickly."

"How many have you whelped?"

"One a year. I got a right to have fun!"

"I heard that on a newscast one evening, years ago, when a reporter interviewed a woman who had never been married and had five or six kids running around—kids that the working taxpayers paid for. It was bullshit then and it's still bullshit. Hit the road, lady. Hit it running and don't look back. Move, you goddamn worthless piece of garbage."

The woman jumped to her feet and took off running. She did not look back nor did she inquire about her "fun" baby.

Linda said, "General, this baby has fleas, head lice, and her diapers haven't been changed in so long she has urine burns from her navel halfway down to her knees."

Ben nodded. "I have despised trashy people of any color all my life. Corrie, have Doctor Chase set up a

44

MASH station near the airport as soon as it is secured. We'll airlift the kids out as soon as possible."

As soon as all the kids were gone, Ben reached down and jerked one woman to her feet. She glared hate and defiance at him. He pulled his .45 from leather, placed the muzzle against the woman's forehead, and slipped the autoloader off the lock position. She jumped at the slight sound.

"How many children have you helped supply to the creepies in L.A.?"

"The who?"

"The Night People. The Believers."

"How . . . did you know we done that?"

"How isn't important. How many?"

"Don't know. Cain't remember. Been doin' it for years."

"Don't you have one shred of decency in you, woman?"

"Fuck you, you son of a bitch!"

Linda looked on in shock as Ben pulled the trigger. The woman's feet flew out from under her and she fell to the cracked pavement, a large hole in the center of her forehead.

Ben stood over another woman. "Get up!"

"I'll tell you!" she screamed, sprays of spit flying from her mouth. "Jesus God Almighty, I'll tell you. We made a deal with them Believer Judges down in Sacramento. We supply them with—" she swallowed hard—"prisoners we tooken and they leave us alone. It's that way all over the state. We live in peace with them and you-all better learn how to do it too. Not just the Believers, but the gangs in L.A. too. You'll never whup them. They's too many of 'em."

"And how many of your babies have you handed over to them?" Ben asked softly.

45

Linda gasped at the question.

The woman sneered at Ben. She knew she was only minutes from death. "The ones that's sickly. The Believers have fine hospitals and such. They raise them up fat."

"Good God, woman!" Cooper blurted out. "The goddamned creepies *eat* them!"

"So?" she said. "What business is that of yours?"

Several Rebels crossed themselves. Jersey muttered, "Suffer the little children unto me, Jesus said."

Ben spat in the woman's face. "Beth, Jersey. Take these . . . ladies out of town and deal with them, please."

"Our pleasure," Beth said, prodding them up with the muzzle of her rifle.

A Rebel walked out of the newly claimed territory and whispered to Ben. Ben nodded his head in understanding. "A few who have surrendered verify that we now have all the children that were in the town," he said to no one in particular. He was thoughtful for a moment. "Corrie, give the orders for all Rebels to evacuate the town. Then order artillery to destroy it and everyone in it."

Smoke spiraled into the sky from the west coast of the state, the interior, and from the east side as Eureka, Redding, and Susanville were brought down by Rebel gunners.

Rebel planes would begin landing as soon as the airport runways were cleared. The children — many of the older ones just taken prisoner confirming the horror story the woman had told Ben — would be flown back to Base Camp One for further medical treatment, and would eventually be placed in foster homes.

"Hideous!" Linda said. "We were so secluded in our little valley we knew very little of what was actually taking place outside of it. This is just . . . mind-boggling."

The bodies of the dead outlaws and their women had been dragged into piles and scooped up by front-loaders, then transported to a mass grave site. All weapons had been gathered up and stacked according to caliber. They would be transported to supply depots and carefully gone over by Rebel armorers.

"Hiding one's head in the sand never really accomplishes anything," Ben said. "Reminds me of the story about the family who had but one child and wanted to protect that child from all the evils of the world. The child was educated at home, all activities monitored and restricted, and never allowed to leave the home compound. On the child's eighteenth birthday, his parents let him go outside the compound for the first time and he died of shock."

"If there is criticism in there, General," she replied, "I accept it for all of us."

Ben shook his head. "No criticism, Linda. Just amazement at your naiveté. I guess you people did what you thought was best. But now you have to face the real world. You witnessed a very small part of it today."

"You mean there is more?" She tried a smile with the light sarcasm.

Corrie walked up. "General, Leadfoot's bunch report that Red Bluff is deserted. A lot of people left there in one hell of a hurry. General Ike reports the same thing all the way down to Ukiah, and General Striganov has scouts out as far south as Interstate 80, just north of Lake Tahoe. Deserted all the way down.

47

But the signs show a lot of people were in that area a short time ago."

Ben opened a map case and carefully studied a map of California. "All right, Corrie. Have Georgi investigate all the towns east of Highway 99. Tell Leadfoot and his people to check out Chico, Yuba City, and Marysville. I think he's going to find them deserted. Abandoned is a better word. Sacramento is going to be our next big one. Tell Leadfoot to stay the hell out of Sacramento."

"Right, sir."

Thermopolis, the leader of the 21st-century century hippies who had joined in the Rebels' fight some months back, walked up. Ben looked around to see if the little con artist, Emil Hite, might be nearby. He wasn't. Ben liked Emil, and the little man was a scrapper, but Emil could be a tad nerve-janging at times.

"Therm," Ben said, greeting the man with the graying shoulder-length hair. "What's up?"

"Ben, I've got an old friend who had a commune not too far outside of Oroville. He was a fairly resourceful fellow. I'd like to take some of my people down there and see if he's still alive."

"I can't stop you, Therm."

"I know that. But if I'm playing the soldier game, I'd like to have the commanding general's permission."

"It's fine with me, Therm. You want some Rebels to go with you?"

Therm thought about that for a moment. He shook his head. "No, I don't think that would be wise. Pasco might misinterpret that as aggression and open fire."

"Why do I get this feeling that your friend will

48

want no part of us?"

Therm shrugged his shoulders. "You're probably right, Ben. But he runs, or ran, a tight ship. No lawlessness, no drugs, everybody works and pulls their own weight if they're physically able. You probably won't like him, but I think you'd respect what he is."

"Okay, Therm. But leave your VW Bugs and wagons here. Take a couple of Hummers with radio equipment so you'll be able to stay in contact with us." Ben smiled and Therm braced, knowing Ben was about to stick the needle to him. "Tie a flower or a guitar or something to the antenna, so this Pasco will know you're only half-converted to reality."

Thermopolis gave Ben a dirty look, nodded his head, and walked off, muttering under his breath about fascists and dictators and the like.

"Better yet," Ben called, "take Emil with you. That would really set you apart."

Thermopolis turned and gave Ben the finger.

Linda had stood quietly, watching and listening to the exchange. "You really like him, don't you?"

"Oh, sure. What's not to like? He thinks I'm full of bullshit and I know he is, so we get along. We've had some spirited debates over the months. He certainly doesn't agree with everything I do, but he's realist enough to know that the Rebel movement is the only thing standing between order and anarchy."

Linda said, "But the East, for the most part, is safe now. He could take his followers and leave, go back to the commune ways and live in peace."

Ben smiled. "Yes, he could. But he won't. That's why I know he's spouting bullshit. Don't kid yourself, he's in this fight to stay. He'll tell you he's with us to see the country in the only reasonably safe way. Safety in numbers, and all that. But he'll be with us when we hit Northstar, and he'll be with us when we sail for Europe. Part of his motive will be his insatiable curiosity, and another part will be that in his brain, if not in his heart, he knows that what we're doing is right. Brutal and savage, but right." Ben chuckled. "Although he'll never admit it and will argue to his dying day that I'm wrong."

"Just like you would never admit it if you are wrong about him?"

"Of course, I wouldn't. That's why we're friends."

"Praise be to Ben Raines, the Supreme Commander of all forces that are right and just and good on this granite planet!" Emil Hite shouted, bouncing into the perimeter.

"Oh, God!" Ben muttered.

"Once more, justice and goodness has prevailed," Emil said, walking up to Ben.

"Right, Emil," Ben said.

"But we shall be benevolent conquerors. We shall heal the sick and offer solace to the bruised minds of those who have been enslaved."

"Right, Emil."

"The mighty army of Ben Raines rolls on, bringing liberty and justice to all." Emil began to sing the "Star-Spangled Banner." Smoot began to howl in protest. Emil looked at her looking at him. "Tin ear!"

"That's very good, Emil. But you're going to herniate yourself if you keep trying to hit the high notes."

"I've been practicing."

Ben eyeballed Emil's latest getup. Emil had long ago abandoned his flowing robes for military battle dress, but whenever he was outside of a combat area, he also wore a turban and cowboy boots. He had recently begun carrying two pearl-handled, nickel-plated six-shooters, tied down like an Old West gunfighter. But for all his eccentricities, Emil had proven himself in battle, time after time, and Ben respected the little man for that. But he still considered Emil to be a tad off the wall.

"Where's Therm going, General?"

"To visit some hippie friends of his in a commune south of here."

"Oh, neat-o! You think he'd mind if I went along?"

"You can go if he asks you, Emil. But don't bug him about it. On second thought, you'd better stay here. I, uh, need you."

"You need *me?"* Emil rose to his full height of about five-five. "I am at your service, *mon general.* Your wish is my command. Ask, and I will obey without hesitation."

Ben was thinking hard, aware of Linda's amused look. "Uh, right, Emil. Listen, I want you to, ah . . . I want you to make certain that Therm and his bunch check out Hummers from the motor pool and that they have a good radio with them. Also make certain they have enough rations for several days. Will you do that for me, Emil?"

Emil sprang to attention. "Yes, *sir!* I shall see to that at once."

"Thanks, Emil."

Emil whirled around, almost tripping over his high-heeled cowboy boots, and went running off to find Thermopolis.

"Your friend Thermopolis is not going to like this," Linda said.

"He'll get over it." Ben grinned, softening the hard planes of his face and taking years from him. "Besides, he's used to me shoving Emil at him."

Ben looked toward the town of Redding from his position at the airport. The small city was no

51

more. The Rebels had set firebreaks to keep the flames from spreading, then moved back and let it burn.

"It seems like such a waste," Linda remarked.

"There are only so many commodes, so many brass fittings, and so many bathtubs and kitchen sinks we can use, Linda. And we have enough stockpiled around the nation to outfit several million more people, and there are still millions more in empty homes and buildings. And we're also eliminating another place for outlaws to stay. Linda, we have warehouses filled to the overflowing with every part and gidget you could name, and some that you couldn't. We probably have half a million or more car and truck engines. We have enough spark plugs to stretch from here to the moon and back, and enough panty hose to completely wrap the earth."

She laughed out loud at that.

"You see, after the Great War, we started what was probably the greatest scrounging effort ever undertaken by humankind. Since so many of us were ex-GI's and ex-intelligence officers, we knew where the underground storage facilities were all over the nation. We filled them up. The Rebels have all the gold, all the silver, all the precious gems, all the great paintings . . . you name it, and we have it."

"And it was your idea?"

He shrugged. "Part of it, I guess. Excuse me." He waved for Corrie to come over. "Corrie, have Leadfoot establish a CP at Beale AFB outside of Marysville and wait for us there. I know where there are some goodies to be had there. Providing somebody else hasn't got them."

Linda glanced at him. "I thought you said your storage facilities were all filled up."

Ben smiled. "These are sealed chambers, concrete and steel bunkers, set deep in the earth, that contain weapons, equipment, and MREs."

MR . . . what?"

"Meals, Ready-to-Eat. Wouldn't you like a break from Doctor Chase's highly nutritious and nearly totally unpalatable homemade goop?"

"Not to take anything away from the doctor, but yes, I would. What does he put in that stuff?"

"It's his secret. His lab people won't even tell me. Which is fine. I'm not sure I want to know."

"General, you want to know a truth about Doctor Chase's field rations?"

"Sure?"

"They taste like shit!"

Ben threw back his head and laughed. "Welcome to the Rebels, Linda."

Chapter Four

The Rebels pulled out the next morning. Vultures were circling high in the sky, sensing there was food far below them, but unable to spot the buried bodies with their sharp eyes.

The convoy traveled as far as Red Bluff, and Ben ordered the Rebels to stand down and start cleaning up the town. "Nice-sized little place," he remarked, after inspecting the town. "And the airfield is in pretty good shape. This would make a dandy outpost. Corrie, see if you can raise Thermopolis on the radio."

After a moment, she handed him the mike. "This is Eagle, Therm. Did you find your lost peace-and-love generation?" He winked at Linda as he said it, envisioning the frown on Therm's face.

"Yes, I did, Eagle."

"Thank you for reporting in, Therm."

"Sorry about that. I truly am. I just forgot."

"Therm, I won't belabor the point. But I was about to send troops in after you. Some of Pasqual's bunch might have gotten hurt."

"Pasco!"

"Whatever. Therm, ask your friends if they know where any survivors might be who would like to help us set up an outpost here in Red Bluff. The town is the right size and everything else about it checks out."

"As a matter of fact, they do. Ben, they know where there are about three hundred people living. They're all in small groups and looking to reestablish what they consider to be normal living."

Ben laughed at that. Linda had been listening over the speaker and had a confused look on her face. Ben said, "What Therm means is that these are the types of people who get regular haircuts, in addition to liking life under rules and regulations and saluting the flag and things of that nature."

"He doesn't like an orderly life?"

"Of course, he does. For a commune to work, they have to have rules and regulations too. He's just needling me." Ben lifted the mike. "Send them on their way, Therm. We'll be waiting for them."

"That's ten-four, Ben. Pasco says they are basically good people for straights."

Ben laughed. "I'd like to meet Pasco."

"He says thanks, but some other time."

"Okay, Therm. You can all go on back to listening to that horrible music."

"How in the hell did you know? . . . Oh, never mind. Old Hippie out."

Linda looked at him. "How *did* you know what they were doing?"

"I guessed. But don't ever tell Thermopolis that."

The first of the survivors in that area of northern California began arriving late that afternoon. They by no means appeared to be a beaten-down bunch, for they were well-armed and carried their weapons like combat-ready troops. They were just tired and very wary. Chase had set up his MASH and was ready to receive them, taking the children first, then the women, then the men.

While the kids were being examined and receiving the first of many inoculations for childhood diseases, Ben met with the leaders of a few of the small groups.

"Pasco radioed us and told us you were in the area," a man said. "We just couldn't believe it. It's been tough, General. Moving every three or four weeks, always trying to stay one jump ahead of the outlaws."

"They are that strong?"

"Sir," another man said, "I'm not being critical, so please don't take it that way. You had to move in some direction; it's only logical that the outlaws would move in the other, getting away from you. They had us outmanned and outgunned. In this area alone there were once—not that many months ago—a dozen settlements, all doing well. Then the outlaws from the east joined up with those in L.A. and San Francisco. I'd say a conservative figure would be between five thousand and eight thousand men, women, and kids have either been killed or captured over the past year."

"You are aware of what the outlaws are, or were, doing with the prisoners they took?"

The man spat on the ground. "Oh, hell, yes! Now let me tell you something that you probably don't know. The largest concentration of Believers in the lower forty-eight is in—"

"The Los Angeles area," Ben said, interrupting with a smile.

The men shared a laugh. "Well, you did know."

"We guessed. The few prisoners we took up in Redding confirmed that. Right before we shot them."

The man studied Ben for a moment. "That's why Pasco will never be a part of your group, General. He thinks you and your people go too far."

"That's his right. There are others who agree with him. And they do not and never will receive any help from us, in any way, shape, or form."

"Pasco knows that. Thermopolis is trying to change his mind."

"What do you think his odds are of doing that?"

The man moved his right hand in a waggling motion. "Not too good, General."

"What's Pasco's problem?"

The man stared and studied Ben for a moment, then stuck out his hand. "I'm Les Word."

Ben shook the hand. Hard and callused.

"Why does Pasco have to have a problem, General?"

"Isolating oneself away from any type of open society tells me a lot. And the Rebels do have an open society. A dozen things come to mind, Les: dropout drug users wanted by the law, when there was a law; malcontents; a land-baron mentality; benevolent king . . . which one fits Pasco?"

"Which one fits you, General?" Les asked with a smile, no back-down in the man.

"Oh, even though I didn't ask for this job—I ac-

57

tually ran away from it for six months—I don't know that any of those descriptions fit me. You see, Les, Rebels know the rules—and in our society there are very few gray areas between right and wrong—and we—*we*—obey the rules. Very rarely does anyone come to me with a legal problem."

"Neat job of sidestepping, General," Les said. "Actually, none of those things you mentioned fits Pasco either. He's really a lot like you. He just places a lot more value on human life—even the degenerate type—than you do."

"And how many times has Pasco been burned believing that? How many of his followers have been killed or wounded or assaulted because of that belief?"

Les smiled faintly. "More than one."

"I don't intend to subject my people to that danger, Les. Let's run it down. Pasco sets up a little empire and isolates his commune from the outside world. The only type of music they will listen to is so-called protest music from thirty or more years ago—not that there is anything wrong with that, I just find it a bit restrictive—their debates are so old and out of step with reality they creak with age. Their generation began and glorified the drug plague that nearly overwhelmed the nation a decade back, and none of them will admit they had anything to do with it. No, Les, Pasco and I have nothing in common."

Les shrugged his shoulders. "He's also afraid that you'll find out where he and his people live and come in after them."

"He's paranoid too. Do you think I would do

something like that, Les?"

"No. And I told him so. You've let the Underground People and the Woods Children alone. I pointed that out to Pasco. He wasn't convinced."

"Then to hell with him," Ben said flatly. "I'm not going to bother Pasco and his followers as long as they leave me alone. There are probably several hundred—or more—communes scattered around the nation, people who just want to be left alone. And I intend to do just that. I most definitely will leave them alone. One hundred percent totally alone and on their own in all respects."

"You won't help them at all?"

"That is correct, Les. Back when the world was functioning, more or less, I had nothing but contempt for dropouts who, for example, when they needed medical attention suddenly decided that maybe they could conform just a little and oh, so magnanimously on their part allowed the conforming taxpayers to pick up the tab. And then they went back to their communes, or living under bridges, or wherever, and laughed and poked fun at the very people and the system that had just helped them by paying their bills. Sorry, Les. People like Pasco and his followers aren't contributing a damned thing to the rebuilding of this nation. They want to step out every now and then and eat the fruit, but they don't want to help in the hard work of cultivating it. To hell with them."

Ben walked away, and Les and the other men looked at Beth and Cooper, standing nearby. "I guess if I say that Ben Raines is a hard man, you're going to tell me that hard men are needed in hard times."

59

Beth winked at him. "And hard women too, Les."

Thermopolis and those who had gone with him to visit Pasco returned the next day. Ben noticed the long-haired and colorfully dressed Therm seemed withdrawn and silent.

Ben walked over and sat down beside him on the tailgate of a truck. "What's wrong, Therm?"

Thermopolis cut his eyes. "You've been a bad influence on me, Ben. With Pasco and his people, I found myself in the unenviable position of defending you and the Rebel movement."

"You didn't have to do that."

"Oh, I know that. But the thing that bothers me is, in many cases—not all, but many—I *wanted* to."

"I've told you before, Therm, there is not fifteen cents worth of difference between us. We both want peace and a chance to live out the remainder of our lives in some degree of happiness and security. The difference between us and people like Pasco is that we're willing to fight and sacrifice for it."

"Maybe you're right," Therm said with a sigh. "But I'll always maintain that Pasco is a good person."

"I won't argue that. I'm sure he has many good qualities just like I have many bad ones. But Therm, nice guys don't win wars. SOBs like me win wars. Real nice gentle sweet people don't make good cops or good CEOs or Chairmen of the Board. Real nice idealistic folks can't run the governments of nations. It takes a person with a cer-

60

tain amount of hard-ass in them to do that. And I knew you had it in you after I'd talked with you for five minutes."

Therm stared glumly at the ground for a moment. "That doesn't say much for me, then."

"That depends on who is doing the viewing, buddy."

Ben gave the orders for Ike to continue down the coastline highway and for Cecil to split off and take 101 down to Ukiah. He told Colonel Gray to take his people down the Interstate, while Ben and his contingent split off and headed down Highway 99, through Chico, Oroville, Yuba City, and Marysville, then finally over to the old AFB. Five and Six Battalions, under the command of Striganov and West, would continue their sweep for survivors and link up with Ben on Interstate 80, northeast of Sacramento.

"There were almost a million people in Sacramento when the Great War hit us," Ben told his immediate team as they rode slowly southward toward Chico. Every little town they passed through showed signs of having been abandoned recently, and in one hell of a hurry. "Flyovers using heatseekers have shown a very large concentration of people in the city. Leaflets we dropped telling them to identify themselves have been ignored. Prisoners have told us the city is filled with creepies. So far this push into California has been a cakewalk. But all that is about to change, people."

"How big was Chico?" Cooper asked.

"A little over twenty-five thousand," Beth said

61

from the center seat of the big wagon. She sat with
Jersey. Corrie and Linda were in the third seat of
the wagon, Corrie with her radio jacked into the
antenna on top of the wagon. "But Leadfoot
radioed that the town is deserted."

"How about San Franciso?" Linda asked.

"We'll take it," Ben said. "But we're going to have
to get close to do it. We won't be able to stand on
the east side of the Bay and shell it—the Bay is
too wide. Our 155 SPs have a range of about
twelve miles. We'll be able to shell in from the
north and south ends, that's all. Once we soften up
those areas, the rest will be block by block and, in
many cases, hand to hand."

"Sacramento?"

"We'll be able to surround it and shell it, for the
most part. L.A. is going to be a real bastard,
though."

"Huge, sprawling place," Beth said. "About sixty
miles wide and forty miles deep."

Cooper whistled softly. "No way in hell we can
surround that place."

"Not completely," Ben said. "But we can split our
forces and attack from three sides. But it's going to
be a very long, bloody, and drawn-out process."

"Is it going to be like the taking of New York
City?" Linda asked. "I've heard so many Rebels say
that was a real tough one."

"L.A. is going to be worse," Ben said.

The advance teams of Rebels waved them
through the deserted and eerily silenced Chico,
then pulled in behind the convoy as a new advance
team took their place; it was on to Yuba City. Like
Chico, the once-thriving town of nearly twenty

62

thousand was a ghost town. In more ways than one. Just before the outlaws and thugs had pulled out, they'd killed all their prisoners rather than have to drag them along. The bodies of dead men, women, and kids were piled in heaps on the sidewalk in the main drag.

"You're seeing another reason why we don't take many prisoners," Ben said to Linda, as he helped her out of the wagon to stand in the deserted street.

A few moans came from the blood-soaked bodies. She jerked away from his grasp and ran to get her medical kit.

"She's got a lot to learn about punks," Jersey said, leaning up against the wagon. "But I imagine she will. If she lives long enough."

The Rebels buried the dead, and chaplain read a short non-denominational service. The wounded were loaded onto trucks for transport on down the road, where Chase would set up a MASH unit for the evening.

Linda was silent as the long convoy of trucks and tanks and self-propelled artillery and Jeeps and Hummers and APCs and Light Armored Vehicles (LAV) named Piranhas rumbled on through the town.

Had any outlaw been so foolish as to remain behind, at the sight of all the Rebel might he probably would have curled up in a nice tight ball and wished for the safety of his mother's womb.

But the Rebels met with no resistance as they rolled through the town and out onto Highway 99.

"Horrible," Linda finally said, gazing out the window at the silent landscape that seemed utterly

63

void of life. "What kind of degenerates are we dealing with?"

"The kind that won't be around much longer," Ben assured her.

Since Thermopolis had already checked out Oroville and found it to be deserted, Ben pressed on toward Marysville and Beale AFB.

Leadfoot had established a CP for Ben on the old base, and he met the convoy bitching. "If there's anything worth takin' on this base, General, I wish you'd show me where it is. This place has been picked over a thousand times."

Ben laughed and patted the biker on the shoulder. "Come on." He walked over to a concrete building about fifty feet long and thirty feet wide.

"There ain't nothin' in that place, General," Leadfoot said. "Me and the boys done checked it out."

"And the girls," Wanda reminded him.

"Right."

"Follow me," Ben said, and the others trooped after him. At the smashed door, he said, "See anything unusual about what is left of this door?"

"It's a sure enough big-ass door," Wanda said. "Big enough for a truck."

"That's right, Wanda. Exactly."

Inside the building, Ben pointed to the roof. "See anything unusual about that roof?"

His personal team, with the exception of Linda, had seen it all before. They knew what he was pointing out and remained silent.

Linda looked up. "Why would anybody build a roof like that? Look at those heavy steel beams."

"See those huge eyebolts?" Ben asked, pointing.

"Cooper, bring a deuce-and-a-half up here and run me some chains, please."

The others stood in silence and watched as Ben, on a ladder, threaded the ends of the heavy chain through the eyebolts, then hooked the chains into two holes in the floor.

Leadfoot got down on his hands and knees and looked. "Well, hell! There's heavy steel rods embedded in the concrete. I'll be damned."

"Everybody outside!" Ben yelled. "As soon as that slab is lifted, since we're going to violate SOP in opening it, knockout gas will be released. It won't kill you, but it will drop you to the ground for about an hour. We have to use generators to pump out the tunnels before we enter. Back the truck up, Coop. Let's open it up."

Everyone backed outside and, at Ben's orders, slipped into gas masks. Cooper put the big deuce-and-a-half in grandma and backed up, the chains tightening, and the concrete slab howled in protest at being opened after all these years.

Generators were brought up and the tunnel was pumped out. Ben, flashlight in hand, led the way down the steps into a cornucopia of supplies. Hundreds of crates, sealed tightly and dated, lined both sides of the wide corridor, floor to ceiling, further than Ben's flashlight beam could reach.

"Take what we need for this run," Ben ordered. "Then we'll reseal the opening and cover it, and pick up the rest on our way back."

"How many more of these caches are there?" Linda asked, after having found a long floor-to-ceiling row of medical supplies.

"Several hundred that I know of," Ben said. "I've

65

only found the need to open a few of them."

"How many rounds of ammo you reckon is in here, General?" Wanda asked.

"Several million, I would imagine."

"Jesus!" Beerbelly, one of Leadfoot's men yelled, from a dark end of the corridor. "We got Jeeps and trucks and all sorts of vehicles down here." He walked back to the group. "The big door you pointed out."

"Right. Of course, there are fifty buildings just like this one on the base. Deliberately so."

"How did you know which building to come to?" Wanda asked.

Ben grinned. "I didn't. I guessed!"

Up long before dawn the next morning, Ben, coffee mug in hand and Jersey with him, as usual, went down to the highway to look over the newest addition to the Rebel army. The Piranha LAV, one nasty fighting machine. The Marines had had them in use for a few years prior to the Great War, and scrounging Rebel patrols had found where they had been warehoused. Hundreds of them.

This campaign would be the first Rebel combat test of the LAVs.

The main reason the Rebels had not fielded the Piranhas prior to this was that the crews had to be trained from scratch on the machine. Not only were the Piranhas deadly instruments of war, they were also sophisticated machines, and could carry six infantry personnel into battle in addition to their crew of three.

Some Piranha mounted a 25mm automatic cannon, others were equipped with a 90mm cannon, and still others were refitted with 30mm Gatling guns. The Piranha had eight wheels and four axles, and that made it an 8x8. It could travel on hard surfaces at speeds up to sixty-five miles an hour, hit rivers at speeds up to thirty miles an hour, and swim along at nearly seven miles an hour.

Ben grinned in the predawn darkness. He patted the armor-plated side of the Piranha. "Slick, huh, Jersey?"

Jersey reserved comment; she had something else on her mind. "Since I know damn well you're going to get right in the thick of any battle, General, how many of these things are you assigning to us?"

Ben laughed softly. "Three of them, Jersey. So rest your mind. 25mm, 90mm, and one with 30mm Gatling gun."

Jersey, using a penlight, jotted that down. "I'll hold you to that, General."

Ben chuckled at her antics. She was looking after his safety and he knew it and appreciated it.

"Let me get this straight," Jersey said, flipping a page in her notepad. "This thing we're standing next to has the 25mm Bushmaster cannon, right?"

"That's right."

"It can be fired single shot, or full auto, up to two hundred rounds per minute."

"That's it. Impressive, huh, Jersey."

"We'll see. And I imagine we'll see up close. In addition it has one 7.62 machine gun, one .50-caliber machine gun, and two M257 smoke grenade launchers."

"You got it."

"That's a lot of firepower, General."

"I had the personal safety of my team in mind when I ordered them up, Jersey."

Jersey closed her notepad, looked at Ben, and burst out laughing. She walked away, still laughing.

Smiling, Ben called, "See, this is what I get for being such a nice guy!"

That brought on another round of laughter from Jersey. She waved a hand and kept on walking, heading for the coffeepot in Ben's CP.

The commander of the LAV walked up, a cup of coffee in his hand.

"How do you like the Piranha?" Ben asked him.

"Love it. We put them through their paces on the way out here, General. It's a fine machine and they'll do everything they're built to do."

"Did you have a firefight?"

"Several of them. Bunch of punks hit us in Kansas. We blew them clean off the highway. That 30mm Gatling gun is one mean son of a bitch."

"What was your best fuel-conserving hard-surface speed?"

"About forty five miles an hour. At that speed, we can range about four hundred miles a tank. But we're limited in their use because of the lack of crews for them."

"I understand. We're training as fast as we can." Ben thumped the side of the LAV. "Did our engineers beef up this armor?"

"They sure did. We caught a 14.5 rocket and it didn't even leave a dent. Just rocked us some inside."

Ben nodded his approval. "Get the others ready

to go. We're pulling out at 0500."

The LAV commander was anxious to show his stuff. "Are we spearheading, General?"

"Some Piranhas are. But don't worry, you'll get to see plenty of action."

"How's that, sir?"

"You're with me."

"All right!" the LAV crew chief said. "All *right!*"

Chapter Five

"Where are the eastern units?" Ben asked Corrie.

"Set to go. Colonel West has swung around and is in place just south of the city. General Striganov is holding at Placerville, waiting for orders."

"Ike and Cecil?"

"General Ike is just north of Santa Rosa and General Jeffreys is waiting just north of Napa. All units are ready."

"Get everyone in the wagon."

"They're ready, sir."

"All right, let's do it."

The long column was stretched out on Highway 70. Scouts and other forward recon units were already in place just north of the city, with West's people in place just south of Sacramento.

Ben got in the wagon and shut the door. He looked behind him. Smoot was curled up on the center seat, between Beth and Jersey.

"Give the orders to move out, Corrie. Let's go, Coop."

"What's our position this time, General?"

"Right behind the spearheaders. Get around all these others."

"And here we go," Beth muttered.

Breaking dawn found all Rebel units outside their objectives and ready for the attack. Ben got out of the wagon to stand for a moment in the cool, early morning air. The start of the most ambitious campaign ever undertaken by the Rebels was only seconds away from kicking off.

"Corrie, what does Leadfoot and his bunch report about the airport?"

"Filled with stinking creepies."

"Tell him to take the field." That transmission sent and received, Ben said, "Tell all units to launch attack."

Rolling thunder split the morning as artillery batteries opened up north, south, and east of the city. To the west of Sacramento, Ike and Cecil began their attacks, softening up their objectives with waves of artillery. The ground trembled under the boots of the Rebels as the artillery pounded the city with HE, WP, and napalm, the shells whistling and humming overhead.

Ben waved to his XO. "Take over here. I'm moving my section and securing McClellan AFB." To Corrie: "Tell Dan to get his people moving. We'll link up at McClellan. Dusters and LAVs out. Let's go."

Cooper cut east, with Interstate 80 to the south of them, and headed for the old Air Force base. They crossed Marysville Boulevard and ran into a roadblock they could not breech.

"Get a Duster up here, Corrie," Ben said.

A Duster pulled up and began hammering at the roadblock with 40mm cannon fire. Outgunned, those left alive at the barricade abandoned their dead and wounded and pulled back, cutting south toward the Interstate.

"Let them go," Ben said. "Coop, get us to the base."

Cooper rolled through the east gate of the base, right behind a main battle tank that had pulled ahead of them. The tank busted through a wooden barricade, crushing several creepies who thought they might be able to stop the tank with small-arms fire. They were wrong. The treads left several bloody smears on the concrete and rumbled on.

The tank led the way across what Ben guessed might once have been a parade field, and then brought them into a complex of old buildings.

"Out!" Ben yelled. He bailed out of his side of the wagon, M-14 in hand. "Tuck the wagon behind a building and join us, Coop," Ben said, then grinned and added, "And leave some water for Smoot."

The Husky pup, although battle-hardened and accustomed to loud booming noises, had been trained to get down on the armor-plated floorboards and stay put.

Shots kicked up dirt at Ben's boots and he made it to the door of an old building, Jersey right behind him. He kicked in the door and went in, the Thunder Lizard set on full rock and roll, Jersey's M-16 clattering along with it.

A smelly creepie reared up in front of Ben, his unshaven face a mask of hate and perversion. Ben lifted the muzzle and blew the man's face into several corners of the room. He stepped over the cooling, twitching body and pointed to a closed door.

Jersey nodded and moved to one side of the door, a grenade in her hand. She pulled the pin and held the spoon down.

Ben blew the doorknob off with .308 slugs. The door yawned open and Jersey released the spoon, tossing the Fire-Frag grenade into the stinking room. A few screams gradually faded into silence.

Ben and Jersey hit the floor as the grenade boomed, sending shock waves through the first floor of the building and sending bloody hunks of creepies in all directions.

Ben both heard and felt footsteps above them, on the second floor. He rolled over on his back and pulled the trigger of his M-14, emptying a full clip of lead into the overhead. He slapped in a fresh clip and got to his boots just as Corrie, Beth, Linda, and Coop ran into the room.

"You're late," Jersey told the group. "You missed all the fun."

Linda's face was pale, but she was hanging in, her Remington 870 sawed-off at the ready, a bandolier of shells looped around her waist.

"Next building," Ben said, stepping into the blood-and-gore splattered room and over the mangled body of a creepie.

"This one is still alive," Linda said, looking down.

"Shoot him," Ben told Coop.

Coop's M-16 barked once and the creepie had no more worries on this earth.

Before Linda could recover from her shock at the execution, the team was out the back door and running hard. Beth jerked her along.

Automatic-weapons fire from the second floor of a barracks building kicked up dirt and rocks at their feet as they ducked behind the foundation of a burned-out building.

"Duster up," Ben ordered.

Within seconds, a Duster spun around the side of

the building and opened fire with its 40mm cannon. The old frame barracks began to splinter and smoke under the impacting shells, and the screams of the cannibals inside reached Ben's group. One creep tried to run for safety. Ground fire tore him apart. Another jumped from the second floor. He was riddled with bullet holes before he hit the ground. The building burst into flames.

"Corrie, order all buildings demolished by cannon fire. All capable use Willie Peter."

Main battle tanks began hammering white phosphorus at the old buildings. Creepies with their clothing on fire began running in all directions, screaming as the WP ate holes into their flesh. Ground fire ended their search for safety.

The Rebels took their time, taking it building by building, following the MBTs, the Dusters, and the Piranhas. Behind them and to the south, Sacramento began to burn from the relentless bombardment of artillery.

Inside the besieged city, creepies were frantically radioing to San Francisco and L.A. California was the last great bastion of the Believers, and if they could not stop Ben Raines and his Rebels here, their cause would be lost nationwide. South of the border, in Mexico, the people had banded together, re-formed their army, and were putting Believers up against walls, in front of firing squads. South of San Francisco, creepies began blowing bridges up and down the Interstate. They did not care that they were cutting major arteries; they did not care that the structures might never again be rebuilt. Their only thought was to slow Ben Raines's march toward them. They did not care that they were cutting off their comrades north of San Jose, dooming them. Ben Raines had to be stopped.

The Believers threw up skirmish lines across the state, stretching from the Pacific to the Nevada line. Suicide teams were sent out, their mission: to kill Ben Raines at any cost.

One of General Striganov's radio operators, scanning the frequencies, caught something, backed up, and listened, recording the conversation on tape. Her face paled as she realized the content of the transmission. She sent a runner for General Striganov.

He came at once and listened to the tape, his fists clenched and his face hard. "The bastards! All right. Go to scramble and advise all commanders. I want a screen around Ben at all times. He'll curse and fume and object, but it's the only way. The others will agree with me, I'm sure of that. Go, Neta—hurry!"

The old AFB was declared secure by 1200. The creepie dead were pushed into piles by blade-equipped trucks and set on fire. The stench of burning flesh mingled with the smoke from the burning buildings on the base.

The Rebels had taken yet another step toward clearing southern California.

Ben looked up from a map to see an entire section of Gray's Scouts moving into position all around him. "What the hell is going on here?"

"Colonel Gray's orders, sir," a young Scout said. "He said under no circumstances were we to let you out of our sight."

Ben waved to Corrie. "Get Dan on the horn. I . . ." He turned as Dan's Jeep pulled up in front of the CP and the Englishman stepped out, walking toward him.

Dan neither backed up nor apologized for his actions. He explained his reasons quickly and succinctly. "And there is more, General. My forward recon people are reporting the creepies and outlaws are blowing major bridges on the Interstates all the way across the state, west to east. We're going to be forced to take secondary roads down to Los Angeles."

Ben slammed a fist on the hood of the vehicle. "Damn!" He knew those bridges would never be rebuilt in his lifetime, and possibly never rebuilt at all. Take two steps forward and one step back toward progress and the unrestricted movement of future generations. "They're desperate people trying to buy a little time." He nodded his head. "All right, Dan. I understand the need for all the extra security. I don't like my movements limited, but I understand the reasoning. Let's get reports from all fronts and then call for a face to face with all commanders. We've got to rework our travel plans, so to speak."

Santa Rosa and Napa were burning as Ike and Cecil walked into Ben's CP at the old AFB. Striganov and West had arrived a few minutes before. Ben's kids, Buddy and Tina, were also in attendance. Gunners were still lobbing shells into Sacramento and the city was burning out of control. Rebels had surrounded the city and were picking off any creepie who tried to escape the inferno.

For once, Ben had to sit and listen as others told him what to do.

Cecil Jefferys, second in command of all Rebel forces, laid the law down to Ben.

"I'm shifting Buddy and Tina and their teams to your command, Ben," the black man said. "The section of Gray's Scouts will remain as your security. I won't even suggest that you stay out of heavy combat situations, Ben. However, I can see that you are blanketed with security."

Ben sat, his face impassive.

"I know you don't like it, Ben. But that's the way it's going to be—understood?"

Ben nodded his head.

All present knew that only two people could get away with speaking to Ben in such a manner: the ex-Army Green Beret and the ex-Navy SEAL, Cecil Jefferys and Ike McGowan, men who had been with Ben since the inception of the Rebels.

Cecil turned to Colonel Gray. "I want heavy security around Ben twenty-four hours a day, Dan."

Dan nodded his understanding.

Cecil turned to Buddy. "Buddy, you are to be your father's shadow, understood?"

"Yes, sir," the heavily muscled and handsome young man said. He smiled. "I suppose I can put up with his grouchiness for the duration."

Ben glared at him. "I thought I told you to take that damned bandana off your head and put on a helmet, boy. What are you trying to be, the twenty-first-century Rambo?"

"I have very vague recollections of a movie character by that name," Buddy replied, undaunted by his father's glaring look. "Be that as it may, I am attempting to be no one but myself."

"Hardhead!" Ben grumbled.

"I would say that he comes by it quite naturally,"

General Georgi Striganov said with a smile.

Ben grunted and glared at the Russian. The Russian glared right back.

"All right, all right!" Ike said, standing up, a mug of coffee in his hand. "Let's everybody settle down and work out a battle plan. The blowing of bridges can be discussed after we've taken San Francisco. And we're not going to be able to just walk in there and have the creeps roll over dead. You want to take it, Ben?"

Ben's irritation at his movements being limited had long passed. He saw the need for it and accepted it with a soldier's stoicism. Thermopolis walked in and stood beside Buddy. "You're late," Ben told him.

"I was busy with my afternoon's ablutions," Therm replied. "Hanging one's bare buttocks over a log is uncomfortable. We need more Porta-Potties."

"Fine," Ben said. "Would you like to be in charge of procuring more portable shitters?"

Therm sighed and looked toward the heavens. "Has anything else of great importance been discussed?"

"Father doesn't like my bandana," Buddy said.

"He wouldn't," Therm replied.

"Thank you," Buddy told him. "Perhaps if I had one made of bullet-proof material it would be more acceptable?"

"I doubt it. You'd look too much like a hippie to suit him."

"Goddamnit!" Ike roared. "Will everybody knock it off and let's get down to business?"

"Thank you, Ike," Ben said. He moved to a map thumbtacked to a wall. He pointed a finger at San Francisco and the Bay area. "There is no way we're going to be able to keep the creepies from bugging out south when they figure out what we're doing — or at least a lot of them. We just don't have the forces to do it; we're going to be committed on a lot of fronts. What we can do is prevent them from pulling either north or east. Ike, the bridges at San Rafael and the Golden Gate are yours. It's not going to take much of a force to hold them, but don't spread yourself too thin. I don't want to blow the bridges, but it might come to that. The creepies have probably wired them all to go anyway. We're going to have BART to deal with, the Bay Area Rapid Transit. And we all remember the problems we had with the subways in New York City. I think we'll just use chemicals and to hell with it. Then we'll use explosives to finish the job. Any objections to that?"

Thermopolis summed up the feelings of all. "If it will save Rebel lives, I say go for it." Although he did not mention the possibility of prisoners being held within the city, Therm, like everyone else, knew that in a city, there was no feasible way to get them out without too great a cost in Rebel life. He, like the others, felt that those being held would prefer a quick death to being eaten alive, as many creepies liked their human flesh.

The others nodded their heads in agreement.

Ben made eye contact with everyone in the room, knowing they were thinking, as he was, about any prisoners within the city.

"Okay," he said softly. "I understand. Now then, Cec, you take the Oakland bridges. Georgie, you and Colonel West swing on down here and take the San Mateo and Dumbarton bridges. I'm going to pull my people down and come up through Palto

79

Alto. That's it, people. We start butting heads in the morning."

Ben knew that if the Believers, the Night People—the creepies, as the Rebels had dubbed them—had any sense at all, they would be bugging out of the city right now, regardless of the blown bridges to the south of them. But there was one exit the creepies might think to use that Ben was going to plug. Or try to. He sent for Dan Gray.

"Dan, I want and your people to start working your way over to Half Moon Bay. Blow all these bridges. That will effectively block at least one exit south for the creepies. I'm moving tanks into position now. You can follow them in as far as they go."

"Right, sir."

"Good luck, Dan."

"Same to you, sir."

Dan knew as well as Ben that he could easily get himself trapped in there and be in one hell of a bind.

Ben was staring at the large wall map when Doctor Chase walked in, accompanied by Linda Parsons. Ben turned and smiled at them both.

Chase looked uncomfortable for a few seconds, then asked, "Where do you want my MASH people, Ben?"

"Just behind all forward units, Lamar. Hell, you know that! What's your real reason for coming in here and bugging me?" He softened that with a grin at the crusty doctor.

Chase sighed and rubbed his temples with his fingertips.

"Headache, Lamar?" Ben asked.

"Yeah. Ben, is the city going to be put to the torch?"

"Yes. Unfortunately. I wish it could be saved, but that's impossible."

"And the same with Los Angeles?"

"Yes. Is that what's bothering you?"

"No. It's the highly infectious diseases our people will probably encounter once in the city—cities—proper."

Ben sat on a corner of an old desk. "You have some intelligence you'd like to share with me?"

"Recon brought back some prisoners this morning; they grabbed them last night—you know that. I've had lab people doing blood work. It . . . worries me, Ben."

"AIDS?"

"Well . . . closely related. But resistant to anything we've got. And anything we're likely to have for years. Ben, I'm afraid Los Angeles is going to be the same."

"It's hell fighting in gas masks, Lamar. They restrict vision."

The doctor shook his head. "I don't think it will come to that. But I would advise surgical masks and gloves taped tight on the wrists. As little exposed flesh as possible."

"All right. That will present only a small problem. What else?"

"Anyone with an open wound—however minor—to be used as rear-echelon personnel."

"Done."

"When we establish a toehold, Ben, I would suggest that we use artillery to bring down the city. Try to avoid as much physical contact with the creeps as we can."

"I'll go for that. Fine. I'll have Beth and Corrie send out directives right now."

"Ben?"

Ben met the doctor's eyes.

"I don't want any prisoners taken. No creepies or anyone in the city with them."

Ben arched an eyebrow. For Doctor Chase to suggest something that drastic meant that he was really worried about disease. "Is it that bad, Lamar?"

"Yes. It's that bad, Ben. I want this city destroyed by fire. I don't want anything left, Ben. Nothing."

Ben studied the toe of his jump boot for a moment. He looked up. "Lamar, if you're telling me that the creeps and their associates are infected with some disease that we are powerless to combat, medically speaking, that means that more than likely every creep and associate in this state has the same disease."

"Yes. That is a very good possibility. Carriers, at least."

"Damn!" He turned to Corrie. "You heard it all, Corrie. Get on the horn and advise all unit commanders. They make no moves until we get surgical masks and gloves on every person. Anyone with a wound—no matter how minor—is to pull back to the rear. Get on it, please."

"Do you want Dan to pull out, sir?" she asked.

"No. Tell him to hold up until he and his people are masked and gloved. Tell him to stand down and wait for my orders."

He waited until Corrie had sent the orders out, then said, "I want all our planes, two-engine and above, to start coming in here. Travis AFB is clear. Tell them to land there and come bomb-equipped. Napalm only."

82

"Yes, sir."

To Lamar: "We don't have that many pilots and we don't have that many planes that are equipped for bombing raids. This is going to be quite a jury-rig operation."

"Anything will help, Ben. Los Angeles is what's got me worried. It's such a sprawling place."

"We'll deal with L.A. when we get there, Lamar. Now I'm going to ask a layman's question. How far are we from a vaccine for this disease?"

"Ben, we weren't even close when the Great War hit us. There were so many variants in the AIDS thing, we'd get one whipped and three more resistant strains would pop up. The powers that be back then just would not put the needed money into research; I don't think they realized what a dreadful plague upon the land it really was."

"Or they didn't care. Remember that many of our so-called leaders knew that the power play that led to the war was on the way."

"It's moot now, though, isn't it?"

"Unfortunately. Well . . . this new development is going to delay the attack for a day, maybe two."

"This is also going to let the creepies and the outlaws grow stronger," Buddy pointed out, speaking for the first time since Chase entered the room.

"I know," his father said. "But with this new twist, it can't be helped. Corrie, have our scanners picked up any word on the whereabouts of Khamsin, Villar, and that bunch?"

"Not a peep, sir. Wherever they are, they're maintaining strict radio silence."

"That tells me they're so weak in number they don't want us to find them. We'd wipe them out. We really creamed them in the mountains. We had to have cut their numbers by a good sixty, seventy percent. Maybe more than that. We certainly buried and burned a lot of bodies."

"And then the remainder just drop off the face of the earth?" Chase said. "That doesn't make any sense. Unless they all decided to go straight for a change, and that doesn't seem a very likely probability to me."

"Oh, no, Lamar. They're holed up somewhere, keeping their heads down. You can bet on that. And what is worse is that they'll rebuild quickly. You know as well as I that there are thousands of thugs and punks just waiting for an opportunity to link up with a gang. Sometimes I honest to God think there are more crud than decent people left. Sure appears that way at times. No, we'll just deal with one problem at a time. That's all we can do."

"Like about a million creepies in the Los Angeles area?" Buddy said.

Ben smiled. "Not that many, son. But for sure, we're going to be outnumbered—again."

Chapter Six

Ben stood on the edge of the tarmac at Travis AFB with his mouth hanging open and watching his own new — or old — air force come winging in.

He shook his head, closed his mouth, and turned to Ike. "Ike, where in the hell did the pilots come up with those planes, for Christ's sake?"

Ike laughed and slapped Ben on the shoulder. "They found some of them in museums over in Nevada. The rest came from the old Confederate Air Force in Texas."

"Good God, Ike!" Ben said, laughing as he watched another plane make its approach and come gracefully in for a landing. "That's a B-17!"

"Yep, it sure is. Only two of them in existence — that I know of — and we've got them both. They're both well over fifty years old."

"Oh, yeah," Ben said. *"Well* over fifty years old." He chuckled as he watched two B-25's touch down on the runway. "Ike, what a hell of a way to run a war."

"Yeah, but you know, Ben, that half of our pilots used to be jet-jockeys, but they say they'd rather fight with these old jobs. Look yonder," the Mississippi-born-and-reared Ike said, pointing. "P-51's comin' in."

"And those?" Ben asked, his eyes to the sky.

"Beats the hell outta me, Ben."

"P-40's," Doctor Chase said. "The old Flying Tigers. Hot damn, boys! That is a beautiful sight for these old eyes, I'll tell you that."

"Those planes are over sixty years old!" Ben yelled.

"That's our air force, Ben," Ike said, grinning.

"They should certainly strike fear in the hearts of the creepies," Ben said drily. "If for no other reason than fear of them falling out of the sky and *landing* on them."

Ike got a laugh out of that, then said, "Oh, they've all been reworked, Ben. Hell, there isn't an original part on any of them."

"How about bombs that will fit the racks?"

"Well now," General Georgi Striganov said, walking up and hearing the question. "I must admit, that is a, well, slight problem."

"I'm not sure I want to hear this," Ben said.

"We sort of had to do some home boy engineerin' when it came to that," Ike said, smiling. "But we believe it will work. We'll see in a couple of days, won't we?"

Ben shook his head. "This is going to be good. I can just feel it."

"It will probably revolutionize modern warfare," Ike said, trying to keep a straight face.

"I'm sure. Let's have a practice run." Ben pointed across the tarmac to a field. "Right over there. Now."

Ben watched the bombs leave the bomb bay and hit the ground, reasonably close to the target. The bombs bounced but did not explode.

He looked at Ike. The ex-SEAL grinned. "I think we may have screwed up just a tad. But nothin' that we can't correct."

Ben nodded his head and sat down in a camp chair, thinking that this was a hell of a way to run a war.

The second practice bombing run went off without a hitch—except the bombs missed the target—and Ben smiled as the old World War Two planes came roaring in, dropped their payloads—this time the bombs exploded—and soared gracefully back into the skies.

Many of the Rebels in Ben's command had gathered around, seeing for the first time in their lives the planes that had helped to win a war that was over, for many of them, decades before they were even born.

"They're prettier than jets," one remarked. "It just seems like that's really flying!"

"Do you remember World War Two, General?" a Rebel asked Ben.

Ben laughed and shook his head. "I'm afraid not. I wasn't born when that war was going on. My war was Vietnam. Hueys and Dust-offs and B-52's. Hell, Doctor Chase just barely remembers World War Two, and he's as old as dirt."

Lamar glowered at him while the young Rebels laughed. When the laughter subsided, Chase asked, "Ben, how about the guns on those old Flying Tigers?"

"They had to be reworked or replaced. We couldn't find ammo for the originals. The .303's were pulled off and 7.62's were put in their place. We can't use the synchronized propeller gun at all. The P-51's have six machine guns. All in all, it's going to be a very interesting campaign, I'd say."

Chase said, "All the troops have been assigned gloves and masks."

"Then we jump off in the morning."

Early morning fog still hung low over the coastline when Ben gave the orders to move out. The mighty machine of war called the Rebels surged forward as the Rebels' air force took off from Travis AFB. B-17's, B-25's, P-51's, and P-40's. The old planes that had helped to win the war to end all wars were back in action. And the pilots were not above hamming it up. They wore leather jackets, white scarfs, and baseball caps. Ben had wanted them in more protective headgear, but they were in such high spirits, he decided against making them wear anything except what they wanted to wear.

The bombers roared over the city, dropped their payloads, and returned to base to load up again while the fighters staffed the city streets with machine-gun fire. Since many of the pilots had been crop-dusters before the Great War, they took chances that few World War Two pilots would had ever thought of taking. They tilted their fighters on the wingtips and roared between the tall buildings, machine guns spitting and hammering out lead. They didn't inflict many causalities flying that way, but they sure scared the hell out of a lot of creepies.

Ike, Cecil, Georgi, and West got into position around the city while Ben and his people were stalled between San Jose and Palo Alto and Dan's bunch pushed on toward Half Moon Bay.

It was hard going for those south of the city, for the creepies were grouped en masse against such a move. Dan and his bunch made it across the maze of Interstate interchanges and headed for the Pacific, while Ben and his contingent had to slug it out for every yard gained.

Ben called for Tina. "Kid, take your people and some Dusters. Cut west through what's left of the Stanford University complex. Take Sand Hill road and try for the Interstate. Plug it up."

"Right, Pop. I'm gone." She kissed him on the cheek and ran yelling for her teams to link up.

Ben turned to Corrie. "We've got to punch through and establish a toehold, Corrie. Order main battle tanks in and have them buttoned up tight. I'll use the outside phone."

When the tanks lumbered into position, Ben ran to the side of one and opened the phone box. "Lower your muzzles and blow me a hole through this crap," he ordered. "Then form a protective line for us to follow. Use HE."

Half a dozen of the steel monsters lined up, lowered the muzzles of their main cannon, and blew a hole large enough for an aircraft carrier to move through.

The tanks moved forward, the Rebels following.

The creepies, hoping to swing around and trap Ben, did exactly what Ben wanted them to do.

They swung around and closed off the rear—or thought they did.

"Order the LAVs and Dusters up," Ben said to Corrie. "A and C Companies face the rear, B and D to the front."

The Rebel companies swung around and caught the creepies in a box. The LAV Pirahnas and Dusters pulled out from hiding and went to work. Heavy cannon fire caught the creepies by surprise as Rebels poured out of the LAVs and added automatic-weapons fire to the carnage. When the creepies tried to retreat to the north, they ran into Ben and his rear-facing Rebels.

The Rebels then turned the littered streets into a slaughterhouse.

Over the rattle and boom of battle, Corrie said, "Tina met heavy resistance in the college complex. She punched through and is almost to the Interstate."

"Okay. We've got a toehold. Dan?"

"Colonel Gray is on Highway 92 and is driving hard toward the Pacific."

"Tell him once there to push on up to Moss Point and secure Half Moon Bay airport so we can resupply him at that location. We've got to secure the San Carlos airport, and we've got to do it by tonight. Tell all units to start laying incendiary charges in the buildings behind us. Torch it all down but leave us a rathole in and out. Then get me Ike."

Corrie gave the orders, then handed the mike to Ben.

"Ike here."

"What's your twenty, Ike?"

"Sittin' on the north side of the Golden Gate."

"Can you cross it?"

"That's ten-fifty, Eagle. The creeps have it all wired to blow."

"Just as we thought. They're so single-minded they don't realize that by doing that, they're trapping themselves. Stand by, Ike. Corrie, get me Cecil."

"On the horn, General."

"How's your bridge looking, Cec?"

"Heavily mined."

General Striganov reported. "No way across, Ben. It doesn't leave us many options, does it?"

"No. I'm afraid it doesn't, Georgi. Stand by."

With the rattle of gunfire, the crackle of flames, and the thunder of artillery in the background, Ben muttered, "One of the greatest tributes to engineering ever built."

"Sir?" Corrie asked.

"The Golden Gate Bridge, Corrie. We'll not see the likes of it again in our lifetime. Get me Ike, please."

"You don't want to do this, do you, General?" Corrie asked.

"No, I don't, Corrie."

"General Ike on the horn, sir."

"Ike, blow the bridge. Cecil, Georgi, blow them. Cut the bastards off, then swing around and link up with me."

"That's ten-four, General," the commanders reported in, none of them liking the decision anymore than the man who gave the orders.

The shelling began almost immediately. The exploding rounds activated the charges placed by the

Believers. The charges blew, rocking the morning with destructive thunder. Huge spans of the bridges shattered, breaking off, then slowly dropping into the Bay, sending wild geysers of water high into the air.

"Get me a report from Tina, Corrie."

"She's in position, sir. Blocking the Interstate at Woodside Road."

"Did she report finding anything of value left at Stanford University?"

"Negative, sir. The place had been virtually destroyed. Indications are that all the books were burned."

Ben shook his head in disgust. "Naturally. The first to go are the intellectuals, then the books. Control the minds, and you control the masses. Corrie, tell Georgi and his people to pour on the coals and get in behind us here. When he gets into position, have him spread his people out from 101 to 280, and then give the orders for this command to move out. We've got to take the airport at San Carlos."

Ike intercepted the orders and was on the horn immediately. "Goddamnit, Ben!" he yelled. "If Georgi and West get in a bind, you and your people could be trapped over there."

"Possibly. But not for long," Ben radioed back. "You and Cec burn it all, Ike. Start your push south and search and destroy. Anything left, the . . . bombers," he said with a smile, "can napalm it."

"That's ten-four, Ben," Ike radioed. He didn't like it, and Ben knew it, but Ike would do it.

"We've hit heavy resistance, Ben!" the Russian

called in. "For your safety, you must hold what you have until we can punch through and get in behind you."

"That's ten-fifty, Georgi. We've got to have the airport under our control and the runways cleared by late this afternoon. I'll see you when you get here." Grinning, Ben tossed the mike back to Corrie before Georgi could start roaring like a bear with a thorn in its paw. He turned to Cooper. "Get the wagon up here, Coop. Fall in behind the tanks. Grab your equipment, Corrie. Let's go."

The Rebels stayed between Bayshore Freeway and the Junipero Sierra Freeway and slugged it out with the creepies. The creeps had them heavily outnumbered, but the Rebels had far superior firepower. Ben's people advanced, very slowly, fighting for every foot of ground gained.

Across the Bay, huge columns of smoke began pouring into the air as Ike and Cecil pushed south, burning everything in their path. The Rebels had the search-and-destroy tactics down to perfection, using incendiary charges their lab people had devised that threw white phosphorus and napalm upon exploding. Four charges, separated and placed two inside and two outside, would effectively burn a city block. For added insurance, the prop-driven bombers and fighters came in right on the Rebels' heels, dropping their payloads of napalm, adding more smoke and fire to the inferno that sent plumes of smoke reaching toward the skies.

General Georgi Striganov split his command, taking his personal battalion first west, then turning north and cutting up under Ben, leaving the troops of the Russian Rebet and the French-Canadian Danjou spread out west to east, to block any escape from the creepies trying to flee the flames. As the first of Cecil's troops reached Rebet and Danjou's position, they swung west and once more joined Striganov, beefing up the general's forces.

Dan and his people had reached the Half Moon Bay airport and were hanging on while Tina sent two squads over to Highway 35, blocking that final southern escape route for the creeps.

Ben radioed his daughter. "How's it going, kid?"

"We're hanging on by our fingernails, Pop," she told him. "But for a while it was touch and go. The creeps have been coming at us in human waves. Or subhuman waves," she amended. "I think we're firm now."

"Hang tough, kid," Ben told her. "I've ordered West and his people to push to your location with battle tanks spearheading. He'll split his people and send half over to beef up Dan. Can you hold for an hour tops?"

"That's ten-four, Dad. Can do."

Ben knew the mercenary, West, was in love with Tina, and she with him. Colonel West would be brutal in his advance to get to Tina. The westernmost positions of the Rebels would be secure in an hour.

Ben radioed Ike and Cecil. "We're in pretty good shape here, boys, and getting better. So slow your advance and do the job right the first time. I want everything from Oakland to San Jose put to the torch." He paused for a few seconds, then lifted the mike, sealing the fate of the creepies and anyone closely aligned with them. "No prisoners."

Cecil halted his forces, stretching them out west to east from Alameda to the Warren Freeway, and waited for Ike to join him. He radioed the pilots and told them to take a break until Ike linked up with him and the drive south could be resumed.

Ben halted his drive north and told his tired Rebels to grab a few minutes rest until everyone could get in place. He knew that would give the creeps a chance to regroup also, but his people were weary and needed a break.

Linda came to him carrying two mugs of coffee. Ben accepted one with thanks and took a sip of the hot brew. He looked at the woman. Her face was grimy from the smoke and sweat of battle, but she was hanging in. That was all Ben could ask and expect of anyone.

She looked across the strip of street that had, for the moment, become the unofficial no-man's-land, and was surprised when Ben said, "It won't take long for the wildlife to return to this area."

She cut her eyes to him. *"Wildlife?"*

"Oh, yes, Linda. This entire region is a very important feeding and nesting area for migratory birds on the Pacific flyway. Once we're out of here, their numbers will increase—I hope."

She shook her head and smiled. "Ben." She used his first name for the first time—and that did not escape Ben—as she pointed across the wide area littered with the broken and bloody bodies of stinking creepies. "There are only God knows how many Believers north of us in that city. And you're thinking about *wildlife?"*

Ben sipped his coffee and smiled, amusement in his eyes. "Oh, you'll get used to me, Linda. In

95

each state we reclaim, I set aside several areas for the wildlife to run free — as God intended them to do. A place for wolves and panthers and mountain lions and bears and other predators to once more take their place in God's way of balancing herd populations —"

A burst of gunfire from the creepie side of the street broke into their conversation. A Rebel tank clanked around, lowered its cannon, and put an end to the gunfire. A creepie staggered out of the rubble and a Rebel cut him down with one shot.

"Then you're opposed to hunting?" Linda asked, after a sip of coffee.

"Oh, no. Not at all. Never have been. Back before the war, in many instances, it was necessary to keep the animals from starving to death. But now, with the human population cut by probably sixty percent, sport hunting is no longer necessary. Hunting for food is another matter entirely." He looked up and lifted a walkie-talkie. "Creeps setting up on the roof of that building ten o'clock from my position in front of the bank building. Blow the top off that building, please."

Linda could not help but notice that he gave the orders with about as much emotion as she'd once used in ordering a hamburger at a fast food restaurant.

Four main battle tanks lifted the muzzles of their cannon and the entire top of the building was blown away. Mangled bodies of creepies were tossed into the air and fell spinning to the street below.

"General?" Corrie said, moving to his side. "Colonel West has reached Tina's position."

Ben checked his watch and smiled. "Damn! He must have grown wings and flown over there. Ain't love grand? All right, Corrie, tell the troops ten more minutes and then we butt heads again."

Thermopolis walked up, after darting and dodging his way through the unprotected areas of the street. The aging hippie did not like all the killing, but despite his bandana, now covered by a helmet, and his colorful clothing, now replaced by battle dress, and his penchant for arguing with a stump, he knew that if peace were ever to once more reign over this land, thus enabling him to take his followers back to the commune, the common enemy must be destroyed. Therm and his group, now battle-tested, had proven to be fine soldiers.

"Rosebud is taking care of Smoot and Chester," Therm said, referring to his wife and to Ben's husky and Dan's mutt. "I pulled my bunch up close. They're grouped on both sides of the street directly behind this position."

"Good," Ben said. "As soon as the tanks have loaded up full we'll take another block. You've learned tactics quickly, Therm. You'll make a fine commander."

"That'll be the damn day," the hippie said promptly.

Ben smiled.

"Everyone reporting in position, sir," Corrie said, after acknowledging the radio calls.

Ben looked at his watch. "Five more minutes. Corrie, check on Dan, please."

"More tanks just busted through to his position, sir. The airport is secure."

"Good. Tell the transport pilots to warm their

engines and get ready to resupply him. Advise Dan they are now under his orders and to take it from this point."

"Yes, sir."

The transport planes would fly first south, then cut west around the fighting, and once over the Pacific, would turn northeast before making their final approach to the small airport.

All major arteries out of the city of San Francisco were now blocked by the Rebels. The creepies could use the sea to escape, but Ben, knowing how shortsighted they were, doubted if the leaders of the Night People had worked up any plans for that eventuality.

There were no bridges left connecting San Francisco to the mainland. To the north and east of the city, flames and smoke faced the creepies. To the south, Ben Raines and his Rebels were massing.

Inside the city, the Believers were frantically radioing for assistance, all the while knowing there was no escape for them and no help coming. Their pleas were met with a cold and uncaring silence from their comrades to the south. Every group living outside the city that had been aligned with them had fled south, setting up skirmish lines to slow the Rebel advance once the city by the Bay was finished and that damnable Ben Raines turned his army southward.

"All right," Ben said. "Let's do it." And the Rebels opened fire with small arms, mortars, cannon, and rockets.

From the Pacific eastward to the San Francisco Bay the land exploded in flames and smoke and death as the Rebel gunners laid down a field of rolling artillery fire. Ben and his forward contingent moved north another burning block. They ignored the cries from wounded creeps. It was not difficult for them to do. All had seen firsthand the savagery and brutality of the cannibalistic tribes called Believers. The wounded creeps had very quickly learned to still their cries for help. Their pleas for mercy got them quick and cold compassion from the muzzle of a Rebel weapon.

Everything in the Rebels' path was put to the torch as soon as it was cleared of enemy troops. Only the roads were left intact. The smoking rubble left no place for the creeps to hide. When they tried to run, they were cut down; if they remained where they were, hoping to avoid Rebel detection, they were either crushed to death under the treads of tanks or burned alive.

The Believers practiced a barbaric and savage way of life, and the Rebels gave them exactly that on their way to death. Many of the creeps had heard how ruthless Ben Raines was. Most did not believe it. Most expected to be taken prisoner and housed and fed and their wounds attended to. Then, when the Rebels had left, the creeps could resume their hideous way of life.

The creeps soon learned, very quickly and quite painfully, that Ben Raines had absolutely no intention of allowing their way of life to continue. Many of the creeps began to curse their leaders for getting them into this predicament. But their leaders did not do it. Just as with the criminal who tries to blame society for his misfortune, that worn-out excuse was not acceptable. They were forced to face the fact that as individuals they were solely to blame.

Two more blocks were taken, and Ben and his battalion linked up with Tina and West at Woodside. Behind them, what was left of Menlo Park was obscured from view by the flames and the smoke that soared into the skies.

"All artillery up to this position," Ben told Corrie. "All planes capable of carrying payloads resume dropping napalm on the city. Group all my people on 101. We're moving toward the airport right now."

Corrie relayed the orders and Ike came on the horn. "Lots of creepies over that way, Ben."

"There won't be in about two hours," Ben told him. "Let's go, people. My next CP will be on the tarmac of the San Carlos airport."

Chapter Seven

Heavy machine-gun fire stopped the advance of Ben's team in Redwood City.

"Forward observers out," Ben ordered. "And tell them to get it right the first time. We're too close for mistakes."

They were so close that the ground beneath their feet began to tremble as the 105's and 155's pounded the target area just ahead of them. With a range of twelve miles, the huge 155mm self-propelled howitzers dropped in high explosives with deadly accuracy. The 90mm cannon that some Piranhas were equipped with began barking and biting as the 81mm mortars rained in death. The air over the heads of the Rebels began howling and fluttering and screaming as the deadly mail started arriving in the city.

With one long block turned to bloody rubble, the FOs called in corrections and the Rebels moved forward as the gunners corrected elevation and began a new onslaught. The creeps were shoved back, back toward the burning city north of them.

"We're going to shove them all the way back into the city proper," Ben told those around him. "Then we're going to seal it off, west to east, and start tossing incendiaries in on them. But we've got about twenty miles of hard slogging to go before we can do that."

Beth was doing some fast figuring with a hand calulator. "The city is about eight miles wide and about that deep, if we plan to push all the way up to Daly City. Our artillery will handle that easily."

Ben studied an old map of the region. "Let's take another block, gang."

The Rebels clawed their way through the rubble that littered the streets. Ben and his contingent stayed along 101 while General Striganov and his people crossed over and started up 280. Rebet and Danjou and their battalions began punching up the area between the two main highways.

It was grim, slow work. Artillery would soften up a block, then the Rebels would move forward, working building to building, house to house, oftentimes engaging in very close combat. Since the creepies were so highly infectious, and Ben did not want his people needlessly exposed to some dreadful, uncurable disease, he soon called a halt to the advance, along all fronts.

Ike and Cecil were across the Bay, slowly burning their way south, destroying everything in their path.

"Get Georgi on the horn for me, Corrie," Ben said. "Something's got to give here and it isn't going to be us."

The Russian who had once been a mortal enemy of the Rebels came on the radio. Years back Ben and Georgi had fought each other from the Mississippi River to the northern California coast.

"We're going to have to hold up, Georgi. We just can't risk infection. Some of our people are getting blood-splattered from close-in fighting. Hold what

102

you've got until we can get flame-tossers up here for the troops and give those tanks with the capability time to fuel up."

"I am in complete agreement, Ben. I'll stand my people down immediately."

The Rebels broke for a well-deserved rest while trucks ran the burning and rubbled streets bringing in backpack flamethrowers for the troops and mix for the tanks.

"Still plan on making the San Carlos airport by this afternoon, General?" Cooper asked.

"You bet, Coop." A dozen main battle tanks rumbled up, hatches closed. Ben used the outside phone on the lead tank. "You flame-equipped?"

"That's ten-four, sir."

"Spearhead us." He hung up and turned to Cooper. "You bring the wagon up, Coop. I'm going ahead on foot. Let's go!"

His team spread out behind the tanks and followed them in. The bodyguards assigned to protect Ben could do nothing to stop him. How do you tell the commanding general he can't do something? They fell in with him and surged forward.

The rattle of machine-gun fire came from a building with a faded sign, SPORTING GOODS, painted on the front of the bricks. The slugs howled off the armor of the MBT and the tank clanked around, lowering its cannon. The muzzle spewed liquid fire, engulfing those inside in flames. The screaming of the torched lasted only a moment as their brains cooked and their heads exploded from the buildup of steam inside the skulls.

"Mop up!" Ben shouted, and a team lanced the smoking interior of the old building with automatic-weapons fire.

"Ben!" Linda yelled. "Up the street. North. They're charging us."

Several hundred yards away, the street was clogged with running, screaming creepies, howling their fury as they came in a suicide charge.

A dozen .50-caliber machine guns, a dozen 7.62 machine guns, a hundred M-16's, one shotgun, and one old Thunder Lizard—caliber .308, in the hands of Ben Raines—began yammering. The Believers came in waves of rage and perversion and died in bloody piles of stinking filth.

"Up on the tanks," Ben shouted, jumping up and crouching behind the commander's cupola. "Let's go!"

The tanks all had bags of sand and dirt piled and secured around the turrets, the Rebels jumped on and crouched down as the tanks lumbered forward. They all tried not to listen as the steel treads of the fifty-plus-ton tanks crushed any life left out of the piles of creeps in the street.

They crossed another street and came to a halt. Steel railroad tracks had been welded in sections, completely blocking the street.

The tank commander opened the hatch and poked his head out. "Go around it, General?"

"Negative. It appears that's what they want us to do. The other streets seem clear, so they've probably got them mined. Use HE and punch through."

The commander clanked his hatch shut and Ben hollered, "Get down, people—down!"

From a half a dozen tanks 90mm and 105mm cannon roared and the barricade was ripped apart. Ben cut his eyes upward and then slid off the tank and grabbed up the phone. "Elevate your cannon. The creeps are waiting for us on the rooftops with satchel charges."

Ben stepped out of the way, his team with him, and ducked into the storefront of an old building. The tanks swiveled into position and the street was filled with a deafening roar as the cannons howled. Several Big Thumpers were brought up. The 40mm fully automatic Thumpers began spitting out anti-personnel high-explosive rounds at an astonishing rate of fire. Bodies of creepies began falling off the rooftops and crashing screaming down to the rubbled streets.

"Every other tank use fire," Ben ordered. "Torch the buildings from the ground up and give the bastards a hotfoot. Troops stay behind the tanks. Give me a report, Corrie."

The woman spoke calmly into her headset as the Rebels remained behind the protective bulk of the huge tanks. One creepie charged and Linda gave him some double-ought buckshot in the guts. The creepie folded up and hit the street, howling his life away.

Ben watched her. Linda's face was pale beneath the grime of battle, but she was hanging in as she pumped another round into the sawed-off shotgun.

Ben shouted over the din of battle. "Corrie, tell the troops to seek cover and have the TCs back up their tanks. Let's let artillery bring it down."

Once Ben and his contingent were secure, or at least behind cover, the tanks backed up and added their cannon to the incoming shells. Row after row of buildings began coming apart in explosive flames. Teams working Big Thumpers moved into position and began lobbing rounds into the area that Ben suspected was mined. The 40mm rounds proved him correct as the concussion of the exploding grenades touched off the mines that were to have killed the Rebels.

Ben walked from the storefront into the building itself. Long ago it had been a drugstore. The pharmaceutical section of the store had, of course, long since been looted. Poking around in the rat-and-mouse-chewed remnants of the vials and bottles, Ben found hundreds of pills, precious antibiotics, years out of date. The stupid and greedy people who had looted the store had taken only that which would make them high, or low, depending upon what perverted kick they had been seeking. Uppers and downers—Ben recalled the old slang terms for them. The looters had taken nothing that would have fought infection. So much for the mentality of looters. Ben had always held the belief that once a curfew had been established in an area, looters should be shot on sight. This just reinforced his opinion.

Ben squatted down in the rubble as Linda and Thermopolis and Corrie joined him.

"They took everything to get themselves high," Therm said, poking around the mess with the toe of his boot. "But nothing to help maintain their health. Not even vitamins."

"They weren't concerned about their health when we had a more or less civilized and productive society," Ben said, standing up. "I never understood why law-abiding citizens ever put up with them."

An amused look passed over Thermopolis' face. "Would you have put them up against a wall and shot them, Ben?"

"The pushers, yes," Ben responded quickly. "But not the addicts. Not unless they committed a serious enough crime to feed their habit." He stared at

Thermopolis. "The Rebel philosophy is still to shoot those engaged in illicit drug manufacturing."

"Yes, I know. Ben, did you ever stop to consider *why* people take drugs?"

"Oh, yes," Ben said, as the battle raged outside the trashed store. He smiled. "Like you, Therm, I have an opinion on nearly everything. Whether it is correct or incorrect is yet another story." Ben looked away as a very slight sound came from behind a closed door to his right. The others seemed not to notice it. He shifted his M-14. "Escapism. Unable to face reality. Wanting everything their neighbors had but knowing they would never have it for one reason or another. Laziness. Greed. In many cases the same applied for those who drank to excess. The only difference was, alcohol was legal. For a brief period in my life, I drank to excess. That was just before the Great War. But I didn't do it because I was afraid of reality. I did it because I liked the taste—I still do. It helped me sleep—it still does. And it was legal. It still is. When I can afford the luxury, I still enjoy a drink or two before dinner. Dinner being what it is in the field," he added with a smile, "it helps to hide the taste."

The closed door suddenly burst open and a creepie with a pistol in each hand screamed out. Ben gave the Believer a burst of .308 slugs. The lead knocked the stinking cannibal backward and dumped him in a bloody, torn pile on the floor. He looked up at Ben and with his last breaths, cursed him.

Ben kicked the pistols away from the man's reach. "But after I grew out of my adolescence," Ben said, resuming the conversation as if nothing of any importance had happened, "I never got behind the

107

wheel of a car after I'd been drinking excessively, or in any way endangered the lives of others." The creepie died. "As you have no doubt observed, Therm, during your months with us, any Rebel who drinks to excess and then attempts to drive is punished. The first offense is a mandatory six months in the stockade. It gets progressively harsher. Killing someone while driving drunk is murder, not manslaughter."

"People should be allowed one mistake, Ben."

"Not when they take the life of an innocent person, Therm."

Thermopolis grunted and shook his head. "I would say that you are a hard man, Ben. But you'd just reply that it's a hard time."

"And you'd be right, Therm."

The Rebels hammered and clawed and scratched their way block after block through the small city. Dan, now reinforced, had bulled his way up Highway 1 to just outside of Pacifica. Georgi had slammed his way to just north of Palomar Park on I-280. Tina and her Scouts and West and his mercenaries had advanced up to the junction of Highways 35 and 92.

"Dan is up there all by his lonesome," Ben radioed. "Tina, you and West beef him up. Rebet, pull your people up and reoccupy the area Tina and West are leaving. Danjou, hold what you've got and advance as we do."

As the Rebel troops were shuffled around, plugging up holes and advancing as they did, Ben's people stood down for a well-deserved rest. Beth guesstimated they were about five miles from the

San Carlos airport.

Ben gave his people fifteen minutes to resupply, go to the bathroom wherever they could find a private place, grab a smoke, catch their breath, and then he ordered his people back up and pushing north toward their objective.

Tina and West got to Dan's position just in time. A human wave of creepies tried a bust-out down Cabrillo Highway and the Rebels proceeded to stack them up like broken, bloody sticks of firewood on the Interstate spur.

Cursing and screaming and howling their hatred for Ben Raines and anyone associated with him, a mob of Believers charged Georgi's position on the Junipero Serra Freeway. The Russian asked for no quarter and he and his people sure as hell weren't going to give any. The charge was thrown back and broken, leaving the Interstate and the streets around it littered with bodies and slick with blood.

Working with backpack flamethrowers, his people torched the infectious bodies and burned them crisp, removing all danger of airborne infections. The odor of charred human death clung close to the ground.

Other creepies left the freeway and tried a bust-out through Rebet's position. They didn't make it.

Those Believers on the east side of the embattled area had given up any thoughts of attempting to bust through Ben's territory.

Across the ever-narrowing Bay, Newark and Fremont were now smoking, with huge fireballs leaping into the skies, darkening them with thick smoke, as Ike and Cecil continued to put the area to the torch, working south.

Ben called his son, Buddy, to his position. "Take

your Rat Team and the bikers, son. Take four Dusters and spearhead us to the airport."

With a grin and a nod of his handsome head, the young man ran shouting for his people to mount up.

With the quick little Dusters leading the way, driving four abreast up the Interstate, twin-mounted 40mm cannon capable of spewing out 240 rounds per minute yowling at full auto and .50-caliber machine guns yammering, the Dusters cleared the way, leaving behind them torn and crushed bodies.

A mile from the airport exit, the speadheaders hit a tangle of trucks and cars that blocked the Interstate. Buddy radioed back to his father.

"Exit the highway and get a toehold on the airport, son. I'm right behind you. MBTs will crash the blockade after seeing whether or not it's wired to blow." Ben waved down a Piranha, jumped in, and told the startled driver to get the hell moving toward the airport. Cooper and the others of Ben's personal team piled into vehicles and fell in behind the Piranha.

Several more Piranhas joined Ben's little convoy. Some of these were equipped with 90mm Mecar cannon, while others were equipped with twin-mounted 30mm Gatling guns. The Piranhas pulled in front of the one carrying Ben and began spearheading the drive. The creepies had nothing that would compare with the twin-mounted Gatling guns. They had light mortars, but the convoy was traveling so fast the mortar crews could not make adjustments fast enough to fire with any accuracy. They tried leading the convoy, but the drivers would just exit the roadway, dodging the rounds, then swing back on at the next ramp.

110

Buddy had called back the locations of the hidden pockets of creepies behind machine guns. The 90mm cannon of the Piranhas and the 105s of the MBTs left the machine-gun nests tangles of smoking metal and bits of torn flesh.

"General!" the driver of the Piranha yelled over his shoulder. "Your radio operator says that Buddy is on the tarmac and meeting heavy resistance."

"Pour on the juice," Ben yelled. "Get us there."

The spearheaders reached the airport and Ben bailed out, M-14 in hand, waving for Cooper to follow him as he ran on the edge of the tarmac, heading for the protection of a group of buildings. Unfriendly fire began kicking up dirt at his heels as he ran. A 90mm gunner got the range of the machine gun tracking the general at the same time another Piranha, equipped with a Bushmaster 25mm cannon, did. Between the two of them, not only was the machine gun silenced, but the whole front of the building was torn with cannon fire.

Ben ran in through the back entrance of an old building, the M-14 set on full auto. Creeps spun around, firing automatic weapons, and Ben hit the deck as the lead howled over his head and punctured the wall behind him.

He rolled quickly and grabbed a grenade from his battle harness, pulling the pin with his fingers — he'd seen men lose teeth attempting to Hollywood-it-up by jerking the pin out with their teeth — and chunked the Fire-Frag in the direction of the Believers.

The mini-Claymore blew, and seconds after the explosion sent shrapnel flying, Ben was on his knees, the old Thunder Lizard bucking in his hands. Creepies were knocked back, bloody, smoking holes in their chests, the dust popping from their garments as the slugs impacted.

"Comin' in, General!" Jersey called. "From the rear!"

"Come on in!" Ben called, ejecting the empty clip and filling the belly of the M-14 with a full one.

His team set up positions near the center of the building and began clearing the place of creeps.

"Corrie," Ben called. "Tell the tank and APC commanders to set up left and right of this building. There is a heavy concentration of fire coming from directly across the tarmac."

The front of the building cleared of all living creepies, Ben ran forward, Linda by his side. They plopped to the floor and Ben bi-podded the M-14 and looked at the woman. "Do you wish for the tranquility of your little valley, Linda?" He grinned at her.

"I'd be lying if I said I didn't."

"Someday, Linda. Someday future generations will be able to live without wars, without fear of thugs and punks. But it won't be in our generation, I'm afraid."

There was that sudden, silent, and usually nerve-tightening lull in the battle that almost always meant a counterattack was in the works.

"But it will be because of what you and the Rebels have done, won't it, Ben?"

"I pray so, Linda. When I pray, and I do pray, I pray for guidance and—"

Long bursts of automatic weapons fire cut Ben's statement short and sent them both hugging the dirty floor, belly and face down. The slugs kicked up bits of splintered wood and punched holes in the walls.

Ben raised his head and spat out dust from the dirty floor. "Goddamnit! I guess I haven't prayed enough lately."

That statement and the expression on Ben's face caught Linda just right and she burst out laughing. It was infectious, and Ben started laughing as what he had just said came home to him.

Jersey, crouched behind an overturned and battered old desk, looked over at where the pair lay. She smiled and shook her head in amazement.

Corrie and Beth and Cooper laughed and grinned at each other and winked.

It had been a long, long time since Ben Raines had really laughed.

Ben had finally buried Jerre in his mind.

Ben looked at Linda and said, "That remark was rather stupid, wasn't it?"

"Let's just say I needed a good laugh."

"Me too, Linda. Me too."

Tanks on either side of the building opened up with cannon and machine-gun fire, and that made conversation impossible as the rounds began creaming the building across the expanse of the body-littered tarmac.

Other Rebels began arriving at the airport and setting up, filling the air with lead.

Corrie was studying the other side through binoculars. "The creepies are bugging out, General!" she called.

Neither Ben nor Linda heard her. They were too busy kissing each other while the battle raged all around them.

Chapter Eight

The San Carlos airport was secure and Ben had set up a CP in another building, after Rebels had scooped out the debris and fumigated the place. The Believers did not take the practice of personal hygiene very seriously. If they bathed at all, it was no more than once a year. Any building previously occupied by the creeps smelled like an overflowing cesspool.

Because of the knowledge that attempts on Ben's life would certainly be made, security around him had tightened. The area around the airport had been cleared for two thousand yards in all directions, all buildings burned to the ground and bulldozed level.

Ben halted the ground advance for that day, but the old prop-job planes continued their relentless drops on the city throughout the night. The thunder of bombs impacting rumbled almost constantly. The city was burning out of control and the Believers trapped inside could do little except die.

The creepies cursed God, cursed the fates,

cursed each other, and most of all, cursed Ben Raines . . . then died. But they weren't dying in large enough numbers to suit Doctor Chase and his medical people.

Tanker trucks carrying water rolled in and the troops took a bath—albeit a cold one—for the first time in several days. It had reached that point— well known to any combat veteran—where the Rebels could smell themselves. It was past being merely odious—it was downright rank.

Hot food was brought in (heated MREs, but that was better than nothing), and the Rebels relaxed for a time.

Cecil and Ike were mopping up in San Jose and putting the city to the torch. The winds had shifted, now blowing from west to east, and that gave the Rebels on the ocean side of the battle some relief from the smoke.

Lamar Chase had joined Ben in a drive-through of the secured area, and later over dinner, he voiced his approval of the Rebels' method of disposing of the bodies by fire. Chase took a bite of his own lab people's concoction, grimaced, and grabbed for the hot-sauce bottle.

"What's the matter, Lamar?" Ben asked. "I thought you told me this slop was good."

"I never said it was good. I said it was nutritious. You want a shot of hot sauce?"

"Please."

The hot sauce was used by nearly everyone to mask the sometimes awful taste of the pre-packaged meals.

"Any qualms about destroying the city, Ben?" Lamar asked.

"No," Ben was quick to reply. "No more than any other city we've put to the torch."

Ben had read the casualty reports: seventeen Rebels dead, more than a hundred wounded; many of those wounded had minor wounds and would not require evacuation back to Base Camp One. But with the danger of infection from the creepies running so high, anyone with wounds, no matter how minor, would be placed on rear-echelon duty and kept off the line.

"It's firm, Ben? You have decided not to enter the city?"

Ben nodded his head. "Los Angeles is going to be a bad one, Lamar. There is a chance, a slim one, that we can gain a hold fast enough that will enable us to use artillery to bring it down. But even with that, we're going to have to enter that city and take it block by block, street by street. Those gangs down there are much better armed than anything we've faced in a long time—not counting Villar and his bunch. I've got a hunch those punks down there have shoulder-fired rockets capable of bringing down planes, so our air force just might be grounded. That's after we get there. Scouts report a lot of barricades in our way, all the major bridges are blown, so it's going to be a problem just getting down to Los Angeles."

There was something else on the doctor's mind, and Ben knew it. But Chase would get to it in time. The doctor asked, "What is your estimate of time for wrapping up here?"

"Four to five more days. We're going to push as far as Daly City and stop there. Let the big guns take it from that point. When we feel the city is gone, as we backtrack, we'll blow bridges and overpasses and exchanges. We won't be able to kill all the creeps, but those left will be damn few."

The doctor shook his head. "No, Ben. No. You've got to kill them all. You've got to eradicate this scourge right down to the last person. They're walking time bombs, disease factories. You should see blood samples under a microscope. It's the scariest thing I have ever witnessed."

"I'm going to ask a layman's question," Ben said. "Why then don't they all just drop dead?"

Linda took it. "Because for whatever reason, and we don't know the answer to it, they seem to have built up an immunity. It may, probably does, work on the same principle as a person who has been stung by bees so many times or bitten repeatedly by poisonous snakes. They either get so much venom in their system they die, or they grow immune to it."

"I suppose we could grab enough of them to take their blood and reduce the levels of whatever it is in there and then start experimenting and . . ."

Linda sighed and Lamar waved a hand, silencing Ben. "Leave the medical side of this campaign to us, Ben. You stick with soldiering. I thank you for the suggestion, but it doesn't work . . . quite that way."

Ben shifted his gaze from Linda to the doctor. "Okay. Then drop the other boot, Lamar."

"Chemicals, Ben. You know how I hate it, but in a case like this, it's the only way to be sure."

"I said after the last time I'd never use them again," Ben reminded him.

"I know. I know. It's not an easy thing to live

117

with. But we didn't know then what we know now."

"They would work here, Lamar. But the Los Angeles area is just too big. It would take months—working around the clock—to produce enough gas to neutralize that entire area. We're talking about hundreds of square miles down there."

"Then we're going to have to be damn careful when we assault that city, Ben. There is no vaccine for what the Believers carry in their bloodstreams. Our researchers and technicians down at Base have thrown up their hands in frustration. And we have the best people in the known world. It's worse than trying to come up with a cure-all for cancer. There are hundreds of types. Same with this"—Lamar lost his temper and his professionalism—"goddamn shit!"

Ben had lost his appetite. He pushed the plate from him and rolled a cigarette, very much aware of Doctor Chase's look of disapproval at his smoking. Ben secretly thought that Chase's idol of years back must have been the Surgeon General C. Everett Koop. Ben smoked about five cigarettes a day: one after a meal, and usually one after some very tense situation. He sighed as he lit up, hating even the thought of chemical warfare.

But he knew Lamar was right. Any person with an ounce of compassion would certainly feel sorry for a rabid dog. But no one in their right mind would try to comfort the animal by petting it. One put it out of its misery by destroying it.

"All right, Lamar," Ben said. "I'll give the orders. But damned if I have to like doing it."

* * *

So those in the city would not be tipped off that anything other than conventional warfare was in store for them, Ben continued his push at 0600 the next morning.

He ordered Dan Gray to hold what he had in Pacifica, then sent part of Ike's troops up to seal off the road linking Interstate 280 with the spur that fed south of the city. He left Cecil the unenviable job of torching and mopping up south, and pulled Ike up to his location for a powwow.

"Depending on the winds, we're going to slow-push up until we're even with Dan's position," he told Ike. "That will put us just south of San Francisco. We'll take our time doing this so the transport planes can get the chemicals and our vaccine for them to us from Base Camp One. On the morning of the drop, providing the winds are right, we'll begin a pullout just at dawn. I want easterly winds to blow this out to sea. I will not okay a drop until that happens. And I don't give a good goddamn if that takes a month."

Ike didn't argue that point. He shared Ben's concern with wildlife and the environment. The smoke was a nuisance, but it did very little, if any, lasting damage.

Ben said, "Our next staging area will be at Hollister. All major bridges are blown on the coastline highway, 101, and all Interstates east of us. So we'll have to take secondary roads down to the Los Angeles area. It'll be slow going. Cecil has already sent troops down to Hollister to secure it and clear us a bivouac area."

Ike studied a map and shook his head. "Man,

it's gonna be a bitch getting down to L.A. We're gonna have to take more twists and turns than a nest of snakes."

"Yes. I've already begun ordering non-combat personnel and non-essential vehicles out of this area, heading them south toward the staging area. Planes carrying chemicals left Base Camp One this morning."

Ike nodded his head. "Lamar is pretty shook up about this plague, as he calls it."

"More so than I've ever seen him," Ben agreed. "But something else, Ike. If it's this bad here, what in the hell are we going to be facing in Europe?"

"Whatever it is, we've got to beat it," the ex-Navy SEAL said. "We've got to stop it before it spreads. And that means the cities will probably have to come down; and what a blow to future historians that will mean. Maybe we can avoid it. I don't know. But I imagine it's the same over there as it is here. The rural areas are clean while the cities are cesspools. We'll know next year, won't we?"

"Yes. Hopefully." Ben walked to a wall map of the world thumbtacked to a wall. "If there are ships seaworthy after we finish the Northstar campaign, we'll sail from there and go through the Panama Canal—if it's still open. If not, we'll have to go cross-country and sail out of the East Coast." Ben waved those thoughts away. "Use this down time to go over all vehicles, Ike. Scouts report these secondary roads we'll be using are real axle-breakers in spots."

"What's the ETA on the chemicals?"

"They'll start getting here this evening. They'll

120

land and make their drop from the Moss Point airport."

Ike nodded his approval. He knew Ben had chosen that airport in case of an accident. It was the airport furthest away from the majority of troops. He studied the map and mentally noted that the Rebels were meeting less and less resistance in their drive north. Thus far, they had bulled their way up to San Mateo on 101, and just past that point on Interstate 280.

Corrie spoke up. "Meteorology on the horn, General. They say we will have a brisk wind out of the northeast commencing approximately 0700 hours day after tomorrow. The winds will remain reasonably stiff for most of the morning. They say if you're going to make the drop, that is the time. For in this section of the country, at this time, the winds can be very erratic."

"Thank you, Corrie, and thank them for that report. Ike, get your people moving south. Quietly. But get them out. This stuff has a life of only a few minutes, but if the winds pick up, no telling where it'll drift in those minutes. Have every person in your battalion draw the injectable vaccine and make sure they know how to properly use it."

"Right, Ben. See you, partner."

Ben stared out the window for a moment. "Corrie, advise those pilots who will make the drop to stay in touch with weather. I want them flying by 0645 on drop day. If the winds change as predicted, they will make their drop immediately and then get the hell out."

"Yes, sir."

"Bump Cecil and tell him I want him out of his

sector and moving south by no later than 1800 hours tomorrow. Make damn sure that Dan, West, and Tina are the *first* to receive the vaccine kits. As soon as the last plane takes off carrying the chemicals, I want them injected immediately and out of that area. By early that morning, the creeps will know something is up when the bombs stop falling. And you can bet your boots they've got people close enough in to see Dan's bug-out."

"Right, sir."

"Have West's men start laying explosives on the bridges and overpasses heading south out of Pacifica. Blow them behind them as they pull out." Ben walked to a window and stared out. "Now all we can do is wait for the winds to change."

Twelve hours before the chemical drop was to commence, the area just south of the city began to resemble a smoking ghost town. Only those personnel who were absolutely essential remained behind. And that did not include Doctor Chase.

"Raines!" the doctor bellowed. "Who in the goddamn hell do you think you are, telling *me* to clear out?"

"The commander of Rebel forces, that's who. While you were up poking your nose close to the front, I ordered all your people to pack up and clear out. They got. Now you're next. So pack up and git!"

"Get me my XO!" Chase hollered at Corrie.

"I just spoke with him," Ben informed him. "He and the MASH units are halfway to Hollister, Doctor."

Chase glared at him. "Raines, you're an ass-hole—you know that?"

"I've been called worse. Now clear out of here, Lamar. You're needed down south and you damn well know it. Stop being so bullheaded."

"What if there is a counterattack and you suffer causualties, hardhead?"

"We have combat medics here and evac planes to get them to surgery—*down south.* That's why you're needed down there, you old goat."

"Ha! For your information, I quit doing surgery except for emergencies a year ago, Raines. So you don't know as much as you think you do."

"Well, then," Ben said with a smile. "If that's the case, perhaps I should send your butt back to Base Camp One and get you out of my hair here."

"Try it, Raines," the doctor said. "You just try pulling rank on me. I'll quarantine your ass!"

Linda stood with her mouth open, watching and listening to the men have at it. Jersey walked over to her. "Don't pay any attention to them. They've been doing this for years."

"Who usually wins?"

"The one who hollers the most."

"I . . . see, I think." She cleared her throat. "I have a suggestion, gentlemen."

Ben and Lamar shut up and looked at her.

"Why don't you *both* go south?" she suggested sweetly. "That way, the Chief of Medicine and the Commanding General would both be safe if something were to go wrong."

"Now there," Lamar said with a smile, "is a very sensible young lady. How about it, *General* Raines?"

"I'm needed here," Ben said stiffly.

123

"To do what?" Lamar challenged him, grinning. "Crank the planes' engines? Tell the pilots what time it is? You going to show them how to operate the bomb-bay doors, maybe? If you just have to give orders, you can radio them from Hollister." Lamar chuckled and added, "Got you, Raines!"

Ben glared at Linda. "Thank you very much for that marvelous suggestion."

"You're certainly welcome," she said with a smile. "Shall I have Cooper bring the wagon up?"

"Oh, by all means, please do."

"Hee-hee-hee-hee!" Lamar giggled.

"Oh, shut up!" Ben said.

"Sore loser!"

The little con artist, Emil Hite, stuck his head into Ben's CP. He took one quick look at the expression on Ben's face and beat it back outside. He looked around for Thermopolis and walked over to him.

"The general doesn't look too happy, Therm. What's the matter?"

"He lost an argument with Doctor Chase. I think we're getting ready to bug out south."

"Suits the hell out of me. All this smoke is really aggravating my sinuses."

Therm could not hide his smile. "Why don't you ask the Great God Blomm to heal them?"

Emil grinned. "Sure. And at the same time, I'll expect to see a herd of elephants flying by."

"It was a good scam, Emil. Even though the majority of your followers knew all along that you were full of shit."

Emil shrugged. "Sure they did. I knew that. Oh, well, I'll think of something else. I always have."

"Why not play it straight?" Therm suggested. "Who knows, you might like it."

"Why don't you cut your hair?" Emil countered. "Who knows, you might like it."

Thermopolis chuckled. "Touché, little friend."

"Am I?"

Thermopolis frowned and looked at the man. "Are you what?"

"Your friend?"

"Of course, you're my friend. There really isn't a mean bone in your body, Emil. You're kind to animals, don't harm the environment, you're nice to anybody who treats you the same, and while you might argue it, the truth is you work harder at getting out of work than you would if you held a regular nine-to-five job. If such a thing even exists anywhere in the world anymore."

"I like to con people," the little man admitted, as he adjusted his turban. "I've been doing it all my life and I'm pretty good at it. But I'll tell you something, Therm. I like what I'm doing now even better."

"The fighting?"

"Well, to be honest, yes, that's part of it. I'll admit that there is a certain type of high to be had in combat. But no, it's the fact that for the first time in a long, long time I'm really contributing something toward the good of all. Ben Raines is human; he has faults just like all the rest of us. But he's trying to do what he believes is right for all the good people of the United States . . . hell, the *world!* I don't agree with everything he does; no Rebel does, is my belief. But he's on the right track, and they know it, I know it and you know it

125

too, Therm. There have been too many excuses made for criminals for too many years. Look around you, pal. There is every race and every religion represented in the Rebels. And yet, I haven't heard the terms nigger, spic, wop, greaser, kike, or slope spoken since I've been a part of this movement. And that's what it is, Therm, a movement. It's a great gathering of like-minded people all willing to put their lives on the line to make this world a better place for those who are willing to follow just a few simple rules."

Therm looked at the man as Emil wiped a tear from the corner of his eye.

"I get emotional just thinking about it." Emil walked away, humming "God Bless America."

Ben Raines has another convert, Therm thought. Another basically good soul willing to lay down his life for the cause. Ben Raines is the damnedest man I have ever encountered in my life. He always has to be in charge, whether or not he really wants the job. He is cruel and compassionate, benevolent and ruthless, farsighted and shortsighted, opinionated, yet with the intelligence to admit when he's wrong . . . although not often, Therm noted.

Sort of like someone else Therm knew.

It startled him when he realized he was thinking about himself.

Chapter Nine

"Everything on delayed scramble." Ben gave the order from Hollister. He rolled another cigarette.

"You're smoking too much," Lamar chided him.

"Shut up," Ben said.

Lamar walked away. He knew when to push Ben and when to leave him alone. He joined Ike, lounging against the fender of a Hummer, drinking a cup of coffee.

Lamar pointed at Ben. "That man can be as surly as a wolverine."

Ike grinned. "Why do you think I'm over here?"

0600. The morning of the chemical drop on the city of San Francisco.

"The wind is beginning to shift," Corrie told Ben, lifting one earphone to hear his response. "Weather people say it will continue in that direction at least until mid-morning. Conditions will be most favorable for a drop in fifteen minutes."

"All right," Ben said. He was reflective for a moment. Then he sighed and said, "Tell Dan and his people to bug out. Advise the pilots there has been a change in scheduling and to get the birds up right now. Tell Dan to monitor the pilots."

Ben began pacing the area around the communications van. Nobody said anything to him except Corrie.

"Bugging out, General," she advised. "The winds have settled and are now blowing directly toward the west at ten to twelve knots."

Ben stopped his pacing. "Have Dan and his people used the vaccine?"

"That's ten-four, sir. They have injected and are all safe."

"What's Dan's twenty?"

"Colonel Gray is just south of the town of Montara. He ordered West and Tina out an hour ago. They are both well south of the drop area and are moving toward this staging area."

"Buddy, the bikers, the Scouts?"

"All standing clear and injected, sir."

Striganov, Rebet, and Danjou were at the staging area.

"Order all personnel to inject, Corrie."

She clicked on a loudspeaker and gave the order.

Ben broke the seal on a syringe and popped himself in the leg. He looked around him. All Rebels in sight were injecting themselves.

"Tell the pilots to drop their payloads as soon as they are over the target," Ben said quietly.

"That's ten-four, sir. Squadron leader has acknowledged the drop order."

"God have mercy on any prisoners left alive in that city," Ben muttered. He shook his head. "And God have mercy on me," he said under his breath.

* * *

In the burning and smoking city, creepies had left their cover and crawled out of basements and buildings as soon as the bombs had stopped falling on them, some hours before. They stood in the ruined streets and wondered what was going on.

Over the crackle of burning wood, they heard the droning of approaching aircraft and ran for shelter.

But no bombs fell, only canisters that did not explode as they impacted with ground. The canisters hissed out an invisible and slightly sweet odor.

Within seconds, the throats of the Believers began closing and their nervous systems began shutting down as paralysis seized their bodies. They lay on the rubbled streets and in their filth-covered lairs and huddled in basements and died as the gas silently touched them.

In the communications center of the cannibalistic sect called the Believers, a dying radio operator got off one last message that chilled those monitoring south of the city, and especially those in the Los Angeles area.

"Gas!" The creep gasped his last message. "He's killed us all. Ben Raines is using poisonous gas. There is no one left. The gas . . ."

The speaker went silent. As silent as the once-great city by the Bay.

The Judges, the rulers of the cannibalistic order called the Believers, were advised of Ben Raines's latest move. They cursed him while they dined on strips of fresh human flesh just cut from screaming prisoners. When they had vented their spleens and filled their bellies, they called for a meeting of all gang leaders who operated in the sprawling area of southern California. There were some seventy gangs in the area, ranging in size from fifty to a thousand or more. They were different only in dress, the headbands or the clothing denoting each gang.

This was the last bastion of creepies and their followers or sympathizers in the lower forty-eight. Thousands of perverted degenerates whose territory ranged from the Pacific east to the state lines of Nevada and Arizona and south to the border of Mexico. They were well-armed, with heavy machine guns, mortars, rockets, flamethrowers, artillery, and just about anything the Rebels had with the exception of tanks and extremely long-range artillery.

This was their territory, from Los Angeles down to Tijuana and east to what was known as the zone, a region where force was the ruler and brutality the order of the day. The punks were going to defend it. They had nowhere else to run. Ben Raines and his Rebel army had managed to bring some degree of law and order and stability to all the other states.

Ben's intelligence on the population in this area was sketchy at best, for no outsider had ever managed to penetrate the area and live for very long. There were gang-run and Believer-run slave and breeding farms all over. There were drug manufacturers, drug dealers, and drug users. There were slavers and slaves. Pimps and prostitutes. The entire area, from Los Angeles south and east, was one huge criminal operation. From the Pacific Ocean to Nevada and Arizona and south to Mexico was a gigantic outlaw land, where violent death, rape and perversion, slavery, and cannibalism came as easily as breathing.

And those who called it home were preparing for war.

At the staging area in Hollister, Ben ordered flyovers of what remained of the city by the Bay, using heat-seekers. The word came back: There was nothing left alive in the city.

"Napalm it," Ben ordered. "For however long it takes to burn the bodies. Blanket the city with fire. Destroy it. Bring what remains down."

This time, every plane that could be bomb-equipped was put to use. The pilots spent all that day and the following night dropping napalm on the already burning city until they were certain the flames would spread and eventually destroy anything left. From China Basin to Great Highway, from San Jose Avenue to Jefferson Street, there was nothing but fire and smoke and death. After twenty-four hours of relentless bombing, the pilots flew down to the old Lemoore Naval Air Station, some one hundred and seventy-five miles to the southeast. There, they would carefully go over their planes, refuel, and wait for the next call from Ben Raines. A platoon of Rebels had secured the old station and cleared the runways. They reported back that the air station had been deserted upon arrival.

The next morning, the long Rebel columns began winding their way south toward Los Angeles. Ben took Highway 25 out of Hollister, a route that would abruptly end some sixty miles to the south. From there, it would be a state road down to the Sierra Madre Mountains. One long, slow pull from Hollister.

Ike took a route that put him — most of the time — between the coast and 101. That route would end at San Luis Obispo. From there, he would work his way down through Santa Barbara, Ventura, Beverly Hills, and into Los Angeles.

Georgi and West would travel east to the middle of the state before cutting south. They would split up just south of the China Lake Naval Weapons Center, with the Russian taking 14 down to the city, and the mercenary taking route 395 into, eventually, San Bernardino.

All of the Rebels expected many, many delays and detours before they reached the City of the Angels.

Ike hit his first obstacle just west of the Sierra de Salinas Mountains. His column had to backtrack and then take an unpaved road through the Los Padres National Forest.

Ben hit his first detour about twenty-five miles south of Hollister. The creeps had blown a bridge, forcing Ben to get off the secondary highway and traverse a dry riverbed. That little move cost him most of a day.

Cussing in half a dozen languages, Georgi Striganov and his forces hit a pocket of resistance between Highways 5 and 99 and were held up most of the day while dealing with them. The Russian and the mercenary dealt with them very harshly, and before late afternoon began to cast long shadows, they left the dead Believers and their outlaw cohorts behind them, their bodies still smoking after being torched.

Cecil was attempting to parallel — as much as possible — Interstate 5. He and his troops could exit just north of the city in the Angeles National Forest.

To keep love interest as widely separated as possible, Ben had assigned Tina to Ike's group, doing so after discussing it at length with West. The mercenary had thought it to be a wise move. Buddy and his Rat Team were Ben's constant shadows, and Dan and his Scouts were also attached to Ben's direct command.

The bikers, named the Wolfpack, and several platoons of forward recon people ranged out in front, spread over half the state, slowly working their way south, the long-range eyes and ears of the Rebels.

Ike found several pleasure craft, with fiberglass hulls, that had been hoisted up out of the water for repairs at a marina. He had them lowered into the water, checked them out, and crewed them with ex-Navy men, with the orders to get down to Santa Catalina Island, take it — quietly, if possible — and set up a listening post there. The island lay some twenty miles out from the L.A. metropolitan complex and could possibly be a great asset in the taking of what was soon to be a sprawling battleground.

"Wouldn't those islands be used by the thugs and creeps in the city?" Linda asked.

"I doubt it," Ben told her. "Those types of

people aren't inclined towards work of any kind and they don't have much imagination. Keeping a large-sized pleasure craft up, so I'm told, is a time-consuming operation. Oh, after the Great War, some of them probably used boats as pleasure toys. Then when the boats started sinking, or the engines quit, they lost interest. It would surprise me if anyone is living on those outer islands."

Beth walked up, a notepad in her hand. "We made forty miles today, General. General Ike is bivouacked in the Los Padres National Forest. General Cecil made about forty miles, and General Striganov is bivouacked near the Sequoia National Forest."

"Thank you, Beth. Have you any word from the forward recon teams?"

"Ike can expect trouble at the south end of the old Hunter Ligget Military Reservation. General Cecil will have a fight in Coalinga, and we'll have a pretty good scrap when we hit Highway 46. All units have been advised."

"Thank you. Get some chow and relax."

Linda studied Ben in the fading light of late afternoon. So far he had kissed her, and that was that. She didn't know what her reaction would be when, or if, Ben tried to take matters further—although she had a pretty good idea how it might turn out.

She had heard rumors about Jerre, and about their stormy relationship, and how she had died. She knew Jerre had borne Ben's children, and that they were back at Base Camp One. She had also heard about the many other women in Ben's life, and that he had really loved only one of them: Jerre.

Ben was smoking his pipe, sitting in a camp chair. Linda got the impression that his mind was a thousand miles away. Or more specifically, about four hundred miles away, in the general area of Los Angeles.

She walked away quietly, thinking that Ben probably would not notice her departing. It would not take her long to learn that Ben missed very little that went on around him.

Buddy came to his father, opened a camp chair, and sat down.

"Where have you been, boy?"

"Talking with some Woods Children who came out of the deep forests across the state."

"How'd you find them?"

"I didn't. They found me."

Ben thought about that, sensing something was up. "It must have been very important news for them to leave the woods."

"They thought it was. Father, Sister Voleta is still alive."

The young man almost never spoke of the woman as his mother. Buddy had long ago realized that she was the epitome of evil and would have to be destroyed. But destroying Voleta, founder and ruler of the savage and vicious cult known as the Ninth Order, was proving to be very difficult.

Ben fought back a quick surge of rage. He calmed himself and said, "God*damn* that woman!

The Woods Children are certain of this?"

"Yes. Absolutely. Their network reported that she had both legs amputated and was horribly burned and disfigured, but that she is alive, gaining strength, and filled with more hate than ever before."

"Damn! Where is she, son?"

"Michigan, unless she has shifted her headquarters recently. And her followers are growing in number."

"Well, we have an outpost in Michigan. What do they report?"

"They report nothing and they never will. They have been destroyed."

"By Voleta?"

"Yes."

Ben sighed heavily and knocked the dead ashes out of his pipe. "Son, I am becoming awfully weary of that woman. She is like an albatross hanging around my neck."

"*The Ancient Mariner*. Yes. I read it. I understand what you mean. But getting to her is not going to be easy. According to the report I received, she is in the process of rebuilding her empire and is constructing numerous hiding places, all of them underground in deep woods. Michigan, Kentucky, Missouri, Maine. Probably more than that, but those were the ones told to me."

"Estimated strength?"

"Several thousand, and growing."

"So are we."

"Yes, fortunately. I am told that Seven and Eight Battalions will be ready for the field in approximately six months."

"That's correct. When we sail from this country, we'll leave behind four battalions of field troops, plus the battalion in place at Base Camp One. How are things over in the Woods Children sector?"

"Stable." He smiled. "It's difficult for me to keep referring to them as "children" since many of them are now young men and women. They have schools and medical facilities and are doing quite well. They asked me if you wanted them in this fight for southern California?"

Ben shook his head. "No. They'd be totally out of their element in this fight. In the woods they're awesome fighters. But this is going to be urban warfare. Have their dreams to become as one with the animals materialized?"

"To a large degree. They are not flesh-eaters and the animals seem to sense that. They are also united with the Underground People. Together, they make up quite a force. Thugs and outlaws have tried to overwhelm them several times. I don't think that any of those who entered the woods with hostile intentions ever came out. Neither have trappers," he added dryly.

Ben grunted. He had always felt — even as a boy — that most trapping was unnecessary and very cruel. He had never particularly given a damn what happened to trappers. "Are you going to have a second meeting with the Woods Children?"

"Yes."

"Tell them I wish them well and thank them for this information."

Buddy rose from the chair.

"Son?"

137

Buddy turned to his father.

"Who, or what, do they worship?"

Buddy smiled, knowing what his father had on his mind. "The Almighty. A great spirit in the heavens."

"That's a relief. Thank the Lord they've stopped building altars to *me*."

Buddy slipped away into the darkness. He did not tell his father that those who lived in the timber and under the ground still held Ben Raines in the same awe and adoration as they did the invisible Almighty. His father just could not understand that all over the nation—and according to what Buddy had learned, and had not shared with his father, in pockets all over the world—people felt that Ben Raines was slightly more than a mortal flesh-and-blood man, very close to being a god—or at least a man who had caught the attention of the gods above and had a pipeline to them.

Ben Raines just could not understand that it had become *his* dream to take a shattered nation and rebuild it. The young man knew that his father considered himself to be a soldier/philosopher and nothing more than that. Many others had had the same dream, but it was Ben Raines who'd actually formed the army of Rebels and put them on the march. It was Ben Raines who'd taken the nation, state by state, and reclaimed it from the outlaws and thugs and punks and warlords. Ben Raines who was the driving force behind the rebuilding. Ben Raines who had physically jerked up the nation from the ashes and held it there until he could get the props under it. And it was Ben Raines who would not be satisfied until the

138

entire world was free and safe and once more a productive place.

Ben Raines just did not understand that he had dreamed an impossible dream and brought it to light and made it reality.

Buddy shuddered at the thought of anything happening to his father. For if the unthinkable happened, the entire load would quite possibly be placed on his shoulders, and the young man knew he was not ready for that. Not for a long, long time.

If ever.

Chapter Ten

Ike reported that he had hit his first skirmish since leaving the city, and would be tied up for several hours at the south end of the old Hunter Ligget Military Reservation. Cecil was hanging back about a thousand meters north of the town of Coalinga, using artillery to bring the defenders to bay.

"We'll push on down to the crossroads and see what's in store for us there," Ben said. "From here on in, main battle tanks take the point. Corrie, what do the Scouts report about this unpaved road straight through to Parkfield?"

"As far as they went, they reported it bumpy but passable."

Ben studied the map for a moment. The shortcut looked inviting. Maybe just a tad too inviting. The uglies would know that forward recon people would check out the road for at least some distance. So if there was an ambush planned—and Ben felt sure that was what lay in wait for them—it would come at the very end of the shortcut.

"Too good to be true, gang," Ben finally said, thumping the map. "Ten-fifty those orders. We'll take the long way around and completely bypass Parkfield. We'll take this little spur down here at Paso Robles and pick up 58 at Creston. Tell Leadfoot and his Wolfpack to spearhead the tanks. They'll leave the main column and cut back east here at San Miguel, come up behind our ambushers, and give them some grief."

"Yes, sir."

"Tell them no heroics, Corrie. Tell them to go in fast and get out fast."

"Right, sir."

Moments later, the sounds of motorcycles cranking up drifted to Ben. The bikers now all rode the big Harley-Davidson motorcycles. They carried submachine guns, grenades, and sidearms. They were a wild bunch, but totally dedicated to Ben Raines and loyal to the Rebels. They had needed a second chance at life, and Ben had given it to them. They all to a person would die for Ben. The bikers dressed as they pleased, and Ben let them, for more than one reason. The bikers could go into enemy territory and look and behave exactly like the enemy—at least for a while. They had done so several times, returning with valuable information.

The bikers roared out, anxious to get into a good fight.

"Mount up, people," Ben ordered. "Let's go see some new country. We'll take it slow. We don't want to get too far ahead of Ike and Cecil."

The long column stretched out, cutting southwest and heading for San Miguel, some twenty miles away. The road was in bad shape, but not as bad as Ben had feared. This road had obviously not been used very much since the Great War, with most traffic staying with the Interstates and better-known roads.

At San Miguel, the bikers had tied one of the yellow bandanas that all Rebels carried onto the city limits sign, a signal that the town was clear.

The beautiful old historic mission, the Mission San Miguel Archangel, had been destroyed. Ben had been expecting it. The Rebels had seen a lot of churches and missions destroyed over the years. The people, survivors of the bombs and the deadly gas of the Great War, had lived through that only to see a deadly rat-borne plague strike that further cut the population. Many had blamed God, and had taken their misery out on the clergy and the churches.

"Stupid damn people!" Ben muttered, standing in front of what was left of the old mission. He shook his head and walked back to the wagon. "Let's go, Coop. Corrie, tell the forward people we'll bivouac just as soon as we cross this spur. Tell them to find us a place on 46. We'll wait for Leadfoot and Beerbelly there, and see what Ike and Cecil are doing."

The main column did not swing over to the Interstate to check out Paso Robles. Ben sent the Scouts in with some Dusters to give the town a once-over while the long column turned west and pulled over at the bivouac site.

Ike had smashed the resistance at the old military reservation and was personally escorting a few prisoners over for Ben to interrogate. Cecil had punched through at Coalinga and was bivouacked a few miles south of the town. Georgi and West had just begun their turn south and had pulled over for the night in the Owens Valley.

Ben decided that the battalions west of the Russian and the mercenary would stay put the next day, allowing those troops to their east to pull even with them.

Ben's CP for the next few days would be an old ranch house just outside of a small town that had once been called Whitley Gardens. The coffeepot was on when Ike pulled in with the prisoners and shoved the first one into the den.

"Stand there," Ike told the sullen-faced young man. "And keep your mouth shut until you're told to speak."

"Fuck you, fatso!" the punk told the stocky Ike. He closed his mouth and his eyes widened in fear as Ben picked up a .45 autoloader from a desk and clicked it off safety. "Hey, man!" the punk hollered. "I got rights, you know?" He coughed, a deep, racking cough.

"You have only what I decide to give you," Ben told him, his voice low and very cold. "Whether you live or die is solely up to me. Whether I hang you, shoot you, stomp you to death, or let you live is my decision, and mine alone. Do you understand all that, you worthless piece of shit?"

"You Ben Raines, ain't you?"

"Yes."

A dark stain appeared on the young man's crotch, dampening his very dirty jeans. He bobbed his head up and down. "Yes, sir. I sure do understand where you comin' from." He coughed again, and Lamar studied him intently.

"Good," Ben told him, laying the .45 back on the desk, cocked but not locked. He waved a Rebel forward.

The young man watched as a briefcase was

143

opened; it contained a strange-looking object. Microphones were set up and the volume tested and adjusted. The operator of the equipment looked at Ben and nodded his head.

"This is a voice/stress analyzer," Ben told the punk. "Our scientists have vastly improved upon the old models, which used to be called psychological stress evaluators. Our people tell me that this machine is eighty-five percent accurate in showing the operator whether or not a subject is lying. Now let's get all the bullshit out of the way. I'm going to ask you a number of questions. Everything you say is being recorded. On that machine, and on tape. Now, you know my name; you know a lot about me. Believe every bad thing you ever heard about me."

"I heard a bunch of bad things about you, General. How you—"

"Shut up! If you lie to me, I'm going to kill you. Right here, in this room, without hesitation. Do you understand that, punk?"

"Yes, sir!" he almost screamed the words. "Ax me anything you like. I'll tell you anything you want to know."

In another building, Dan Gray was interrogating another prisoner, using the same methods.

Ben stared at the young man. "What is your name?"

"Henry Gavin." Cough.

"Fine. Henry, how many people live in or around the Los Angeles area?"

"Thousands and thousands, sir. I don't rightly know the exact number." Cough.

"You have lived in that area?"

"Yes, sir. I live there. I was borned there.

Twenty-five year ago."

"Borned there," Ben said softly. "Where are your parents?"

"I don't know. Dead, I reckon."

"Don't you care where they are?"

"No." Cough. "Why should I? All they ever done was make me go to school and beat me when I hung out with the Dukes."

"Who are the Dukes?"

"My gang," he answered proudly. "See this red headband I got? All Dukes wear red headbands. We're one of the toughest gangs in the city."

"And that makes you proud?"

"Damn right." Cough.

"I suppose you and the Dukes and the rest of the gangs have been active in cleaning up the city, caring for the sick and the old and very young, and setting up schools and hospitals and so forth?"

"Huh?" Henry blinked. "Hell, no! Who wants a bunch of dumb shit like that?"

"Who indeed?" Ben muttered. "Who is the leader of the Dukes?"

"Rich." Cough.

"Rich . . . what?"

"I don't know. Just Rich."

"How many people belong to your gang, male and female?"

"About five hundred or so. About three hundred men and the rest is chicks. That don't count the slaves, of course."

"The slaves? Explain that."

Henry coughed and shrugged his shoulders. "Slaves is slaves. We use them for entertainment. We fight them like chickens or dogs. To the death. We bet on them. Every gang has their favorite

145

slave-fighter. We buy them through barter, steal them from other gangs, snatch them from out in the zone."

Ike shook his head in disgust. Doctor Chase had a savage look in his eyes. Ben cleared his throat and took a sip of water. He had a very bad taste in his mouth. For years an animal-rights activist, Ben had always felt that people who made animals fight for sport — much less humans — were mean-spirited, low-moraled assholes. "The zone, Henry. What is that?"

"It's a no-man's-land."

"Go into more detail, Henry."

"The gangs control everything from Ventura down to Tijuana, then east along the border over to Mexicali, then north up to Interstate 10; everything back west to the ocean. The zone is anything that ain't under our control." Cough.

The Rebel commanders exchanged glances. "Tell me how you get along with the Believers."

"They leave us alone, we leave them alone. We swap them slaves for stuff. Dope and things like that. In case of trouble, we all band together to protect each other's turf."

"How do you people survive? How do you eat? What do you eat?"

"Slaves grow gardens for us. We have cattle and hogs and chickens and shit like that. When a slave gets too old or wore out to work or fuck or suck, we give him or her to the Believers." Cough.

Lamar Chase glanced at Ben. The men shook their heads in disgust. Ben said, "Henry, you're a real prince of a fellow."

"Oh, well, thanks. Sure." Cough. "I'm known as bein' pretty cool."

Ben sighed and said, "Do you know all the gangs in the territory?"

"No way, man. They's too many of them. But I know all the main gangs."

"Run them down for me."

"Well, okay. Let me think." Cough. "Chico runs the Swords. They wear black and red. Manuel is boss of the Mayas. They wear blue shirts. Bull bosses the Busters. They wear green. The Fifth Street Lords is run by a dude name of Hal. They dress all in black. Dicky is the main man of the . . ." Cough. ". . . Blades. They wear silver. Sally runs the Mixers. Purple is their color. The Angels is headed by Josh. They dress all in white. They look kinda stupid. Ruth fronts the Macys. Tan is their color. Chang is the boss of the Tokyos — black headbands. Fang is boss of a real big gang called the Hill Street Avengers. Brown headbands. Guy name of Brute is head of the White Men. They dress in hot pink."

Ike almost spilled his fresh mug of coffee. *"Hot pink!"*

"Yeah. They're a bunch of fags, but they're allright guys. Mean as hell if you crowd them." Cough. "You want me to go on, General?"

"Please do," Ben said. "It's fascinating."

"Thanks. Leroy is the head knocker of one of the biggest gangs. They're called the New Africans. Black and green is their color. Carmine bosses the gang called the Women. Bunch of dykes. They wear yellow. Cash runs the Surfers. White and blue. Jimmy fronts the Indios. White and red. Stan's bunch is called the Flat Rocks. Yellow headbands. The Boogies is bossed by Ishmal. They wear turbans. The Skulls is run by Junkyard.

147

They all wear black leather gloves. They's a whole bunch of little-bitty gangs scattered all around the fringes of the territory and the zone. Can I have a drink of water?" Cough.

Ben nodded and one of Henry's hands was unchained. He drank two glasses of water, went into a fit of coughing, and the hand was once more chained.

"All right, Henry. Tell me what kind of weapons you people have."

"All kinds, General. Machine guns, rocket launchers, grenades, mortars—anything we could grab from the military bases all around the area." Cough.

Ben drummed his fingertips on the desk. "Has any large force ever tried to overrun you people?"

"Hell, no!" Henry said with a laugh. "No, General. And you people ain't gonna make it neither. You and your army is gonna get chewed up." Cough. "All these good-lookin' cunts around here is gonna make for fine barter."

Jersey laughed at him.

Ben stared at the punk for a moment. "Get him out of here and chain him someplace. Keep him away from people. The bastard has fleas jumping all over him."

"And that's not all he has," Lamar added.

"The one I interrogated was slightly more erudite," Dan Gray said. He and Ben were comparing notes on the prisoners' remarks. "They have been studying our tactics for years, so it seems. And those in the city are highly organized. It's going to be a tough campaign. They've practiced their plans many times and each gang knows what to do. They also know that we don't have the chemicals to neutralize such a large area. A conservative guesstimate would be thirty-five thousand of the enemy."

"I was going to say fifty thousand," Ike said. "Trained, well-armed, and ready for a fight."

"Yeah," Ben said, leaning back in his chair. "Well, we've got to reclaim the old military bases first thing, once we're in the area. The caches of weapons and supplies have probably not been found. Georgi and his people will take China Lake and Fort Irwin while West moves down to reclaim Twentynine Palms. Cecil will occupy Edwards. Ike, you and yours take Vandenberg."

Corrie stuck her head into the room. "Leadfoot and the Wolfpack have reported in, sir. They creamed the ambushers. The Pack suffered two minor wounds. They took no prisoners."

"Tell them to come on back, Corrie."

"Yes, sir."

Lamar entered the room and poured a cup of coffee. He had a very grim look on his face. "All right, ladies and gentlemen, here it is. Our prisoners, all of them, have advanced syphilis and tuberculosis. You have all been inoculated, so there is little danger for any of you. However, I have ordered booster shots for all Rebels. It's going to take a day to get the vaccine in here, and a couple of days to get everyone popped. So stand your people down, Ben. And roll up your sleeve. And that is a direct order from the Chief of Medicine."

Ben did not question the order. He and Lamar loved to argue and yell at one another, but when it came to health matters, Ben was no different from any other Rebel. He did what the Chief of Medicine told him to do.

The medical research people down at Base Camp One had taken the vaccine BCG, widely used in halting the spread of TB, and improved on it. The vaccine was basically weakened tubercle bacilli which were injected into the skin, then followed by injections of various drugs such as ethambutol, rifampicin, thiacetazone, and poyrazinamide, and sometimes streptomycin, isioniazid, and para-aminosalicylic acid. The reasons for the varied combinations was because the disease could grow resistant to repeated doses of the same drug.

"How do you suppose Leadfoot and that bunch roamed around like the wind for all these years without contracting some dreadful disease?" Linda asked, helping Lamar inoculate.

Dan smiled at her. "Leadfoot and his bunch are far from being stupid, Linda. Believe it or not, there are a couple of Ph.D. types among them. And several holders of master's degrees. I believe the one called Frank actually taught at one of America's more prestigious universities."

"Stanford, I think it was," Ben said. "He was an associate professor, I believe. Frank is a good man. He just took a wrong road for a brief time. What Dan was going to say, Linda, is that most of those people are pretty good medics in their own right. They've all read up on what medicines to take and so forth. And they all knew a great deal about herbal and folk medicines. I had a bad case of diarrhea one day, and didn't have anything at hand to help me. Axehandle went out into the woods, came back with some blackberry roots. He boiled them and made me a glass of hot tea. I've had better-tasting liquids, but it stopped my diarrhea."

Ben grimaced as Linda popped him with the needle, then swabbed the injection point with alcohol. "You'll live," she told him.

"I'm not sure I will," Dan said, after Doctor Chase had popped him. "Lamar has the touch of someone repairing anvils."

The Rebels rested, cleaned already spotless weapons, and waited for the entire army to be inoculated. All of them, from the Scouts to the cooks and back again, had been briefed as to what lay ahead of them in southern California. They were under no illusions. This was to be the toughest fight they had ever endured. Outnumbered meant nothing to them. The Rebels were almost always outnumbered.

Those prisoners that Ike had captured were turned loose and told to go somewhere, make their peace with God, lie down, and die. Doctor Chase said that there was no way any of them could live another six months.

"Won't they spread the disease?" Ben asked.

"I pumped them full of medicine. It certainly won't cure them, but it will somewhat reduce the danger of them spreading the tuberculosis. The syphilis is another matter. I did what I could for that, but it's my opinion that Gavin will not live another sixty days. Lab results show extensive brain infection. His motor reactions are already severely affected. None of them will be alive six months from now."

"Why don't we just cordon off the area down

there and let them all drop dead of diseases?" Jersey asked, considerable heat in her tone. "Serves those guys right if their whosis rots off. Damned bunch of rapists and slavers."

Lamar looked at her. "Remind me to always stay on your good side, Jersey."

Ben said, "We just don't have the personnel or the time to do that, Jersey. That might take years. Too bad, though. It was a good idea."

"You people are vicious," Lamar said. "What's a nice, gentle man like me doing in the company of such heathens?"

He was booed and hissed out of the CP, leaving with a grin on his face.

On the night before the long columns of Rebels were to resume their push toward the south, Ben stayed up late in his CP. Those they would be facing in the southern part of the state had rockets, several different kinds of rockets. The old prop-job planes of the Rebels could not hope to evade any kind of Stinger or surface-to-air missiles. So that grounded the planes. He made a note to have Corrie radio the pilots first thing in the morning and have them stand down in any kind of combat role for the duration. They wouldn't like it, but they would see the reasoning behind the orders.

He killed the low flame under the coffeepot and rinsed it out, then checked his watch. Midnight. Time to go to bed and get his customary four hours of sleep. Very rarely did Ben sleep more than five hours a night, usually less than that.

In several days, the columns would be nearing the territory of the gangs in southern California, and Ben expected the first real heavy fighting of this campaign to begin. Ben had expected the area around Monterey to have been heavily populated, but Ike had reported nothing stirring. Fort Ord had been destroyed, and the lovely old towns on the Monterey Peninsula burned and deserted.

Ben sat on the edge of his camp cot and unlaced his boots. What had he left out? What had he forgotten? He went over every aspect of the battle plans in his mind, picking at them, worrying with them. He could not think of anything that he and the other commanders had not touched upon.

He heard footsteps on the front porch. They were friendly footsteps or his guards would have opened fire. Since the assassination plots against him had surfaced, security was very tight around Ben.

A knock on the door.

"Come in if you're friendly," Ben said.

Linda walked in, carrying a small bag in her hand. She sat down beside him on the edge of the cot.

"You having any reaction to the booster shots, Ben?"

"Just a slight fever yesterday. It's gone."

"I guess by this time tomorrow, the whole camp will be talking about my coming over here."

"Oh, it won't take that long. News travels fast. Give it an hour, tops."

They stared at each other for a moment. Linda said, "This is a very narrow cot, Ben."

"It's a warm night. We could always go outside."

"There are fifty people out there guarding you! I don't want an audience, thank you."

"You plan on getting kinky?"

153

Both of them laughed softly.

"Tomorrow," Linda said, "I wish you would request a larger cot."

"I shall certainly do that."

She reached over and turned off the lantern.

Chapter Eleven

"Heads up," Ben told the forward recon teams just as they were about to pull out. "This is the day we're probably going to meet our first real resistance. Make a mistake and you're not only dead, but other Rebels will die as well. Okay? Take off. We'll be an hour behind you."

Ben turned to Corrie. "Advise all units to move their recon teams out, please." He waited while those orders were relayed, then said, "Tell all drivers to start their engines and check out any bugs. We're going to be pushing hard this day. I'd like to be sitting on Interstate 5 by this afternoon."

Beth glanced up at him. "Interstate 5? I thought we were pushing south to 101 and Ventura."

"That's what the creeps and crud think too," Ben said with a smile. "That's why I talked on an open frequency the other day. We'll leave Highway 33 just south of Maricopa and cut through the northern edge of the Los Padres National Forest, coming out on the Interstate east of Tejon Pass. Just a slight change of plans, that's all. Let's keep the creeps and crud off balance whenever we can. If the Interstate

155

is impassable, we'll take 138 for a few miles, then cut south on a state road. Either way, by this time tomorrow, we'll be knocking on the gates of San Fernando, or damn close to it."

Thermopolis was standing close by, listening. "That will put us ahead of the others," he said. "You plan on spearheading this operation, Ben?"

"Indeed I do, Therm. We're going to hit the northern edge of the enemy's territory so damn hard they'll all have a headache for days."

Therm's wife, Rosebud, was studying an old map of southern California, using the beam of a tiny flashlight. "That is one *huge* area. New York City is going to seem like a walk in the park compared to this place."

"Well, dear," her husband told her, smiling, "you always wanted to see southern California."

The look she gave him closed his mouth.

"Sweep the area for anything you might have left behind," Ben told them. "Have yourselves another cup of coffee. Then get ready to mount up. Let's go make boom-boom with the creeps and the crud."

"My, you do have a way with words," Therm told him.

The columns rolled out just as dawn was streaking the eastern skies with faint light. Forward recon teams, from the Pacific Ocean east to the desert, reported that all barricades in front of them were unmanned. It appeared that everyone had abandoned them and headed back to the city to dig in.

"Good move on their part," Ben said. "They'd be losing personnel unnecessarily by leaving small groups behind to face us. We're not dealing with a bunch of idiots . . . despite the names of the gangs. We'll pull over just as soon as we hit 58 and radio-check all the other units."

"We'd better do it now," Corrie said. "I've got Ike on the horn. But we'll lose contact with him as soon as we're on the east side of these mountains."

"Good. Ask him if he's met any sign of resistance."

"That's ten-fifty, sir," she said. "San Luis Obispo is a burned-out ghost town. No signs of recent occupation. Cecil reports that Bakersfield is in ruins. There are survivors there, but they all ran away and hid at his approach. They appeared to be badly frightened and very disorganized. He is proceeding over to Edwards Air Force Base and making good time."

"Can you make contact with Georgi and West?"

"Negative, sir. Not with this radio. We'll have to use the van when we stop."

Ben halted the columns at Highway 58 and made contact with Georgi.

"I am investigating what is left of the China Lake base now, Ben," the Russian said. "But it has been picked over very carefully. I can find nothing of any practical use."

"That's ten-four, Georgi. Call it off and move out."

Ben's unit cut over, picked up Highway 14, and moved slowly toward the town of San Fernando. Ike slammed his way down 101, and pulled up short when he was suddenly bogged down in a firefight just south of Santa Maria. Georgi was highballing it toward the San Gabriel Mountains, and West and Cecil had linked up and cleared George AFB between Highway 395 and Interstate 15.

Ben had pulled in every tank he could crew for this campaign. He had old Pattons, Sheridans, and Walker Bulldogs. His people had modified APCs, adding more armor plate and adding another 20mm Vulcan Gatling gun to the M113's. The M113's were seldom used for troop transport, since the interior was usually loaded down with ammo. With both Vulcans working simultaneously at full rock and roll, each Vulcan was capable of spitting out up to 3000 rounds a minute.

Ben's forward recon teams radioed back. "They're waiting for you, General. We've spotted mortar pits and heavy machine-gun emplacements."

"Stay where you are," Corrie said, relaying Ben's orders. "Tanks up."

Cooper pulled in behind an MBT and Ben got out. The hatch popped open. "Let's open the dance, Sergeant," Ben told the commander. "They've ignored our surrender terms and have chosen to fight. I'm tired of pleading with these bastards to give it up. So let's give them a taste of what they're in for."

"Right, sir," the TC said with a grin. He spoke into his headset. "Get into position, boys and girls. You've got the range. Let's start some fireworks."

Two dozen tanks began shelling the edge of town, using a combination of rounds: WP, HE, and napalm. Ben leaned against the fender of a vehicle and waited. After the entire area in front of them was blazing, for ten blocks running east and west, Ben gave the orders to cease fire.

"Mop it up, people," Ben said. "Bring me some of these crud. Let's see what we've got."

Not much, was the general consensus.

"Can you comprehend and speak English?" Ben asked one young man. Like the others, he wore a denim jacket, with one sleeve shorter than the other.

"Yeah, I can talk, Pops," the punk popped off. "You got your hearin' aid plugged in?"

Ben gave him the butt of his M-14 to the mouth. A short, brutal stroking. Rotten teeth shattered and lips were pulped. The punk lay on the street and looked up at Ben, this time with real undisguised fear in his eyes.

"You would perhaps like to try this conversation one more time, asshole?" Ben asked.

"Yes, sir." The punk had managed to push the words past swollen and bloody lips.

"That's good. Much better. You will have to learn to respect people of my advanced age. We get testy at times. Now then, the name of this misbegotten bunch of dickheads is?"

"The Bandits, sir. My mouth sure hurts somethin' awful . . . sir."

"That is one of life's little tragedies, boy. How many in your gang?"

"Couple of hundred. Was. Sir. I guess you cut us down some."

"I guess we did at that. Do you know who I am?"

"I reckon you must be General Ben Raines. Can I get a rag from my pocket and wipe my mouth?"

"Why, sure you can!" Ben said, knowing damn well the punk was going to try for a gun.

The craphead came out with a derringer and Ben shot him in the belly with the M-14.

"How . . . did you know?" the punk gasped, both hands clutching his shattered stomach.

"Magic," Ben told him. He kicked the derringer away and turned to a medic. "Get a blood sample. Let's see what he's carrying, other than the obvious fleas and head lice. Be careful with these

159

crapheads."

Ben walked over to stand staring at another Bandit. This one was not nearly so smart-mouthed and defiant after watching what had happened to his fellow Bandit. He had pissed his dirty jeans. "My name's Jimmy, sir. Whatever you want to know, you just ax me. I'll tell you."

"That's very good, boy." Ben pointed. "Five blocks that way—what are we going to run into?"

"The Rats, sir."

"The *Rats?*"

"Yes, sir. You see, to get to be a Rat, you got to eat a dead rat."

"Why would anybody want to be a Rat?"

" 'Cause they bad, sir."

"So is their breath, I'm sure," Ben muttered. He winked at Jersey. "How'd you like to kiss one of those guys, Jersey?"

She grimaced. "Barf City, General!"

"And the Rats control how much territory?" Ben asked.

"The rest of the town till you get to the barricades. They run east and west. Then the Dinks take over."

"The Dinks?"

"Yes, sir. They're worser than the Rats. You'll be able to smell their territory a long time afore you ever get to it."

"And why is that? I'm quite sure they don't bathe regularly, but it must be more than that. You don't bathe either, but fifty feet away and I couldn't smell you."

Jimmy's smile was very thin. He knew there was no way on God's green earth that he was going to leave this area alive. Everything he'd ever heard

160

about the Rebels was true. "The Dinks drags their kills back to their home turf and hang them up so's they can rot. It kinda lets people know they's about to enter an area where they ain't welcome."

"I would certainly get that impression," Ben said. "I've hanged a few outlaws up myself to let them swing and rot."

"Did you torture them a long time before you swung them?" Jimmy asked with a sneer.

"No," Ben said softly.

"You a real candy-ass, ain't you, General? Torturin' is fun. I like to hear people scream and beg for you to kill them."

"Yes, I bet you do," Ben agreed.

"Jesus Christ!" Lamar said. "Lawlessness is one thing. But this is a total breakdown of values, morality, decency . . . everything!"

"You think it's bad here, wait until you get into Los Angeles," Jimmy warned them. "You people ain't seen a damn thing yet. Dead bodies left to rot in the streets and be et by dogs and cats and rats. Screamin' of them bein' tortured all the time. Some chick has a kid she don't want, she just tosses it out in the gutter and lets it die. You'll see. This is paradise compared to what's further down south. And they gonna kill all you candy-ass soldier boys and girls." He cleared his throat to spit on Ben and Ben knocked the punk to the ground.

Ben looked at his son. "Get rid of them all, Buddy."

"Yes, sir."

Ben walked back to his vehicle and got his kit. He poured a cup of water and brushed his teeth and rinsed out his mouth. He had developed a very bad taste in his mouth while listening to Jimmy.

"I knew it was going to be bad," Jersey said. "But nothing like this." Her stomach rumbled. "I got to get me something to settle my stomach after listening to all that garbage."

Ben rummaged around in his kit and handed her a pill. "Try that. Corrie, find out where everybody is and give me a report. We don't want to get too far ahead."

"Right, sir."

"Burn everything in our sector, Dan," Ben ordered. "Leave nothing standing."

"Right away, sir." The Englishman trotted off, yelling for his people.

Four quick shots split the air. Linda walked up a few moments later, her face pale. "Your son just shot those young men, Ben."

"Yes, I know. I told him to."

She opened her mouth to speak, and Ben spoke first. "We don't take many prisoners, Linda. And we'll take none in this area, at least not for very long. Everyone in this area, everyone who belongs to a gang, joined knowing what they were getting into. They knew we were coming months ago. They were warned — by us — repeatedly. They could have left. They chose to stay and fight. We have neither the time, the facilities, nor — and I'm speaking for myself here — the patience to jack around with a bunch of no-goods. I'm not a social worker, Linda, although there are several in the Rebel army who were before the Great War. That should tell you something. Now does that answer any other questions you might have?"

"I guess that pretty well sums it up, Ben."

"Believe it, Linda."

"General!" Corrie called. "West reports a lot of

overpass and bridge damage, and so does General Cecil."

"All right. Acknowledge it. I anticipated that. Where is Ike?"

"On 101 around Westlake Village."

"Tell everyone to hold what they've got. Stand by for a change in plans. I'm going to take a chance."

"This is something new?" Jersey muttered.

Ben heard her and grinned.

Dan and Buddy gathered around Ben as he carefully spread an old map of Los Angeles out on the hood of a Jeep. "Once Ike has established a secure position in his sector, he'll begin advancing and neutralizing the Pacific Palisades area. We'll make very slow advances until Ike gets a toehold in Santa Monica. Then we'll start pushing down to the Ventura Freeway while Cecil drives through Glendale down to the Hollywood Freeway. We just don't have the personnel to effectively cover such a massive area, so it's back to taking chances.

"When Ike, our bunch, and Cecil begin pushing toward a secure position to operate out of, Georgi will be swinging around and covering from here at Pasadena south down to just north of where West will be setting up with the Long Toms. I want West to take all of our long-range artillery — every piece of our self-propelled — and his tanks and get into position along this line. Burn out a five-block area in front of them for security, and then start lobbing in shells around the clock; the rest of us will be doing the same. Tanks spearhead each drive and this is a put-to-the-torch operation all the way.

"Corrie, get in touch with Base Camp One and get me Seven and Eight Battalions in here. Start them coming right now! Fly them in around the

163

clock, with heavy equipment following them in trucks. Roll them, Corrie. They're about to get some real AIT—call it on-the-job training. I want them pulled in close to protect the backs of West's people."

"There are a lot of green troops in there, Father," Buddy said.

"They won't be for long," Ben told him. "We'll hold up any major advances until Seven and Eight are in position. Corrie, have Georgi send some people east to secure this airport at Upland. Seven and Eight will deplane there and move into position."

"Right, sir."

"All right, people. Right now, let's take a few more blocks just to keep in practice. We'll launch the main push as soon as Seven and Eight are on the ground and moving. Send those orders out on scramble, Corrie."

Ben turned to find Doctor Lamar Chase's finger in his face. "I want that extra MASH unit from Base to come in with those boys and girls, Ben. Those are green troops and they are going to get bloodied."

"You took the words right out of my mouth, Lamar."

"That's bull-dooky, Ben, but it sounds good. Just do it."

"No sweat, Lamar. Look, we're going to be pushing hard when we kick this off, so for a time, you won't have a secure central receiving hospital. Everything, *everything*, is going to be up to your MASH people."

Chase nodded his head. "We can handle it. I'll advise my people. We're going to need lots of whole blood, so I'll start yelling for volunteers. Take care of him, Linda. See you around, Raines."

Ben said, "Let's take a couple of blocks, people."

The Rebels spread out, with tanks spearheading, and began hammering their way south. An hour before dark, they had clawed and scratched their way to within a block of the San Fernando airport. Bodies of Bandits and Rats and Dinks, sprawled in grotesque postures of death, littered the trashy streets. Ben had felt all along that this campaign was going to be a tough one, and the afternoon's battles had proved him to be correct. The street punks knew they were literally fighting for their survival. It was stand-or-die time. Ben Raines was not going to take prisoners, and was not going to have programs of reeducation and rehabilitation for them. He was going to destroy them to the last person and then burn the city to ground level and stir the ashes so they could never flame again.

"It ain't right," a Rat bitched during a brief lull in the fighting. "We done run up surrender flags. Ben Raines oughta honor them."

Carlo Mendez, a man who had been a Los Angeles street punk even before the Great War, laughed at the Rat. "Why should he? We had our chance to give it up. Ben Raines is no sobbing hanky-twister. He knows he's got our backs to the wall, and that if he takes our surrender now, as soon as they pulled out, ninety-nine percent of us would go right back to what we were doing before he came. We got us maybe a fifty-fifty chance of winnin' this fight. And pal, we'd better win it. 'Cause we just ain't got no place else left to run.

165

Ben Raines is gonna wipe the earth clean of every-one like us he can find."

"He's a devil!"

Carlo laughed. "Naw, he ain't. He's just a man who don't like punks, that's all. He's a law-and-order type, from his head down to his boots. The world is gonna be different, pal. There just ain't gonna be no place for guys like us in it. It's gonna be a very polite society."

His friend snorted in disgust and spat on the dirty floor. He inched up and peeked over the edge of a windowsill. A Rebel sniper about five hundred meters out put a .50-caliber slug right between his eyes. The street punk died with his eyes bulging in shock, the top of his head and his brains splattered on the wall behind him.

Carlos looked at the mess and shook his head. "Bastards can shoot. And that probably makes you one of the lucky ones, Garcia." He glanced at one of his lieutenants. "We're pullin' back. We can't win this fight with each warlord defendin' his own turf. We got to call a meetin' and make some plans. It can't work this way. Let's go."

"They're bugging out, General," Corrie called. "Forward units report a mass pullback."

"Start dropping artillery in on them," Ben ordered. "Give them everything we've got for a couple of minutes. That will give us about a three-block secure area. Tell the gunners to keep the airport intact."

Corrie relayed the orders and the tanks and mortar crews began lobbing them in.

"The son of a bitch!" Carlos cussed as the shells began dropping in all around him. "He never misses a bet." A shell landed close and knocked the street punk off his tennis shoes. They were good tennis shoes too. He'd killed a dude to get them. Good tennis shoes were getting harder and harder to find. When the dust cleared, Carlos jumped to his feet and ran for his life.

"Secure the airport," Ben ordered.

Tanks surged forward, Scouts and Buddy's Rat Team right behind them.

"Get me a report from Ike."

"He's punched through and is holding along Highway N1."

"Tell him to break it off there and to get some rest. Cecil?"

"Locked in heavy fighting along Interstate 210 just north of Glendale."

"It'll be dark soon. Tell him to hold what he's got. Georgi?"

"He's in control of his sector along 210. Colonel West is beginning his stretch-out move. That's the heavy smoke we see to the east and north."

"Let's don't be too obvious with it. Tell all commanders to shut it down and secure for the night. Come on, gang—let's go see what the airport looks like."

Not bad. There was no lingering stench of the Night People. That confirmed what the prisoners had told them. The Believers were concentrated in the heart of Los Angeles; true to form, they preferred the cities to the countryside.

"Runways are not in that bad a shape," a Rebel reported. "We can have one operational in several hours."

Ben shook his head. "We won't need this one. We'll push south in the morning and try to secure the Hollywood-Burbank airport. By that time, we'll be needing supplies and we'll have wounded to fly back to Base Camp One. Corrie, I want a casualty list all the way around."

Seven dead and twenty-two wounded. Of the wounded, five were in serious condition.

"Transport the dead out of the burn area and bury them up in the mountains," Ben said. They would be buried in unmarked graves, for the criminal element hated the Rebels so, they had been known to dig up Rebel graves and mutilate the bodies.

"Father," Buddy said, walked up. "A group of Woods Children have moved down to the edge of the mountains north of us. They have volunteered to bury our dead in secure places."

Ben did not ask how Buddy knew that, or how he had been contacted. There was a mystic aura about the young man that baffled his father. "I thought I told them to stay out of this fight."

Buddy shrugged his muscular shoulders. "They obviously chose to ignore that directive."

"Tell them thanks," Ben said. "It'll be a big help."

Thermopolis walked up to join the small group on the edge of the tarmac. He wore a grim expression. "I lost a man," he said. "The street punks grabbed him and poured gasoline on him, then set him on fire. We found his body about ten minutes ago." He clenched big hands into big fists. "Goddamnit!"

"Now you see yet another reason why I deal with punks as I do," Ben told him. "I'm really very sorry, Therm. The bodies are being readied for transport up into the mountains. Do you want to go with your man?"

Therm shook his head. "No. I'm needed here. It's just that Santana had been with me for a long time. We worked together before the Great War. He was a good decent human being. Loved animals and loved the earth. He used to work for the Forest Service."

"Why did he leave them?"

"He didn't agree with a lot of their policies. I'll miss him."

Ben thought of all the Rebels, men and women, buried in lonely unmarked graves all over the United States. Border to border and coast to coast. Freedom fighters. "I know the feeling, Therm. I know it only too well."

"Do you ever get used to it?"

"No."

Therm looked surprised, then managed a smile. "You never pull a punch, do you, Ben?"

"Occasionally. Not very often." Ben studied the man's face. "Getting involved now, Therm?"

"Let's just say I'm trying very hard to keep Santana's death from clouding my judgment."

"From becoming emotional about it?"

Therm nodded his head. "Yes. You could say that."

"You lost Tapper and Robin last year, I recall."

"You remembered?" There was a note of surprise in the man's voice.

"I remember a lot of Rebel deaths, Therm. My memory goes back years in recalling the men and the women who died fighting for a dream." Others had gathered around, standing in silence, listening. "Back at Base Camp One, there is a list of all the men and women who have died while serving in my command. It goes back years. The list just keeps getting longer and longer. And in a sense, I keep getting more and more emotional about it."

"You? *Emotional?*"

"Oh, yeah, Therm—me. But I keep it up here." He tapped the side of his head. "Everytime I see some goddamn slobbering punk who refuses to obey even the simpliest of rules, I think of Captain Voltan. Salina, Pal Elliot, my son Jack Raines. And my unborn son who died in his mother's womb after Salina was bayoneted in the stomach. I think of Jimmy Deluce. I think of Sam Pyron and his wife. I remember Valerie, Megan, Al, Abby, Belle Riverson, Badger Harbin. I remember hundreds of Rebel dead, Therm. And I think of all those who stepped up to take their places, knowing the risks involved. I feel like crying when I think of a little boy I found on the road—in Missouri, I think it was—a long time ago. I named him Jordy Raines. He was ten years old, he thought. He wasn't sure. He died in my arms down in Texas, after being shot by a warlord.

"I think of a woman named Rani, and of the kids she took in to raise. And I think of another woman . . . named Jerre." Ben was silent for a moment, and Therm noted the silent rage etched on his face, and his hard, hard eyes.

"I hate punks, Therm. I have hated punks and thugs and trash all my life. They come rich and poor, they come educated and illiterate. But to a person they are what they are because that's what they want to be. Nobody made them take the dope. Nobody forced them to kill and rob and rape and assault. Because, Therm, we all, to a very large degree, control our own destinies. Especially in these times, Therm. Especially now. Now is when the true worth of men and women comes to the fore. Now is when you can see what a person is really made of. Now, more than ever before, there is only black and white and no gray in between. Now, when *everybody* has the opportunity to start fresh, can one truly see what a person is worth.

"The psychiatrists and social workers and sobbing sisters and hanky-stompers can all kiss my ass, Therm. Both now and back when we had a so-called working society. You can take a rose, and you can dip it in shit, but after you do, all you've got is a shitty-smelling rose. You can wrap a punk in ten-dollar words and fancy excuses for his or her behavior, but after you do, all you've got is just another goddamn punk.

"I keep my hate simmering low on a back burner, Therm. With the pot carefully lidded. But every now and then I have to go back and lift that lid and look inside. I have to hear the cries of those innocents who were raped and beaten and enslaved and tortured and killed by punks over the years." He pointed south, toward the sprawling city of Los Angeles and the area all around it.

He turned, looking square at Thermopolis, and his eyes were as cold as Therm had ever seen them. "It makes the killing a lot easier, Therm. A lot easier. Keep that in mind."

Ben walked away, toward his new CP. Jersey swung in behind him, the butt of her M-16 on one hip.

Linda shivered and rubbed her arms as chill bumps rose on her flesh.

The other Rebels who had gathered around were silent.

"I always thought I would like to get a look inside that man's head," Therm said. "Until now. Now I'm just not so sure I'd want to take a look."

Buddy turned away. "Not unless you want to see what Hell looks like."

Chapter Twelve

Ben was up early, an hour before anyone else, except for Jersey and Buddy. He fixed a pot of coffee and opened a packet of breakfast rations. He preferred eating them in the dark so he wouldn't have to look at what he was eating. The planes carrying the first of Seven and Eight Battalions had started arriving just after midnight; the flights would continue for several more days, with trucks rolling twenty-four hours a day from Base Camp One, bringing in additional equipment and artillery rounds.

Ben took his rations and coffee outside, to sit on the curb. He was surprised to see Therm stroll out of the darkness, stop while being challenged by the guards, then walk over to where Ben was sitting. The man carried his own coffee and field rations. He sat down beside Ben.

"We've been together for quite a while, haven't we, Ben?" Therm said, breaking the silence.

"Yes, we have, Therm. We've seen a lot of battles and you've proven yourself many, many times. I still say you'd make a fine commander."

"You probably know that's why I came over this

morning. I've done a lot of thinking since losing Santana yesterday."

Ben hid his smile of satisfaction by lifting his coffee mug to his lips and waiting for Therm to take the conversation further.

"You've saddled me with Emil and his bunch, Ben. Who else do you want me to take?"

"Why . . . gee, Therm. You've really caught me by surprise with this request."

Thermopolis looked at him and then chuckled. "Cut the crap, Ben. You've been trying to make me a field commander for a year and you know it."

Ben smiled. "You get along well with the Wolfpack. They like you and respect you. I'd like to put them under your command. In addition to Seven and Eight Battalions, three platoons of green troops are joining us late this afternoon. Those three platoons are yours. I'll shift some experienced personnel around and assign tanks and other support people to you today. We can call your unit the Peace and Love Battalion."

"Very funny, Raines. Hysterical."

"You can paint some guitars on the sides of the tanks."

"Now, that's not a bad idea."

Ben sighed. "Me and my big mouth."

"It's my command," Therm reminded him.

"That it is."

Wenceslaus, one of Therm's people, wandered out of the darkness and Therm waved him over.

"Yo, man," Wenceslaus said.

"At first light, get some paint," Therm told him. "We have some tanks to decorate."

Wenceslaus choked on his coffee. "We got to do *what?*" he finally gasped.

"I've just been made a battalion commander."

"Say *what?*"

"You heard me." Therm looked at Ben, who was smiling at the antics of Wenceslaus. The man had spilled hot coffee on his hand and was sucking his thumb. "What's my rank?" Therm asked.

"Lieutenant colonel."

"You've got to be kidding!"

"Nope. Get your people together, Therm. Meet me back here after dawn. You'll get a quadrant assigned to you then." Ben stood up. "You remember that line about heavy is the crown?"

"Vaguely."

"You'll soon see what the man was writing about."

"Everything else remains the same," Ben said, wrapping up the meeting. "With the exception of Colonel Thermopolis leaving us and taking his command down to secure the Hollywood-Burbank airport. We will start our move west to the Interstate and clear that while Therm is busy at the airport. The first elements of Seven and Eight Battalions are getting into position now, and West is lining out the artillery. He'll probably begin shelling around noon. Therm, when the airport is clear, you'll proceed down to Burbank and start neutralizing that area. We'll push down to the Ventura Freeway and then cut over to near your position."

Thermopolis nodded his head in understanding.

He wasn't kidding himself a bit; he knew he was being tested. He said a silent prayer to whatever God looks out for old hippies (the same one that looks out for everyone else) that he would be up to the test.

Wenceslaus walked in. "Rosebud and Swallow got those goddamn tanks painted, Therm . . . I mean, Colonel. Whatever. The tank commanders kind of like it."

"See you in Burbank, Colonel," Ben said. Okay, people, let's go."

"That's the way it stands," Carlos told the gathering of street gang leaders. No representative from the Believers was present. The street gang scouts had reported the battle lines being shifted and the arriving of planes from the east. They all knew something big was in the works. They just didn't know what. "The bottom line is, we either stand together, or hang separately."

"Oh, that's lovely!" Brute said. "Familiar, but lovely. And I agree with you, dear boy."

"Shiitt-it," Carlos muttered.

Leroy said, "I ain't tossin' in with no honky motherfuckers. 'Specially I ain't with that goddamn Rich and his Klucker-gang." He looked at Rich. "Why don't you carry your white ass back to Georgia and burn a cross or something?"

"Fuck you, Leroy," Rich told him.

"Let's don't be too hasty about this," Sally of the Mixers said. "Carlos is right. All the way right. We don't stand a chance if we fight these people separately. But united, we've got them outnumbered."

"She's right," Fang said, and Chang agreed with him, as did most of the others.

Ishmal and Junkyard stayed firm with Leroy.

"Talk about me being racist," Rich said.

"Shut up," Bull of the Busters said. "Everybody just shut up for a minute."

"Oh, I just love it when he becomes authoritarian," Brute said.

Bull looked at Brute, open dislike in his eyes. "That goes for you, too, fruit-boots. Now listen up. The way to do this is to take a vote. If the majority agrees to band together, we do it that way. The way it works is like this. Any who don't agree to pull together is out—all the way out. That means you don't get no help from any of us who band together to fight Ben Raines. No help a-tall."

"I'd sooner have to listen to somebody yodel hillbilly music all day than fight alongside some racist motherfucker like Rich," Leroy said.

"Shut your goddamn mouth, Leroy!" Bull shouted at him. Bull stood and stared Leroy down. Leroy ran the biggest gang in the southern California area, but he respected Bull—as much as he could respect any white man—and feared him. Bull was a huge man, and a very powerful and cruel man. He liked to torture prisoners, enjoyed hearing them scream in pain.

"Speak your piece then," Leroy said sullenly.

"Thank you. Now listen up. Raines has got maybe, tops, five or six thousand troops—and a lot of them is cunts, and everybody knows most cunts can't fight worth a shit."

"Fuck you too!" Sally yelled at him, reaching for a pistol. Ruth and Carmine were dragging iron.

"I didn't mean you broads!" Bull quickly yelled, breaking a light sweat. These women would shoot him in a heartbeat and he knew it.

The women holstered their pieces and stared at him.

"Okay," Bull continued. "We got Raines's people outnumbered ten to one, easy. I ain't sayin' this fight will be no cakewalk, but we can whip him. If—*if*—we pull together. Now just think about this, people. We whip Ben Raines and his army, and we rule the nation. Think about that. The whole country out there"—he waved his hand—"will be ours."

That got everybody's attention. Even Leroy and his followers. Leroy smiled and said, "That would mean I could start up a real New Africa and none of us would ever have to look at no ugly white motherfucker again. I like that."

"Yeah," Rich said with a nasty grin. "I like it too. That happens, then I could invade your New Africa and put all you jive brothers back in the cotton patch, where you belong, workin' for whitey."

Leroy and Rich got nose to nose, both of them cussing and shouting threats. Bull jerked them apart. "Cool it, goddamnit!" he yelled. "Somebody make a note that when we line out battle stations, we keep these two bastards as far away from each other as possible."

"I'll put your ass in the grave, honky!" Leroy said to Rich.

"I'll cut your nuts off, coon!" Rich replied. "And

178

feed them to the hogs!"

"We still haven't talked with the Believers," Carmine of the Women pointed out, after Rich and Leroy were dragged to opposite sides of the room.

"They'll go for it," Bull said confidently. "They ain't got no choice in the matter. And even if they didn't, who gives a damn? We don't need them. They need *us*."

"Disgusting people," Brute said.

"We agree on something," Bull said reluctantly.

"You have a plan, Bull?" Chico asked.

"Oh, yeah," Bull said with a smile. "Yeah, I do."

The mighty machine of war called the Rebels surged forward at first light, pushing hard behind the spearheading tanks. And hit no resistance.

Therm stood in the middle of the Hollywood Burbank airport terminal and scratched his head. Not one shot had been fired from either side.

Ike rammed all the way down to Malibu on Highway N1, burning as he went, but encountering no resistance.

Ben had pushed his people south on 170 down to the Ventura Freeway, and none of his people had fired a shot. But they had put everything behind them to the torch.

Cecil had turned his column and was now halted, standing on the edge of what appeared to be a deserted Glendale, wondering what in the hell was going on.

Georgi had pushed over to the center of Pasadena, and there the Russian had halted his advance, sensing a trap not far ahead. "Get Ben on the radio," he ordered. "Get *all* commanders on the horn."

The commanders on network, Therm asked, "What the hell is going on, Ben?"

"For whatever reason, they've pulled back. Everybody just hold what you've got. West, are you ready to commence shelling?"

"Sitting on go, Ben."

"Start dropping them in while we assess this situation. But I think they pulled back to band together."

"That's ten-four, Ben," the mercenary replied. "Seven and Eight Battalions are trickling in, getting in place to our rear."

"Give the punks a great big incendiary kiss, West."

"Will do, Ben," the mercenary said with a laugh.

From miles away, the 8-inch howitzers and the 155's began laying down a killing field of fire. With each gun capable of a round a minute, the earth began to tremble with rolling thunder. Buildings exploded and flames leaped into the air.

"All right, people," Ben ordered. "Let's take some more ground. Corrie, order all the tanks and mortar crews to start shelling."

On a line stretching east from Malibu to the Orange Freeway, Rebel gunners began opening up. Everything with any range at all was put into service, the shells and rockets pounding the earth until the trembling resembled a never-ending earthquake.

Ike had advanced to just west of Topanga Beach, and had still not encountered any resistance. He pulled up and ordered his people to hold up and burn the town.

Ben had vowed he would not commit troops until the area in front of each unit was pounded into fiery mush.

The Rebels began encountering resistance as they advanced, but the relentless artillery barrage was driving the street punks back. The smoke from hundreds of fires had brought visibility down to zero in some areas. The Rebels put on gas masks to help in combating the choking and blinding smoke. The street punks had forgotten that little item.

"All units forward two blocks," Ben ordered, and Corrie relayed the orders.

The Rebels moved out, walking behind tanks and APCs, mopping up what was left of the gangs in the battered and burning sectors. Those street punks who had been assigned the suburbs began pulling back, cursing Ben Raines as they retreated. In the city, the creepies had no place to go. They dug in deeper and waited for the artillery they knew would be coming as soon as General Ike McGowan got into position.

The Rebels' policy was to shell several blocks, using incendiaries, and then stand down and watch it burn. When the flames had subsided to the point where they could advance, they would move forward, establish a new position, and resume their shelling of another sector.

It was slow work. But doing it this way greatly reduced the number of Rebel dead or wounded. And it was frustrating to the enemy, because the Rebels presented few targets. The street punks might catch a glimpse, through the smoke and fire and dust, of a running Rebel as he or she darted from cover to cover, but even that was rare, and the punks rarely scored a hit on a Rebel in that situation.

At the end of the third day of the assault against southern California, Ike had moved into shelling range of west Los Angeles. Ike was using what long-range artillery he had, and using it effectively, standing back miles from the target and dropping them in.

The street punks were being slowly pushed back, but in the city proper, the creepies had no place to go; they could do nothing except die. It was going to take weeks, possibly even months, for the Rebels to win the battle this way, but the one thing the Rebels had was time.

"Goddamn Ben Raines!" one of the Judges, the leaders of the Night People, cursed after days and nights of relentless shelling. The smoke from the hundreds of fires, most of them burning out of control, was thick and choking.

The damn Rebels seemed to be everywhere at once. How Ben Raines managed that, with so few under his command—few, compared to the thousands who were, at least so far, unsuccessfully fighting him in southern California—was a bewilderment to the enemy. The street punks had sent people around to flank the Rebels from the east. They ran into Seven and Eight Battalions, dug in deep and heavily armed, and were thrown back time after time. Rebel snipers, or so it seemed to the punks, were everywhere, and their fire was deadly.

And when the Rebels moved out of a position, they left nothing behind them except burned-out foundations and ashes. There was no place for the enemy to hide or to launch an attack. At night, the Rebels sent up flares at the most unexpected of times, catching the punks as they tried to advance through the ashes, and cutting them down with heavy machine-gun fire.

A bug-out was a possibility, but one that offered little hope to those in the sprawling area. The mercenary, West, had moved his people closer to the city. He was now stretched out, in strategic areas, north to south along Highway 57, with Seven and Eight Battalions moving with him, protecting his rear. It was a very, very thin line, and had the street punks possessed any military knowledge at all, they could have busted through at almost any point. Why they did not was something no Rebel commander could understand.

Perhaps it was because West and Seven and Eight Battalions never gave the punks a chance to rest. The mercenary was savage in both his defense and his attack, burning and destroying as he went. Bridges and overpasses were blown; block after seemingly endless block of long-deserted businesses and homes were burned or still burning. Mines had been laid, from the insidious pressure mines to the horribly devastating Claymores.

And the big guns of the Rebels boomed day and night.

Ben Raines had taken a terrible chance by spreading his forces so thin, but so far, it appeared to be working.

The street punks finally began to realize that

183

while it might take the Rebels six months to smash through, destroying everything and everybody in their path, they would eventually do just that. Ben Raines was not going to come nose to nose with them—not yet. He was going to lay back and use his awesome artillery to pound them to pieces and then send troops in to mop up.

The street punks and the creepies also realized that while they had been terribly shortsighted as to their future, Ben Raines and the Rebels had carefully looked at the long-range picture. They had worked out their battle plans over years of actual combat, and the Rebels made few mistakes.

The booming of artillery never stopped. The cannon and mortars lashed out death and destruction twenty-four hours a day, the rolling thunder becoming a constant.

"I didn't think we could do it," Ben admitted. "I was wrong."

"Chisel that in stone," Doctor Chase said. "Because you might never hear it again. However," he added, "I must admit that we were all wrong."

Few of the Rebels had believed that laying back and using artillery would have worked within such a massive area as they were assaulting. And while they were delighted that it was working, none could understand why those so loosely trapped were not making more of a fight of it.

"They could bust out anytime, at any place they choose," Tina said, studying a huge wall map of the southern California area. "Yet they don't. Why?"

"Maybe they don't know they can," Therm finally said, after the others had looked at each

184

other and shrugged their shoulders.

"Go on, Therm," Ben urged. "Elaborate, please."

The ex-hippie (or perhaps hippie-turned-warrior-hoping-to-become-a-hippie-again-once-this-crap-was-over) was fast becoming a respected commander of troops. He was more cautious than Ben, but he got the job done, and that was all that mattered in the final run.

"For one thing," Therm said, "they can't see us. And with the constant hammering of artillery, they probably believe that their initial estimates of our strength were way off the mark. But there might be another reason. They just don't know what to do."

"Or a combination of both," Buddy said, picking it up. "They've never faced anything like the Rebels before. They've had their own way for so long, they just don't know what to do against such a large and well-organized army."

Ben rose from where he'd been sitting on the edge of a scarred old desk and walked to a boarded-up window, to look toward west Los Angeles. He could see nothing but black smoke rising from the ruins of the burning city. Ike and his people had pushed east to Santa Monica Boulevard and his artillery was pounding the city mercilessly. West had moved in from the east and had put everything behind him to the torch, with the exception of a two-block area running north and south that was under the control of Seven and Eight Battalions. When West advanced a few more blocks, Seven and Eight would put their sector to the torch, then move out behind him. West was now in control of the John Wayne Airport in

Orange County.

It's too easy! That thought jumped into Ben's head. There is just too much going for us that has come too damn quick and too damn easy.

For the moment, Ben kept those thoughts to himself.

Georgi had put Pasadena to the torch. Cecil had torched Glendale and pushed south, almost on a parallel with Georgi.

Everything was just coming too easy to suit Ben.

Therm and his short battalion had been on the edge of Beverly Hills, just approaching the now-fading opulence of the homes of famous movie stars and rock singers, when Ben had called for a meeting of all unit commanders. Therm had left Emil Hite behind (but not in charge) with a contingent of the new Rebels just arrived from Base Camp One. He had left him wandering through a huge mansion that had once belonged to a rock singer who had fronted a band called the Sickening Slime.

Ben turned around to face his commanders. "It's going too damn easy, people. I don't know that anything is wrong, but I have a gut feeling that something is. Let's kick it around. First of all, we know for a rock-solid fact that there are thousands of creepies and street punks in southern California. But we've had more of a fight with a few outlaws and warlords along the way than these people have given us. Why?"

"For a fact, resistance has been extremely light," the mercenary, West, said. "And I will admit I have puzzled over the why of it."

186

"Yeah," Ike said. "Now that you bring it up, nobody on the other side has thrown jack-crap at me. And we all know the creepies can fight. We don't know that for sure about the punks, though."

"I think they can fight," Georgi said. "They just haven't done so as yet. Like you, Ben, I am puzzled as to why they haven't."

"I have encountered virtually no resistance," Cecil observed. "I think we have deluded ourselves into believing those we face are cowards, fleeing before us in fear, when in fact, they are not cowards at all."

"Then what are they up to?" Ben asked the group. "We've got to know before we—I—make a fatal mistake in planning and get a lot of Rebels killed. Have our people out on Santa Catalina Island been able to pick up anything of value?"

"Not much," Corrie told him.

The island had been deserted when the Rebels landed to set up a listening post. So far, all they had learned was that they were all bored with the inactivity of it all.

"The enemy has good communications equipment," Corrie said. "But much of their conversation is gibberish to us. They're using a lot of street-punk talk that just doesn't make any sense to our people."

Ben looked at Dan and smiled.

Dan returned the smile. "I believe I can certainly take care of that little problem."

"See to it, Dan," Ben said. "Lamar, get the chemicals readied for drug interrogation."

"They'll be ready."

Hopefully, there would be prisoners taken this

night.

"Is anybody running low on supplies?" Ben asked. After seeing several affirmative nods, he said, "Stock up, double up on everything. If something heavy is in the works, we stand a good chance of being cut off from each other. And we might be cut off for several days."

Dan left the room to go head-hunting for prisoners.

"One way or the other," Ben said, just before dismissing the commanders, "we are going to find out what is going on. In the meantime, all of you hold your positions and brace for trouble. Just in case."

Chapter Thirteen

The Rebels attempted no further advance against the street punks and the creepies. Dan led a team of Scouts into hostile country to grab some prisoners for interrogation. The Rebels assigned to Ben's command post waited while Ben sat for hours, looking at the big wall map.

"Has to be," he finally muttered. "There is just no other reasonable explanation. Corrie, call Dan and his people back in. Immediately. Tell Dan that is a direct order from me."

"Yes, sir."

Therm was waiting for his trucks to be loaded with fresh supplies and was in Ben's office, drinking coffee and alternately chatting with Cooper and studying Ben—the latter being one of his favorite pastimes.

Ben waited until Corrie had recalled Dan and his Scouts, and said, "Corrie, advise all units to be alert for a sneak attack—possibly a suicide attack, from all sides. That's got to be their plan. All other patrols that are out, tell them to dig in and stay low. If an attack is coming, it's going to be soon. They can't wait much longer."

Therm joined Ben by the map. "If you're correct, we're going to be in trouble."

Ben nodded. "Yeah. You are so right, Therm. Get on back to your command; your trucks should be ready by now. Draw plenty of drinking water. We're going to be cut off from each other for no telling how long."

"See you whenever, Ben."

"Let's hope."

Buddy walked in the CP just as Therm was leaving. Ben brought his son up to date on his hunch.

"I think you're right, Father. They slipped around us and headed north while we were driving south."

"And before West and Seven and Eight could loosely secure this area," Ben said, running a finger from the north to the south, along the eastern edges of the combat zone, "they found a hole and slipped through, out into the zone. Corrie, advise all units we're under a red alert. Get ready. Do it quickly, but not in a panic. Let's don't give ourselves away. Let the punks still think they've got us fooled. We've got to be under observation — all units. It's my belief that if, or when, they hit us, we're going to be hit hard from all sides. That's why there has been no radio traffic of any significance."

"You believe their plan was already worked out before we hit the outer edges of the territory?" Buddy asked.

"Or maybe while we were hitting it. They probably saw that fighting us alone, in separate gangs, just wouldn't work."

"We're going to be cut off from each other for sure."

"Yes. Perhaps for several days. Okay, people, let's get cracking. We've got a lot to do in a very short time."

The Rebels began quietly and quickly bracing for an attack. Snipers slipped into place, all of them equipped with night scopes.

"West and Seven and Eight will probably have a hard time of it," Ben said. "Corrie, tell them to make like this is an Indian attack on a wagon train. Is his CP still at the airport?"

"Yes, sir."

"Pull them in tight. None of us have a place to run so we've all got to adopt a wagon-train mentality and we don't have long to do it."

"Right, sir. General Ike?"

"Ike can put his back to Santa Monica Bay with the assholes coming at him from three sides. He just resupplied, so he's in good shape. Corrie, as soon as everyone is in place and ready, tell them to button up and get set for one hell of an attack. We will cease all artillery at 1900 hours. Forward posts heads up and be prepared to bug out. No heroics, people. The name of this game is staying alive. Every communication will be on scramble and no unnecessary chatter. No smoking, no fires, no lights after 1900 hours."

The Rebels got in place and waited. Darkness began creeping in around them, shadowing the streets. Murky pockets in their line of sight became areas of suspicion.

191

Linda came to stand by Ben's side. "How bad is it, Ben?"

"We've been in worse spots," he said softly, his eyes sweeping the seemingly deserted streets below them. "I let us get overconfident, that's all. This is the final push in the lower forty-eight, and we were too anxious to bring it to an end. I let it happen. It's my fault."

"West's people report movement, sir," Corrie called from across the room. "Enemy coming out of the zone."

"Tell all forward recon people to get the hell back to their units. Right now! It's all going to break loose in a few minutes."

Ben checked his watch just as the artillery barrage stopped. The sudden silence was eerie.

"Now they'll know that we know," Ben said. "They've got too much forward momentum to stop now. All hostile units are committed. They can't stop now. It's root-hog-or-die time for them. And us," he added.

"Ike coming under very heavy attack from all open sides," Corrie called out. "They're throwing everything they've got at him. Rocket launchers, mortars, and heavy weapons in use by the bogies."

"Tell him I said good luck and to keep his lard-ass down," Ben said with a smile. He pinched off the fire from his hand-rolled smoke and stowed the butt in a pocket of his BDUs. He took a sip of water from his canteen and moved to a position at a window, stacks of clips already there. His M-14 was bi-podded.

His personal team got in place, quickly, quietly, and professionally.

Buddy laid aside his Thompson and got behind

an M-60 machine gun.

On the roof of the building, and the buildings surrounding Ben's CP, teams of Dan's Scouts were in place, with mortars, rocket launchers, and .50-caliber machine guns.

"Come on, you sleazy sons of bitches," Ben muttered. "Come tell us about how it was all society's fault that you turned out to be such assholes. Let's rock and roll some." He started humming "Bad Moon Rising."

Dan looked over at him and smiled. He would have preferred "Ride of the Valkyries."

Buddy grinned in the semi-gloom of the room, knowing his father was in his element now. He had never met a man who enjoyed combat more than Ben Raines. The Rebels had long ago ceased any attempts to put Ben behind the lines, behind a desk.

A rocket exploded against the side of the building, on the ground floor, and the early evening was suddenly shattered by the roar of hundreds of weapons, yammering on full auto.

"Flares up!" Ben yelled.

Outside, dozens of flares lit up the dusk, exposing the street punks as they charged the Rebels' positions from all sides. Ben let out a war cry that would have put a Cheyenne chief to shame and opened up with his Thunder Lizard, holding the trigger back. One line of street punks went down as the .308 slugs impacted against flesh and bone.

Ben slipped the empty, popped a full clip into the belly of the old war hoss, and let it bang.

Buddy had pinned down a small band of punks with his M-60 and was making life awfully miserable for them. One stuck his head up just as Buddy was making a return sweep and the punk lost the entire top of his head. His friend squatting next to him received the full compliment of brains and eyeballs. He jumped up screaming in terror and Buddy stitched him across the chest. Now all he had to worry about was facing his Maker, and He was not a terribly forgiving God.

Smoot and Chester were in a box-bed, under the desk, with a flak jacket wrapped around the both of them, secured so they could not slip out of it.

Ben shifted positions and took a quick look out what remained of a shattered window. "Take over here," Ben called to a Rebel.

"Where are you going, Dad?" Buddy yelled over the roar of gunfire.

"To the bathroom maybe. None of your business." Ben hurried low across the floor and out the door of the second-story office, into the hall. But he couldn't shake Jersey, who was staying right behind him.

"Get back to your position," Ben ordered.

"Sorry," she told him. "Where you go, I go. So just lead on."

"Hardhead," Ben muttered.

"Look who's talking, will you? Come on, General. What's going on?"

"Hostiles have infiltrated the building next to this one, that's what."

"And you were going to take them out by yourself?"

"There aren't that many of them."

"How many?"

"Oh, a dozen or so."

"That's good, General. Excellent. Has it ever occurred to you that you are not Superman? Has it?

194

That a lot of people spend a lot of time just trying to keep you alive? Huh. Do you know—"

"Hush up and come on if you're going with me, Jersey." Ben turned his head and grinned at her. "Hell, there're two of us—we've got them outnumbered already."

She gave him a dark look and muttered something under her breath. But she followed him. Jersey would have followed Ben through the gates of Hell.

They slipped down the stairs and paused by the back door. Flares were constantly being fired high into the air, keeping the night bright with artificial light. Ben pulled Jersey close and put his lips next to her ear so he could be heard over the yammer of gunfire.

"We go out the door and cut immediately to our left, keeping between those old garbage dumpsters and this building. That way we'll stay in the shadows. Once across the alley, we toss Fire-Frags in and follow. You ready?"

"Oh, sure. I can't begin to tell you how much I'm looking forward to this."

Ben chuckled. "Let's do it."

They exited the building quickly, Ben in the lead. Working their way past two old dumpsters, they both bellied down on the littered concrete as two street punks ran past their position and into the building across the alley.

"That makes it either fourteen or sixteen," Jersey muttered. "Right?"

Ben smiled and whispered, "We still have them outnumbered, short-stuff. Let's go."

They ran across the alleyway and flattened against the old building, one on each side of a huge paneless window. Ben pulled a Fire-Frag from his battle harness and Jersey did the same. They looked at one another as the sounds of voices came from inside the building. Jersey nodded her head.

Two Fire-Frags were chunked into the ground floor of the building. The door blew off from the concussion of the exploding grenades.

The shrapnel had just ceased bouncing off the interior and the screaming of the wounded had begun when Ben and Jersey rolled into the room and laid down a field of automatic fire, effectively clearing the area of street punks. With their ears ringing from the concussion of the mini-Claymores, Ben and Jersey got their bearings and spread out, covering the only door they could see from the dim light of the flares. It went to the second floor. They could both hear the faint sounds of footsteps above them.

"Goddamnit, there ain't no other way out!" the voice said, reaching Ben and Jersey.

"Take a peek down there."

"You so damn interested, you take a peek."

Ben and Jersey remained silent, crouched behind a pile of junk in the room, their weapons set on full auto, each with a fresh clip. They waited, eyes on the blackness of the open stairwell leading to the second-floor.

A lone figure came cautiously down the steps and stuck his head into the dimness of the room. Ben and Jersey waited. They didn't want just one punk dead—they wanted them all dead.

"Fuller's dead," the punk called over his shoulder. "I can see half a dozen more on the floor. All blown to shit. There ain't nobody movin'."

Several more punks gathered around the first

196

one at the base of the stairs, none of them wanting to take that first step into the ground floor room, but knowing they had to do so if they were to get away.

"They was waitin' on us." Words just reached Ben and Jersey over the diminishing din of battle. "Bull's plan didn't turn out worth a damn. They knew we was comin'."

"This ain't the time to discuss it. You see anybody down yonder?"

"No. I can't see nothin' 'ceptin' dead people."

"Come on."

The punks crowded out of the stairwell and onto the ground floor.

Ben and Jersey opened up, the Thunder Lizard and the M-16 blasting the darkness. The street punks were slammed back against a wall as the slugs tore the life from them. Ben and Jersey ceased fire and waited. A faint moaning came from the piled-up bodies by the stairs.

"That's it," Ben said. "Let's see what we have over there that might be able to talk."

Two were still alive. One of them was hard hit in the guts and dying. The other had suffered only two minor flesh wounds.

"Eagle to Rat," Ben spoke into his walkie-talkie.

"Goddamnit, Dad, where are you?" Buddy's voice held more than a note of irritation.

"In the building just north of your location. Ground floor. Come on over. We have a prisoner. The ground floor is clear. I can't be sure about the other floors, so watch it."

Buddy and Dan and a squad of Rebels were in the building within two minutes.

"This craphead isn't hurt bad," a medic said.

"He's got lots of conversation in him."

"I ain't tellin' you bastards nothin'!" the punk said, spitting out the words.

Dan smiled at him in the gloom. The smile was very much like a cobra before a strike. "Oh, I think you'll be chattering like a magpie before long."

At daylight, the punk was tossed out onto the sidewalk, weaponless, and told to hit the road. He had been wrong. He'd had plenty to say to Dan and Ben. It had just taken a little persuading, that's all.

The Rebels had not physically tortured the young man. He'd been interrogated with the use of drugs.

Sixty thousand punks and creepies," Ben said, after taking a sip of coffee. "Well, I guess that means we do have our work cut out for us. Of course, that was a guess on his part, since I doubt that any census has ever been taken of the current population of Los Angeles."

The fighting had all but ceased, the punks retreating several blocks at first light. The Rebels were still loosely trapped—in a manner of speaking—but the punks were now in that unenviable position of riding a tiger: afraid to turn loose and afraid to stay on.

"Get me a report from all units, Corrie," Ben requested.

"Working on it now, sir," she called. A moment later, she said, "All units holding firm with no ground lost. Reporting five dead and eleven wounded during the night. Several prisoners were taken and their stories match the one told us."

Ben picked up his M-14. "All right, people. Tired we may be, but we've got to take some ground today. The one thing the punks won't be expecting is a counterattack from us this early. Ready tear gas and everybody into masks. We're going to do our best to clear everything between us and Therm. Let's do it."

Tear gas canisters and smoke grenades and shells began raining down all around the area, the choking and blinding fumes masking the forward movement of the Rebels as they counterattacked the street punks.

It was door-to-door and building-to-building fighting, with small arms and grenades, the Rebels offering no mercy or pity to the punks as they staggered out of hiding places, tears streaming down their faces from the gas. The Rebels took no prisoners as they advanced. Knowing this, many of the punks ran from the relentless advance. Ben Raines's philosophy of war was simple. We will give you one chance to surrender. If you do not take it at the time it is offered, you will die. There will be no second chances. It was a hard philosophy, enforced by hard men and women, in a hard and harsh time on earth.

The Rebels brought up flamethrowers, torching as they advanced, the flame-tossers adding a new element of fear among the punks.

Ben stepped into a doorway and came face to face with a street punk dressed all in white, from his funky tennis shoes to the white headband.

He screamed obscenities at Ben.

Ben lifted the muzzle of his M-14 and added a touch of red to the natty outfit.

Automatic-rifle fire knocked out splinters of wood from the old building, the splinters bloodying Ben's face. He wiped the blood away and ran into the building. He cut to one side and hit the floor rolling just as a woman dressed in a bright yellow shirt cut loose with an AK-47.

"Bastard!" she screamed at him, the AK bucking and jumping in her hands.

Jersey appeared in the doorway and stitched the woman with a burst from her M-16, then jumped and rolled inside just as Ben was getting to his knees, his Thunder Lizard howling, the muzzle pointed at a knot of men and women all jammed up in a doorway leading to the outside.

Ben slapped in a fresh clip and cleared the log-jam, the .308 slugs knocking several of the group outside and the rest of them spinning to the floor, their blood staining the dirty floor and the walls.

Beth and Cooper ran into the house, followed by Corrie and Linda.

"Hail, hail, the gang's all here," Ben called cheerfully, his voice muffled through the gas mask. He winked at Linda.

"The man has a sense of humor," Linda said, just as a burst of lead sent them all belly-down on the floor. She crawled to a window, Corrie right behind her, and between the two of them filled the smoky air with lead and double-ought buckshot and some very unladylike cussing.

"Tsk, tsk," Ben said.

Linda and Corrie turned to look at him and he shut up.

A grenade came sailing through a shattered window and bounced along the floor, sending everybody jumping for whatever cover they could find.

In Ben's case, no cover. He was squatting in the center of the big room.

Jersey threw herself on the grenade, covering it with her body. "Get down, General!" she screamed.

Chapter Fourteen

Ben froze, watching as Jersey closed her eyes and move her lips in silent prayer.

Five seconds took ten minutes to tick by. "It's a dud, Jersey," Ben called. "Throw yourself away from it as far as you can."

"I'm too scared to move, General."

"Do it, Jersey. Now!"

She hurled herself from the grenade, rolling on the floor, and Cooper grabbed her, pulling her away.

"Leave it alone, General!" Dan's voice came sharp from the doorway. "Just stay right where you are." He walked to the grenade, picked it up, and threw it out a window. It bounced off a building, hit the alleyway, and blew. "Sometimes they do that," the Englishman said. "Unpredictable little buggers."

Ben got up and walked over to Jersey, putting his arms around her, holding her close. She was still trembling. "What can I say, Jersey?"

She pulled back and grinned up at him. "Well, sir, you could give me a raise."

And amid the sounds of the battle raging outside, laughter rolled from the ground floor.

From Ike's position on the west side of west Los Angeles, to the mercenary's position on the east side of the combat area, the Rebels no longer felt they were trapped, even though they were, in a manner of speaking.

The street punks and the creepies had not only been thrown back, they had suffered terrible casualties during the failed assault. The dead were scooped up and placed in buildings, then the buildings set on fire.

The Rebels resumed their slow, block-by-block taking of the last major bastion of lawlessness and cannibalism and slavery in the lower forty-eight.

Ike and his people were clearing and burning the west side of West Los Angeles, pushing up to the San Diego Freeway and driving hard and relentlessly toward L.A. proper.

Therm, Ben, and Cecil began slowly pushing the punks and the creepies who fought with them south, while Georgi and West linked up and began their slow advance toward the sea. The Rebels who had been on Santa Catalina Island were now, at Ben's orders, linked up with West.

Four long and bloody days after the failed assault by the street punks, Ben told his people to stand down for twenty-four hours and catch their breaths.

While to the uninitiated it might seem premature, Ben knew his Rebels now had the upper hand and were going to win this fight. The street punks had thrown everything they had at the

Rebels, and the Rebels had held and were now once more advancing. The fight was a long way from being over. Weeks of bloody work still lay ahead of the Rebels. But the street punks were going to lose. Ben suspected that even they knew it.

Ben had relaxed the rules concerning prisoners, and had allowed his people to take alive those punks who had come staggering and weeping out of the burning and smoking rubble of war. They were transported north, into the forests and canyons north of the city, and were guarded by the Woods Children. As slaves and prisoners were liberated by the Rebels, trials were held. Any punk who was identified as having killed in cold blood, raped, or tortured was put to death.

Ben had heard horror stories coming out of what was called the zone, and wanted a meeting of his commanders. He had some news for them.

Ike jumped straight out of his chair, yelling. "You're gonna do what? Goddamnit, Ben, that's the dumbest damn thing I ever heard you propose."

Ben sat calmly. He had anticipated the uproar and was ready for it.

"I absolutely forbid it," Cecil said, shaking his head. "No. No. Under no circumstances, no! Reckless on your part and just too dangerous."

The mercenary, West, said, "General, I believe that would be very irresponsible on your part. I'm against it."

Therm said nothing because nothing Ben Raines ever did surprised him.

"Stupid!" Doctor Chase said. "Just plain stupid.

But I'm not surprised that you'd come up with something this half-cocked."

"I might go along with it only if I could accompany you," Dan said.

"You'll be in command of my section here," Ben told him. "And Cecil will be in command overall."

The yelling started anew.

Ben poured another cup of coffee, petted Smoot, who was laying on the desk, and waited it out.

"Ridiculous!" General Georgi Striganov snorted his disapproval. "If anyone at all goes, it should be me."

"I'll take two companies, a complement of armor, and Buddy and his Rat Team. We'll pull out in twenty-four hours."

"You will, by God, take a platoon of my Scouts!" Dan stood up. "And that is something I insist upon, General."

Ben knew to argue with the Englishmen, who was as hardheaded as Ben was, would be futile. He nodded his head in agreement. "All right, Dan. Fine."

Ben was going out into the foreboding and mysterious area called the zone.

"I'll put together a medical team for you," Chase said, knowing the brief argument was over. Once Ben made up his mind, there was no turning him around.

"Well, shit!" Ike said, disgust in his voice. "I'll order flyovers to start immediately."

Ben nixed that. "Keep the planes on the ground," he said, scratching Smoot behind the ears. The husky rolled over on her back and

205

grumbled in contentment. "We don't know whether or not the warlords out there have rockets capable of bringing a plane down. Let's don't risk it."

"Ben," Georgi said, trying one more time. "I wish you would reconsider. That area called the zone is hundreds and hundreds of square miles of hostile territory. None of us really knows what is out there."

"That's why I'm going," Ben replied. "To find out. We do know that there are slave and breeding farms out there, and I'm going to put a stop to them. It's something that will have to be done at some point in this campaign, so let's get it done now. Dan will take over for me here. Cecil is Forces Commander. That's it, people."

The unit commanders filed out, to a person bitching and grumbling and cussing, but all knowing there was no point in arguing further with Ben.

Ben smiled at Linda. "Well, how about it? Ready for a little adventure?"

She returned the smile. "Oh, sure, Ben. I mean, it's been so damned dull around here."

Ben walked the line, inspecting his command just moments before pullout. Five main battle tanks, five Dusters, five M113's, five LAV-25 Piranhas. A line of tankers and supply trucks. Two full companies of Rebels, a platoon of Dan's Scouts, and Buddy's Rat Team.

It was a lot more personnel and equipment than Ben wanted to take with him, but it was better than having to put up with several days of argument from the others. And Ben also knew that his days of just taking off and lone-wolfing it were gone. Too many people depended on him; he had too many decisions to make. This was about the closest that he was going to come to being a lone wolf in search of action.

"The first good-sized town we come to," Ben told Dan, "I'll secure an airstrip for supply planes. Providing there are no surface-to-air missiles out there. I have a hunch we're going to be taking a lot of people out of the zone. And they are not going to be in very good shape."

"You know that I should be leading this expedition," Dan said, trying one more time.

Ben smiled and ignored the statement. "Keep the home fires burning and the feet of the punks in the flames, Dan. I'll be in radio contact. Good luck."

"Good luck to you, sir."

"Mount up!" Ben yelled. "Let's go."

The column headed north, driving through all the still-smoking devastation they had earlier wrought. They cut east until they found a winding two-lane highway that ran through the San Gabriel Mountains. The Rebels bivouacked that evening in the mountains, and were all both pleased and somewhat spiritually moved at the serenity of their surroundings, untouched by all the hideousness and suffering that lay only a few miles to the south.

At dawn, they were rolling eastward, and soon picked up Interstate 40.

"How far do we take it, General?" Cooper asked.

"All the way to Needles, Coop. We'll stop at every town and look it over. Beth, did the vehicles' water tanker fill up last night at that stream?"

"Yes, sir. Filled to capacity."

"That's good. Because it's about to get dry up ahead."

Bone dry. "Like in a desert," was Jersey's comment about the country they were passing through.

Barstow had been destroyed. Little remained of it except for burned-out buildings, and the walls of those structures were pockmarked with old bullet scars.

Barstow had been a thriving community of nearly twenty thousand. Now there were no signs of life.

"Hell of a battle fought here," Cooper remarked. "Several years ago, I'd say."

The convoy had stopped in the center of the burned-out town. "Scouts out," Ben ordered. "Look it over."

No signs of human habitation, they reported back.

The convoy rolled on.

There was nothing left worth salvaging in the tiny towns that had once existed alongside the Interstate. They had all been destroyed and picked over countless times. Carrion birds and rats had picked the human skeletons clean of flesh, leaving the bones to bleach in the sun and be eventually scattered by the desert winds. The Rebels inspected the towns and then rolled on. They made a very dry camp at the southern edge of the Bristol Mountains. Since leaving the northern edge of the sprawling city of L.A., none of them had seen any sign of a living human being. They had seen the fleeting shapes of coyotes darting, seen tracks of wolves once more returning to their rightful place in the scheme of things, and had heard the screams of pumas at night. But no signs of humans.

"It's eerie," Linda said over a second cup of coffee as they all sat around a campfire. "It's like we were suddenly transported to a new world, void of life."

"And technically," Buddy said, warming his hands over the fire, for the nights were cool, "we're not even in what is referred to as the zone."

"I believe that this is called a no-man's-land," Ben said. "And I can certainly see why."

"Tomorrow, Father?" Buddy asked.

"We'll have us a look at Needles, and then cut south, on Highway 95. We'll take that down to Blythe, and from there we'll head on down to Yuma. From Yuma to Calexico. There, we'll have to figure out a route."

"Do we have any intelligence on what we might find there?" a Rebel asked.

"Only what some prisoners have told us, and how much of that we can believe is up for grabs," Ben said. "Outlaws, punks, thugs, drifters, slavers, murderers, human crud of the worst sort. If you can hang a name on the dregs of society, you'll find them where we're going."

"And we are going straight in, right, General?" Beth asked.

"That's right." Ben smiled at her. "We'll just call ourselves . . . ah, well, *missionaries*. Going on our way spreading the good word."

Buddy returned his father's smile. "Are you going to give us bibles to pass out, Father?"

"You already have them, boy. They're just in a slightly different form than the King James version."

Buddy held up his old Thompson.

"That's it, son. Yea, verily, and all that. Amen."

"Somebody drag them out of the road and burn the bodies," Ben said, as he looked down at the dead outlaws who had tried to block their entrance into Needles. "Buddy, take a couple of tanks and a company and secure the town, please. We know they have prisoners in there, so try to take them alive. Corrie, get me Ike or Cecil on the horn."

After a moment, Corrie said, "Cecil is out of pocket. Ike is on scramble."

"Yo, Ben." Ike's voice came out of the speaker. The sounds of artillery booming in the background was strong. "What's your twenty, Eagle?"

"Needles. The town's got some crud in it and we believe they're holding prisoners. We'll take it and move on. How's it going on your end?"

"Moving right along, Eagle. We're advancing three or four blocks a day, pushing the punks and the creepies south. Ben, you might find yourself in a very bad position if you advance further west than Calexico."

"I know. But I haven't made up my mind what we're going to do yet. We'll secure the airstrip at Blythe and bump you from there. Eagle out."

Ben handed the mike to Corrie and listened as a short battle raged within the shattered remains of the small town. Buddy returned, escorting a band of prisoners.

"I knew it!" a woman hollered, as she came within sight of Ben. "I done tol' you and tol' you it had to be him. I tol' you we all ought to run."

"Shut up," a man said.

"Civilians?" Ben looked at Buddy.

"They killed all the prisoners before we could get to them, Father," his son told him. "They just lined them up and shot them."

"Why would they do that?" Linda asked.

"To keep them from talking, telling us all the horrors these crud have put them through." Ben faced the man who had told the women to shut up. "You—what can we expect in Blythe?"

The man spat on the ground. "Screw you, asshole!"

Ben butt-stroked him with the M-14, knocking the outlaw to the ground. Ben placed the muzzle of the rifle against the man's forehead. "I am accustomed to having my questions answered in a civil manner, punk. Now do so."

The outlaw with the busted and bloody mouth spat out broken teeth and lay on the ground, looking up at Ben. Fear crept into his eyes. He had known for years that Ben Raines and the Rebels would someday come; had known for years that he should change his ways and stop his career of lawlessness. And now he knew it was too late. His guts knotted in fear as he realized that death lay laughing at him just around a dark corner.

"I'll be good," he mumbled. "I promise that I'll

211

be good. I swear it!"

The hard eyes of Ben did not change. Contempt for the outlaw touched his face briefly. "You'll be good only as long as the Rebels stay around. So let's don't kid each other. You can live three more minutes, or you can die right now. It's up to you. What's in Blythe?"

The outlaw was shaking in fright. He used to think it funny when his prisoners trembled in fear, crying and begging for their lives. Now he could not find a single amusing thing about it as he pissed his dirty underwear. "You don't strike a very good deal a-tall, General."

"I don't make deals with punks," Ben told him. "It's not a good practice. Speak your piece."

"Fuck you!"

Ben shot him. He walked over to another man. The man dropped to his knees and began praying. He prayed for forgiveness for all the women he'd raped and sodomized. The men he'd tortured and enslaved. The children he'd sexually abused. Jersey listened to him and spat on the ground.

"What's in Blythe?" Ben asked, when the punk paused to catch his breath.

"Texas Jim!" the man screamed, his spittle spraying Ben's trousers. "Jesus God Almighty! You ain't got no right to do this. We human bein's. I'll admit we done wrong, but give us a break. I got constitutional rights, General. I want to see a judge. I want me a lawyer. I got rights under the Geneva Convention. I got—"

A bullet.

The thugs and punks and outlaws and their women began crying and praying and begging.

Ben moved to another man. Put the muzzle of his M-14 on the man's forehead. "The longer you talk, the longer you live."

Linda understood it then—finally, why the lawless feared Ben Raines so. There was no give in the man. None. You obeyed the few laws that the Rebels laid down, or you lay down dead. He was flint-hard and uncompromising. And he was going to win. She knew in her mind that nothing was going to stop him. No woman would ever change him, no man would ever break him.

"Texas Jim is a warlord, General," the outlaw told him, his voice numb with shock and fear. "He's got him a good-sized army down yonder. 'Bout two hundred and fifty tough ol' boys. You know what I mean?"

"I certainly know the type. White trash and assorted other assholes who believe they are above any law. Go on."

The outlaw thought about that as beads of sweat broke out on his forehead. "He be waitin' for you, General."

"You think maybe I should run back to my vehicle and hide my face in fear?" Ben asked.

"I reckon not," the man said slowly. He turned his head to look at other Rebels, gathered around. There was no pity on their faces. They were expressionless. A couple of them were eating rations out of cans. One was stretched out, catnapping in the shade of a big tanker. One woman was brushing her short hair.

"Yuma?" Ben asked.

"That would be Banniger and his bunch. About the same size as Texas Jim."

213

"Calexico?"

"That, I don't know. Things are subject to change from one week to another. That's right on the edge of the zone, so gang leaders come and go. Last I heard they be nearabouts a thousand or more toughs down yonder. You gonna let me live?"

"Give me one reason why I should."

The outlaw hesitated, thinking so hard his eyes bugged out. He had killed and raped and assaulted and in general made life miserable for nearly everyone he had come in contact with for years. He tried to think of some decent act he had done. He could not. He recalled the time he'd been with that bunch when they'd attacked a nearby Indian reservation and killed all the men and raped the women and young girls—and a few boys too. Just to hear them holler and squall. He swallowed hard. "You cain't just line us up and shoot us, General. That wouldn't be right."

"Isn't that what you people just did with your prisoners?"

"Well . . . yeah. But you 'posed to show us mercy. That's the way it's 'posed to work. I mean, after all, I was an abused child."

The Rebels had piled the bodies in a building and then set it on fire. Smoke from the burning town was in their rearview mirrors as they pulled out.

Linda was silent as the long miles rolled by. Finally, Ben said, "Say what's on your mind, Linda."

"The begging of those people back there, Ben,

214

just before they were shot."

"What about it?"

"Doesn't it bother you?"

"Not anymore. It used to," Ben admitted. "But then I have always known that people have a choice of several roads to follow. Nobody forces them to travel any of life's choices. Anytime you have to put a gun to someone's head, to force a promise from them to obey even the simplest of rules, you are dealing with a loser, a liar, and a punk. Our way is very simple, Linda, with no complex legal mumbo jumbo. The Rebel road is wide and free. Be whatever you want to be as long as you obey the few laws we enforce. The other roads are rough and rocky, and violent death at the hands of Rebels is all that's waiting at the end of those narrow paths. And those who choose the lawless routes know it. They always have, Linda. No matter what lawyers and judges and social workers and psychiatrists used to say, the lawless knew what they were doing. And they did it because they had nothing but contempt for those of us who chose to obey the law. I have nothing but loathing for them.

"My God, Linda, we're living in the simplest of times since humankind crawled out of the caves. All one has to do is find an abandoned house and start anew. All one has to do is flag down a Rebel patrol and say, I want to join you. It doesn't make any difference what one was before the Great War. We don't care. We don't look back. Now and the future are all we're concerned with. If you can't live with that, Linda, go on back to your peaceful little valley—what's left of it—and see how long

215

you can survive without us."

She was silent for another few miles. "No, I'll stick it out, Ben. Just give me a little time." She smiled. "You see, I was one of those opposed to the death penalty back when the world was whole, so to speak."

"We have a number of them within our ranks, Linda. But they saw the light, and I suspect so have you, or you wouldn't be here."

"The callousness of it all is still a little mind-numbing. We used to see it in the movies, but we knew it wasn't real. They were actors, and they'd get up and walk off once the scene was shot. But I'll pull my weight while I'm getting accustomed to the Rebel way."

"You certainly have so far, and I have no reason to doubt your ability to do so in the future. Sure, it's mind-numbing, Linda. Unlike the movies or on the pages of a book, here you smell the urine and the excrement after the bullets strike, and sometimes before they do. Few people can face death as calmly as they believe they can."

"So I have discovered," she said, a dryness to her words. "No, Ben, I'm with the Rebels all the way. I'll stick it out."

"Good," Ben said, a pleased note in his words. "You'll make it, Linda. Part of your mind is still operating on yesterday's premise that we have courts and halfway houses and all the trimmings that go with civilization. But we don't. What you really haven't grasped is that all that stands between anarchy and order is a very thin line of men and women called the Rebels. But understand this, Linda. Once we clear the lower forty-

216

eight, the laws we'll set in place will never be what they were back before the Great War. Not as long as I'm alive. Or Buddy or Tina or Ike or Cecil or West or Georgi or Dan, or any Rebel for that matter. We will never allow that to happen. Not again. In our society, right is clearly spelled out, as is wrong, and there is only dark water and quicksand between the two—no gray. No legal jargon, no plea-bargaining, no defendant's tearful pleading that it quote-unquote 'won't happen again and I'm so sorry I got drunk and killed those people.'

"It's bullshit when people say they didn't know they were drunk when they got behind the wheel of a car. They knew. They just didn't care. So why should we care what happens to them? It was bullshit when a hunter killed another hunter by shooting him out of a tree and said he was so sorry but he thought it was a deer or a squirrel. What it was was an irresponsible act by an asshole with a gun. And it wasn't the fault of the gun; someone has to be behind the trigger. It was bullshit then and it's still bullshit when a criminal says that society drove him or her to kill and steal and assault and maim.

"The Rebels, Linda, all of us, would much rather be back in Alabama or Nebraska or Michigan or Louisiana or New Hampshire, farming or tending shop or raising cattle and hogs and watching our kids grow up or doing whatever is legal and moral. But we chose instead to fight to pull this country, and the world, out of the ashes of horror. I'd like to go back to Base Camp One, take off my boots, hang up my guns, and write,

Linda. And I'll do it someday, God willing. I'll have my dogs at my feet and fingers on the keys of a typewriter, and my guns will be cleaned and oiled and in a gun case. And the front door will never be locked and I can leave the keys in my car or truck, and no one will have to worry about some perverted son of a bitch grabbing their kids or raping their wife. Because we don't need those kinds of people, Linda. And whenever anything like that happens in Rebel-held territory, justice comes down swift but fair, and nearly always final.

"There is a line from an old World War Two song: 'The White Cliffs of Dover.' It goes something like this: 'There'll be love and laughter, and peace ever after, when the world is free.' And we're going to see that day, Linda. The Rebels—all of us. A year ago, I wouldn't have said it. But now I believe that. Me and my kids and hopefully my grandkids, and that overaged hippie Thermopolis, and the little con artist Emil Hite, and the Russian and the Englishman and the mercenary.

"We're going to free the world from savagery and oppression and fear. We're going to do it, Linda. We know how now. We've got it down to a fine art. The people with any degree of decency in them either join us actively, set up outposts, or agree to live in peace with all other living beings . . . and that includes animals. Those that won't agree to those terms fight us and die. My grandkids, Linda, if I ever have any, are going to live free and without fear of thugs and punks and assholes. And if I have to die in a ditch somewhere insuring them that right, then so be it."

A mile passed in silence. "Well, shit!" Corrie said.

"What's the matter with you?" Jersey asked.

"The best speech I ever heard the general make and the goddamn batteries went dead in my tape recorder!"

They all spent the next several miles laughing uproariously and wiping tears from their eyes.

Chapter Fifteen

"Buddy is reporting that this Texas Jim outlaw has a tad more than two hundred and fifty men, General," Corrie said.

The column had stopped for lunch on the east side of the Big Maria Mountains, about twenty-five miles north of Blythe.

Ben smiled at that. "Corrie, inform my usually erudite son that a 'tad more' doesn't tell me a whole lot."

"Yes, sir." She bumped Buddy, then turned back to Ben. "He says to try about five hundred or so men in the gang."

Ben nodded his head and looked to Linda as she asked, "Where are all the good, decent people, Ben? Are they like the people I was with for years, hiding out in tiny pockets?"

"A lot of them, yes. There are a lot of good people out there." He waved his hand. "We just have to find them. Punks and crud and scum just seem to naturally come together, like flies on a pile of shit. But we're finding more and more decent people in our travels."

Ben washed down the last bite of his rations with warm water from his canteen and screwed the cap back on. "All right, people," he said, standing up.

"Let's gear up and button down. Playtime is over."

Buddy met the column about a mile north of the town. "The outlaws say we don't have the right to come in here and tell them what to do, Father. Texas Jim said, and I'm quoting directly here: 'There ain't no government and there ain't no laws, and just 'cause your name is Ben Raines that don't spell jack-shit to me.' "

"My, but he does coin a lovely phrase, doesn't he?"

"Yes. Very quaint."

"Prisoners?"

"Not according to the man my team went in, pulled out, and questioned. They've had prisoners, slaves, but they just traded several dozen of them to another group of trash down the road. For drugs."

"Where is this man?"

"He died."

"I see. How unfortunate for him. How are the outlaws armed, son?"

"Assault rifles, grenades, light mortars. According to the thug we questioned, there are no SAMs here or anywhere else in the zone."

"Ben Raines!" The shout came pushing out of huge speakers located at the edge of town. "My name is Texas Jim, and I got this here to say to you and your soldier boys and girls. You bes' carry your asses on away from here, 'fore I decide to kick all your asses clear over into Arizona."

The Rebels all shared a good laugh at that.

"Oh, my," Ben said. "Do you think we should run away and hide, son?"

"That thought did not enter my mind, Father."

"Well, then, how do you suppose I should reply to his challenge?"

"I'm sure you'll think of some highly appropriate answer," the young man said dryly.

"Ummm." Ben feigned deep thought, then snapped his fingers. "By golly, son, I think I've come up with something."

"I knew you would. I have great faith in you, Father."

"Thank you, son. Corrie, tell the tank commanders to crank up their 105's and start dropping in HE and incendiary rounds, please."

Ben let the thunder roll and roar for five minutes, until the entire northern section of the town was blazing. Ben then moved the column up to within a few hundred yards of the edge of town. Buddy handed his father a bullhorn.

Ben lifted the horn to his lips. "Now you listen to me, you redneck asshole!" Ben's voice boomed over the short distance. "You have three choices: stand and die, surrender, or cut and run. Make up your mind, prick!"

The elaborate speaker system of Texas Jim had been destroyed during the first salvo. Using a bullhorn, the outlaw screamed, "I'll kill you someday, Raines! I swear on my mother's pitcher I'll cut your nuts off and do a diddy-wa-diddy on them, you son of a bitch!"

Ben lifted the bullhorn. "You have one minute to respond, armadillo-breath."

Linda cut her eyes at him and started giggling. *Armadillo-breath!*

Buddy was lying by the turret of a tank, behind sandbags, looking at the town through binoculars. "There they go, Father," he called. "They're heading south. I don't understand this, because we're going to have to fight them someday. Why not do it now and get it over with?"

Ben looked up at the young man. "You know anything about herding cattle, son?"

"I can't say that I do."

"I didn't either, until I started writing Westerns, years ago." Ben winked at Linda and walked off.

Buddy jumped down from the tank. "Now what in the hell is he up to?"

"He'll tell us when he's ready," Beth replied.

"I'm a-tellin' you, Banniger," Texas Jim said to the outlaw at his headquarters just over the line at Yuma, "Ben Raines is a-comin' and there ain't nothin' on this earth gonna stop him. He's a devil, man. A devil straight out of hell."

"He's a man, just like us. What we got to do is come up with a plan, Jim," Banniger said. "Mexico is no safe haven for us no more. Not since the people down there rose up and threw us all out. Goddamn greasers. Who'd have thought them stupid peasants would ever do something like that?"

"We can't stop them Rebels, Banniger. They're outnumbered ten, twelve to one over in southern California, and they're steady kickin' ass."

"I know," Banniger said.

"Well, what the hell is we gonna do then!"

"We do some thinking, Jim. That's all we can do."

"We're picking up a lot of transmissions in Spanish, General," Ben was informed. "Garcia is translating and he says there has been a major revolution in Mexico. The people have risen up and reclaimed their country. They're redistributing land and power

223

and are picking up the pieces and putting their country back together." He paused. "They are patterning their laws after the laws being set up in this country by one General Ben Raines."

"It was only a matter of time," Ben said, sugaring his coffee. "We've known there were many survivors down there, and they knew we were up here. But so far, they have not asked for our help. Advise them that we will lend a hand if they need it. And also ask the commanders if they would help us if we request it."

The reply was prompt and courteous. The Mexicans had things under control in most areas and they would be more than happy to assist General Raines in any manner possible.

"Tell them I wish them much success and I will be in touch shortly," Ben said. He smiled. "Well, now, that's one nation we don't have to worry about."

"How does it feel to be so big a part of history, Ben?" Linda asked.

Ben glanced at her, a startled look in his eyes. "I beg your pardon?"

"Georgi Striganov and the Canadians have adopted your method of law enforcement and justice. Now the people of Mexico have done the same. Your plans are to span the globe. You're a part of history, Ben."

Ben grimaced. "Just don't start putting up any statues yet," he said sourly.

"Why get so grumpy about it, Ben? It's your concept."

"It isn't *my* concept, Linda. It's been the concept of free-thinking men and women for years. The goddamn lawyers and civil rights groups—and I'm not talking about racial issues here—screwed it all up for the majority of people. A very small power-hungry minority of people at the federal level ran the lives of millions."

"And in the end, you won't be doing the same, Ben?" she asked softly.

"Me? Hell, no! You still haven't grasped the big picture, have you, Linda? There will be a small bureaucracy in our government; that's almost unavoidable. But it will be kept small. There will be police and deputies, but the chiefs and sheriffs won't be elected in some popularity contest, they'll be appointed on the basis of their ability to do the job. And they won't have much to do. Look, the Rebel way is this: If a person puts a fence around their property, and posts No Trespassing signs, that person is telling *everybody* to stay the hell off and out. And it doesn't make any difference if the gates are open or closed. You walk on that property and get hurt, that's your problem. Somebody sticks a gun or a knife in another person's face and gets killed, the case is closed after a very brief investigation. The Rebel concept is based on common sense and damn few rules. That's why so many people can't live under our system. It's too simple for them. They just seem unable to grasp the fact that Big Brother is, for the most part, out of their lives."

"But the children . . ."

Ben waved her silent. "Unlike the system of old, Linda, children are taught from kindergarten on that rules are made to be obeyed, not broken. It sounds very totalitarian, but it really isn't. Our system is built on respect for the other person. It's taught in our schools. We don't teach rumor or myth, we teach solid fact. If it can't be proved, we don't teach it. We neither teach the Big Bang theory nor Creationism. That's something we leave up to the parents. Ignorant people just can't make it in the Rebel system, neither can pompous, arrogant people. Trouble-makers and bullies don't last very long. We have a few basic laws; everything else is decided by town meeting. That's because what is good for an outpost in New Mexico might not be so good for an outpost in upstate New York. It's a simple society, Linda. And the great thing about it is that it works."

"But not for everybody, Ben."

"That's certainly true. Small-minded and petty people can't make it in this society. People who won't respect the rights of others can't make it. People who delight in spreading vicious gossip have a tough time. People who like to belittle others don't last long."

"But what happens to those people, Ben?"

"We don't care what happens to them, Linda. We don't have time to try to reeducate them. Maybe later, but not now. Ours is not a perfect system, far from it. And it will moderate in the severity of punishment as the years go by and our educational system discharges more and more graduates of our system. Schooled from kindergarten through high school and college to respect others, the land, and the animals that live on it."

"Some might call that *brainwashing*, Ben."

"Some already have, and it is to a degree. But if respecting the rights of other law-abiding citizens, being good caretakers of the land, and seeing to it that entire species of animals are not wiped out due to man's greed and ignorance is brainwashing, I'll accept that accusation."

226

Linda smiled at him. "You know something, Ben, you missed your calling."

"Oh?"

"You'd have made a dandy politician!"

The entire camp was yelling and cheering and making bets as Ben chased her around the bivouac area, hollering how dare she call him a goddamned politician! But as the saying goes, he chased her until she caught him.

Ike, Therm, Cecil, Georgi, West, and their forces continued to hammer at the street punks and the Believers in the Los Angeles area. Each day dawned with new ground gained. Two blocks one day, four blocks another, one block the next; but always an advance, with the Rebels blowing up and burning everything in their path as they fought on.

The Rebels under Ben's command stayed in Blythe for several days, cleaning up that area of the town that had not been destroyed by artillery, and clearing the small airport. Survivors were flown in from months of rehabilitation and reorientation at Base Camp One. The men and women and kids were a far cry from what they had been when the Rebels rescued them from various outlaw and warlord strongholds around the nation. They were now a fit and healthy and determined bunch. Never again would they allow thugs and punks and outlaws to overwhelm them.

"It's your town," Ben told them. "Your area of control. Good luck."

The town leader was running up the flag of the Rebels as the column rolled out the next morning, heading for Yuma.

In Yuma, Texas Jim and Banniger had rallied their men. But it wasn't for a fight. Not yet.

"We got to beat the Rebels," Banniger said. "We got to stop them. But we can't do it here. Them Rebels over in Los Angeles is kickin' some ass, boy."

"We can't do it here, we can't do it nowhere," Texas Jim said dejectedly. "We been beat. We just got no place else to go. Banniger, I was talkin' to an ol' boy on the shortwave the other night. Bubba had about two hundred and fifty men in his gang. They was rollin' through Georgia, havin' their way and samplin' Southern pussy. They was about fifty, sixty miles south of what's left of Atlanta when they come up on this real pretty little town, all neat with lots of gardens and stuff like that. Folks livin' clean and dressin' fine and all that. Bubba and his boys rolled into town and before anyone of them could blink, they had the shit shot out of them. Bubba's got fourteen men left in his gang. It was one of them Rebel outposts they hit. Them townspeople jerked up the wounded and them that surrendered, had a trial—*that day*—and hanged 'em. Just like that, Banniger. They didn't even blink doin' it. Bubba said they buried them in a mass grave, unmarked."

"Say all that's on your mind, Texas."

"The day of the outlaw is over, Banniger. We got no place left to run. Raines is killin' anyone who don't kowtow to his rules. It's over."

Banniger was a bit smarter than Texas Jim, and he knew that Raines was not killing anyone who disagreed with the Rebel philosophy. Raines was simply withholding Rebel aid to anyone who did

228

not come under the hard and narrow umbrella of Rebel thinking. That wasn't anything new; that was just good politics. But Texas Jim was correct in part of his thinking. The day of the outlaw was over in the lower forty-eight. Banniger had been closely monitoring the Rebel movement for over a year. He had good shortwave equipment and had charted the Rebel course whenever they did not talk on scramble.

Banniger knew all about Lan Villar and Ashley and Khamsin and Kenny Parr. And he had him a pretty good idea where those ol' boys were heading, and it was Alaska. He'd bet his life on it, and was about to do just that.

"All right, Texas," Banniger said. "What do you think we should do?"

"Run," the outlaw said. "Gather up what is ourn and git the hell gone from here."

"And go where?"

"I ain't got no idea, Banniger."

"I do."

"You do?"

"Yeah. Raines didn't let you and your boys leave without a reason, or hadn't you thought about that?"

"I thought about it. I don't know why he done it."

"He's herding us, Texas. Or so he thinks."

"Herdin' us where?"

"West. You notice that he's in no hurry?"

"Yeah, I did. So?"

"This is so. Raines is givin' his main army time to clean out the Los Angeles area. Then punks up there ain't got but one direction to go, south. Now if the street punks and them gawdawful cannibals is bein' pushed south, and we allow ourselves to be pushed west, where is that gonna put us, Jim?"

Texas Jim had to ruminate on that for a couple of minutes. Get his directions all straightened out in his mind. He frowned and chewed at a dirty thumbnail and finally said, "In a damn box, I reckon."

"That's right. With the Mexican forces south of us, sealin' off the border like they been doin,' and the Rebels north and east of us, if we allow ourselves to be herded, where would that leave us?"

Texas Jim sighed heavily. "Drown-ed in the damn ocean," he said glumly.

"That's right. And I ain't got no desire to become shark bait. Do you?"

"Hell no! But where does that leave us to go?"

"Alaska."

"*Alaska!* Jesus Christ, man. It's cold up there. We'll freeze our asses off."

"Would you rather have your ass shot off by a Rebel bullet?"

"Puttin' it that away, no. You ever et blubber, Banniger?"

"Can't say as I have."

"Me neither. But I seen pitchers of it. It didn't do nothin' for my appetite."

"If Ben Raines gets hold of you, you gonna lose your appetite forever."

"That there's a pure fact. We bes' take some women with us, Banniger. There ain't no women up there neither."

Banniger laughed at him. "Get your boys together, Texas. We're pullin' out."

"When?"

"Right now, partner, right now."

230

Some very weary-looking and badly used men and women met the Scouts at a small town just a few miles north of the Arizona line. The Scouts radioed back to the main column and waited for Ben.

"Texas Jim joined Banniger and they pulled out several hours ago," a man told Ben. "We've been slaves here for a couple of years. Some of the people here for longer than that. We were sure that we'd be killed, but Banniger just turned us loose. He said that he didn't need any more marks against him in General Raines's tally book."

"He headed east on the Interstate, General," a woman said. "But we found this in his headquarters." She held out a well-worn map.

Ben took it and carefully unfolded it. A map of Alaska. He studied the neat handwriting on the map edges. Ben leaned up against a fender and slowly nodded his head. "It makes sense," he said, handing the map to Buddy.

Buddy glanced at the writing and grunted. "Now we know where Villar and Khamsin and the others are heading."

"If we can believe the writing on the map, yes. And it's probably true. Banniger was in such a hurry to pull out, he forgot about this map. Well, they don't have anyplace left to go in the lower forty-eight, unless they wanted to link up with Sister Voleta."

Buddy shook his head. "I can't imagine they would want do to that."

"Neither can I. They're thugs and outlaws, not crazy. All right, so now we know what is waiting for us in Northstar." He looked at the ragged and physically abused group of men and women. "What is

231

left of Yuma?"

"It's intact, General. It's dirty and trashed but still standing."

"Could you people make a go of it if we resupplied you and got you all set up?"

"We would give it our best, General. But I can guarantee you this. You arm us, and no bunch of thugs and punks will ever again overrun us."

Ben chuckled. He'd heard this story many times before. And he knew the answer to his question. "So you people were all pacifists after the Great War, eh?"

The man's smile, and the smiles of those around him, held no humor. "We tried extending the hand of peace and friendship to any who came our way. It looks real good on paper. In practice it was a royal fuck-up!"

Ben laughed and patted the man on the shoulder. "Come on. We'll get you all fed and outfitted and have the medics give you all a good exam. I think you folks are going to fit right in."

Ben and his contingent of Rebels stayed in Yuma for four days, while the medics checked over the newly freed people and determined who needed what in the way of medicines. Many of the ex-prisoners were in bad shape, both mentally and physically; those would be sent back to Base Camp One for hospitalization. The Rebels cleaned up the small airport and got a runway in shape.

Ben made no effort to chase after Banniger and Texas Jim. He knew, or at least had a pretty good idea, where they were going, and he would deal with them later.

Ben wanted to clear the lower forty-eight of as much human crud as possible before he started giving a lot of thought and planning to Alaska and beyond. Sister Voleta and her Ninth Order took up some of Ben's mental time. The woman had a way of pulling thugs and perverts and deviants to her like metal shavings to a magnet. Ben decided that would be work for the battalions he left behind.

Buddy and his Rat Team, working with Dan's Scouts, had gone out and brought back valuable information concerning the enemy that lay to the west.

"Corrie," Ben said, after listening to his sons report, "see if you can patch me through to the HQ of the Mexican army."

"No problem," she told him. "I have their operating frequencies." It did not take her long. "A General Payon waiting, sir."

"General Payon, General Raines here. I congratulate you on restoring order in your country and look forward to working with you."

"Thank you, General Raines. We are moving along swiftly. As you have been. We will both succeed with a little bit of luck and many smiles from God. And now, sir, how may I be of assistance to you?"

When Ben finished, General Payon chuckled. "It is truly a fine plan, sir. A fine plan. And you have our full cooperation, of course. I will begin moving troops into place immediately."

Ben smiled as he handed the mike to Corrie. "Now, you bastards," he muttered. "Let's see you get out of this box!"

Book Two

Liberty is a beloved discipline.
George Homans

Chapter One

In the battered and burning area of Los Angeles, Leroy looked at the messenger and felt a churning in his guts. If what the man reported was true, they were all screwed and about to be kissed during the screwing . . . by the kiss of death.

The Rebels were slowly and methodically closing in on them. Each new dawning brought the law and-order bastards and bitches another block or two or three closer, on all sides. The smoke was thick and choking all around them. And it seemed like the thunder of artillery and the booming and crashing of incoming shells never stopped. A lot of the street punks were folding up mentally under the constant attack. Some had committed suicide, others had surrendered, still others had gone crazy as the pressure got to them.

"Let's go see Junkyard and Ishmal," Leroy told his bodyguards. "We got to figure out something, and we ain't got a whole lot of time left to do it."

The punks still held a lot of territory. But it was

shrinking day by day. Rebels were stretched out west to east along Interstate 10 and north to south along Interstate 710. The south and the west were still open, but Ben Raines and his people and the Mexican Army lay to the south, and to the west was the Pacific Ocean, and now that bastard Raines had covered that too.

Most of the street punk leaders were in attendance. Most of those who were not in attendance were dead.

Ruth of the Macys said, "Some of my people seen boats this morning. Big boats layin' off shore."

"Yeah, they're there, all right," Cash of the Surfers said. "Mexican gunboats. Big ones. They come up and got into position last night."

"We're screwed!" Hal of the Fifth Street Lords said. "And I ain't gonna surrender. Too many freed prisoners would be happy to testify against me. I'm dead either way it goes."

"Yeah," Jimmy of the Indios agreed. "We're dead if we stay here, and dead if we surrender. The Rebels overran my turf and grabbed the slaves I had. You know they're singin' like birds. I wouldn't last five minutes."

"None of us would," Sally of the Mixers said. "So let's don't even talk about surrender. But goddamnit, I don't want to die! It ain't right what Ben Raines is doin'!"

"Sure ain't," Josh of the Angels said. "What Raines is doin' is agin the law."

Brute looked at him, disgust in the gaze. "Idiot! Ben Raines is the law. He's the *only* law in the United States."

"So what do we do?" Dicky of the Silvers asked.

"That's why we're here," Leroy said. "To come up

with a plan."

Rich was not in attendance. But he did have a spy present. He would know everything that went on. And if he could do it, he was going to toss Leroy, Ishmal, and Junkyard to the lions . . . in this case, the Rebels.

Artillery started booming after an hour's respite, the shells creaming another two-block area to the north and to the east. Cigarettes were lighted with trembling hands. The bombardment was getting to them all.

Everybody started coming up with plans. But none of the plans were worth a damn.

Finally, when everyone had wound down, Leroy said, "The Rebels have to have a weak spot. It's up to us to find it and do it damn quick."

"The Rebels ain't got no weak spot," Carmine of the Women said, pointing out what she felt to be the truth. In fact, the Rebel lines were so thin they had plenty of weak spots. "But what they got is a system that's workin'. And it don't look like we got any defense against it.

"There is one way," Brute of the White Men said softly, his words just audible over the crashing of artillery rounds. "Maybe it would work." He outlined it, and most of the street punk leaders turned down the suggestion.

"It would work," Stan of the Flatrocks said. "But I don't like it."

"I don't like it either," Bull said. "But we may have to do it anyways. Now tell me this, Brute. If we got out, where would we go?"

"Where Raines would least expect us to go. North into Canada and maybe on up into Alaska."

"Alaska!" Leroy shouted. "That's your ass, blueboy. I ain't carryin' my ass up there to freeze off."

Brute faced the gang leader. "To tell you the truth, Leroy, very few of us really give a damn where you go. You're crude, ignorant, and a racist."

"You don't talk to me like that, faggy."

"I just did, Leroy," Brute said with a smile. "And if you don't like it, come on and take your best shot."

Bull watched it all with a smile. He'd known Brute for years, and knew the man was just as tough as any among them. His sexual preferences were a little weird, but no one with any sense would sell him short on courage . . . not and live to tell about it.

"When this is over, I will," Leroy warned the man.

Brute put one hand on his hip and with the other hand, gave him the finger.

That made Leroy so mad he picked up a chair and threw it out a window. He and his bodyguards stormed out of the meeting. Leroy stood outside and calmed down. Problem was, he thought, what Carmine said was right. There just didn't seem to be a way to stop the damn Rebels. They just kept on coming. They would shell and burn two or three blocks, and then lay back and wait to see if anyone tried to punch through. Then they would move forward, and do it again and again. Slowly, slowly, the noose was tightening around the necks of those inside the burning city.

Now the whole Mexican Army was stretched out from Mexicali to Tijuana, blocking that southern escape route. Too bad, Leroy thought. Mexican pussy was good. He sighed. And now Mexican

240

gunboats were out in the Gulf of Catalina, and the damn Rebels were everywhere else.

Leroy cursed Ben Raines.

So maybe that damn fag had a good idea. But *Alaska?* That just didn't appeal to Leroy at all.

"General Payon's army is in place," Corrie informed Ben. "All roads leading into Mexico are blocked and heavy patrols are at other strategic locations. A few punks and creepies might get away, but not many are going south."

"Thank you, Corrie. Now patch me through to Cecil, please."

"Go, Ben," Cecil said, coming on the horn.

"Cec, I spoke with General Payon. They had the same problem with their politicians down there that we had up here. Just one massive network of misinformation. Mexico City is gone. It took a direct hit and will be hot for centuries. That much is fact. But the rest of the country is all right. General Payon is temporarily in charge and is patterning the laws after ours. They've been busy with punks and thugs and crud and Night People, and they're dealing with them the same way we did: with extreme prejudice."

"Ike informed me the Mexican gunboats are offshore now, in force, and have been in touch with him. They're prepared to stay for as long as it takes. It looks like we've finally got a handle on this situation."

"For a fact, Cec. I'm going to shove off in the morning and start an easy push west. General Payon says his people are dug in and ready for a fight."

241

"That's ten-four, Ben. Central Los Angeles is burning. Ike is in control of the old Los Angeles airport. There is nothing left between Manchester Avenue north to the mountains. Everything else has been put to the torch. My bunch, Ike, Georgi, Therm, and Dan's command, is stretched out along I-10. West and Seven and Eight Battalions are spread out north to south along I-110. We're closing the pincers, Ben. There is no place left for the punks to run."

"Then they've got to pull a desperation move, Cec. They have no choice in the matter. Be alert for that. How about the creepies? Have they linked up with the street punks?"

"What's left of them, yes. And speaking of what's left, Ike reported finding what appears to be the HQ of the creepies—the Judges' chambers, so to speak. There must have been quite a pocket of methane directly under the building. An HE round hit it and the whole damn block went up. It was a pretty good bang. Ike's people found a lot of bodies, but no way for us to know how many of the Judges died."

"Do you have any kind of overall body count?"

"Adding what we guesstimated just before you left, Ben, I'd say close to twenty thousand have died. I would guess that between two and three thousand have slipped out and split."

Ben paused for a moment. "Cec, do you want to try another attempt at surrender terms for them?" Ben could feel the weight of twenty thousand shot, burned, and blown-apart bodies on him, and he knew that his other commanders were experiencing the same emotion.

When Cecil spoke, there was a weariness in his

voice. "And do what with them, Ben? Rehabilitate them? How? Where would we house them? Weeks before we hit southern California we offered them surrender terms. They refused. We got on the edge of the city and offered them terms again. They refused. To hell with them, Ben. I wouldn't believe anything these bastards said if they were standing in the middle of a bible factory."

"All right, Cec; then that's the way we'll play it. We won't offer them surrender terms again, but if they throw down their guns and walk out under a white flag, we'll honor it on the spot and try them."

"All right, Ben. But I'm going to wait a few minutes before passing the orders. You might change your mind."

"Eagle out."

Jersey was looking at him when Ben turned around. "We've given them half a dozen chances to surrender, General. That's ten more than they would have given us."

Ben looked around him, his eyes touching each member of his personal team, and also his son. "Say what's on your mind, people."

"No surrender," Buddy said.

"They're scumbags, General," Beth said. "They're slave traders, drug dealers, murderers, and cohorts of cannibals. They'll not surrender to me."

"Me neither," Cooper said, in a rare moment of standing up to the general. "I'll shoot every damn one I see, armed or unarmed. They're worse than the Nazis I've read about."

"I see," Ben said softly. "Is this the sentiment of everyone in this command?"

"Yes, Father," Buddy said. "It is."

Ben nodded his head and looked at Linda. She shook her head. "A small part of me says to show them some mercy. But a much larger part of me says that I could never trust one of them. Not after hearing what *all* of the ex-prisoners have to say about them."

"All right," Ben said, his words soft. He looked at Corrie. "Take it off scramble and patch me through to all commanders, please."

She handed the mike to him. "This is Ben Raines. Take no prisoners. Repeat: take no prisoners. That is a direct order." He handed the mike back to Corrie. "Let's get packed up, people. We shove off at first light in the morning."

Ben's orders made it, in some repects, much easier for the Rebels on the line. No one ever disobyed a direct order from Ben Raines.

In the ever-shrinking area controlled by the street punks and the creepies, the battle halted for a few moments after Ben had spoken. There, among all, it was a time for much retrospection and what-ifs. But after a few moments, most of the street punks reached the usual conclusion that what they were was somebody else's fault—not theirs. It was society's fault that they were not made chairpersons of the boards of large corporations the instant they dropped out of school. They shouldn't have been sent to jail just because they raped or mugged or killed. The women should have given up that pussy on demand; the people should have handed over their money on demand; if they'd done that, then they wouldn't have been killed. Hurt, maybe, but what the hell? That's the breaks.

The street punks had arrived at this juncture of their lives not because of anything they had done, but because of society. After all, in the words of a less than logical song of decades past, during one protest period or another, they hadn't asked to be born, so society sure as hell owed them something—right?

It had never occurred to most of them that society had offered them all a great many things: free schooling from K through 12—and in many cases through college—if they had the drive to see it through. The right to choose their own paths. The right to vote. The right of free speech. They all had the same rights as anyone else. They were just too goddamn sorry and lazy and worthless to take advantage of it.

"It ain't right," Jimmy of the Indios said. "They ain't gonna give us another chance."

Brute of the White Men and Cash of the Surfers looked at each other and smiled. Cash said, "We had our chances, Jimmy. Zillions of them. But we blew them all every time one was offered to us. There ain't no point in whining about it now. Now all we got to do is die."

The area controlled by the street punks and the creepies had shrunk dramatically. The Rebel commanders had reached the point where the danger to their troops had lessened considerably; most of the work was up to the artillery. On the three landlocked sides of the area, gunners pumped in round after round, on a twenty-four-hour basis, the rolling and killing and burning thunder never ceasing. Fires from hundreds of out-of-control blazes lit up the night sky and smoke was so thick even during the day it was difficult to see. The last major bastion of lawlessness, perversion, cannibalism, and horror in the lower forty-eight was only a few days from being destroyed.

The leaders of the street gangs and a representative from the Believers called for a last-minute meeting. Even Rich was in attendance.

"We got to bust out," Leroy said. He was calm and in control of himself, even though he still despised Rich. He spread a map on the table. "Right up here is the Rebels' weakest point—at least from what I could see. Brute, your plan was a good one. We got to take it. I . . ." He paused as the artillery stopped.

"What the hell?—" Fang of the Hill Street Avengers said, the sudden silence loud in the room.

A radio operator answered the frantic calling on his radio, then turned to the gang leaders. "Our forward people say the Rebel planes is warming up. You know what that means."

"Gas," Stan said. "The bastards is gonna drop gas in on us like they done in Frisco."

"Hold it!" Bull yelled, as the gang leaders started to panic. "Just hold it for a second. If it's gas, and I'll bet it isn't, there ain't no way any of us could get far enough away to do any good. So just calm down and wait this out. Let's see what develops."

They waited. They were jumpy and wide-eyed but they waited.

"The Rebels is shiftin' people around," the radio operator said. "They're pullin' back to the east of us. They've left Highway 107 south wide open."

"That don't make no sense," Dicky of the Blades

said.

"Yeah," Ishmal of the Boogies agreed. "Why would they do something stupid like that?"

"The Russian son of a bitch is pullin' out too," the radioman yelled. "They're gettin' into trucks and leavin'. The Rebels is all shiftin' around. The Russian is headin' back east on the freeway. What the hell's goin' on?"

Leroy's lips peeled back in a snarl as his eyes touched Rich, who was smirking at him. "Why don't you tell us, white boy?"

"Okay, I'll do that. But if you're thinkin' gas, forget it. Unless you fart. Look here, boys. The Rebels is tryin' to sucker us south. They've left a buffer of ten or twelve blocks of no-man's-land between us and them, all the way around. And a line of Rebels north of us, stretched out west to east. And it has to be a thin line. That's our ticket out of here, boys. That's where we slide through."

"For a honky, you ain't but half stupid," Leroy said. "You right. We got no choice in the matter. We got to head north."

"But not all of us," Bull said, speaking the damning words.

"What you mean?" Ishmal asked.

"All of us pulling out would be a dead giveaway," Brute said. "But it isn't as dismal as it sounds."

"It ain't?" Sally asked.

"No, dear, it isn't. The fair way to do this is to draw lots."

"I don't need no property," Junkyard said.

Brute sighed. "Dear God," he whispered. "I have cast my fate to the winds, and am on a vessel crewed by cretins." He cleared his throat. "We will draw straws, cut cards, or toss pennies to see who

247

goes north and who heads south."

"Oh," Junkyard said.

"Now then, any move we make had best be started tonight," Brute continued. "Those of us heading south will pretend to be taking the bait offered by the Rebels. When you get halfway between L.A. and San Diego, cut straight east, break up into small groups, and disappear. Get rid of your gang colors and bury them. Forget them. Occupy farm houses and chew tobacco, hum hillbilly music, scratch at yourselves and look outdoorsy if Rebel patrols find you. There is a good chance many of us will make it. All who elect to go to the barren and hostile wilderness, a.k.a. Alaska, will rendezvous . . . oh, let's see . . . in Central Nevada as quickly as possible. Everyone agreed on that?"

"We got shortwave equipment," Bull said. "Our rendezvous code word will be . . . what? Come up with something, Brute."

Brute smiled. "Miami."

"That's a good one. Let's start cuttin' the cards."

"What are we gonna do out *there?*" Ruth of the Macys asked, waving her hand toward the countryside. "I ain't been out of the city in years. What the hell is out there?"

"Ben Raines," Josh said glumly.

Chapter Two

The Rebel planes had taken off, some of them to resupply Rebel units, most of them to take freed prisoners to Base Camp One for medical treatment. The Rebels loosely surrounding the small area of the city still in hands of the street punks took a break to bathe, eat hot food, change into clean uniforms, and rest. Rest the body and the ears, now that the artillery had fallen silent.

"You know that a lot of them will bust out of the city tonight," Buddy said to his father.

"It can't be helped, son. We're down to only a few artillery rounds per gun. We've used thousands of rounds during this assault and the factory back at Base One can't keep up with the demand. It'll be at least a week before the supply can be built up."

"Take a guess, Father. How many of the punks who bust out of the city will settle down and stop their lawless ways?"

"Not many. Percentage-wise? Five to ten percent, maybe. These are hardcore punks."

"They're sure to find out about the outlaws

gathering in Alaska."

"We'll have a fight up there, for sure. But we'll have all winter to gear up for it. When we pull out for Northstar, we'll be fully prepared. Even better prepared than we were for this assault."

Darkness had settled softly over the land, and the Rebels camped between Yuma and Mexicali rested. Ben sat outside his tent, waiting for Corrie to tell him the punks were bugging out of the city . . . and in which direction they were heading. He'd made a mental bet with himself that some would head south, and some would head north. How far south they would go was something he could not know. But if he were in their shoes, he would take the bait and wait until they were in a very isolated area, then cut hard to the east and try to find a hidey-hole.

Using a flashlight, he studied a map. They would break east between Oceanside and Del Mar, splitting up into small groups and taking that maze of county roads that led over to 78 and I-15.

"Punks are bugging out, General," Corrie called. "Heading south."

Ben did not ask for numbers; there was no way to tell. "Corrie, have Seven and Eight Battalions stay in position and order West to leave immediately. Head straight down I-15. Tell him we are leaving within the hour and by dawn will be in position just east of Escondido on Highway 78. He is to leave the Interstate at the junction of 76 and spread his people along that route. I'll spread my forces on either side of Santa Ysabel. Advise General Payon of our plans and order all personnel to break camp."

The Rebels were accustomed to abrupt changes in plans, and in thirty minutes they were ready to go.

"Take the Interstate to El Centro, Coop," Ben told him. "Then north to Brawley and west on 78. Are the Scouts out, Corrie?"

"Should be five miles ahead of us now. West is on his way, pushing hard."

"Let's go, Coop."

They had just over a hundred miles to travel, on roads they were unfamiliar with, and through territory that was unknown but presumed hostile. They could make no more than thirty-five miles an hour, and in many instances, much less than that. Tanks spearheaded the drive and tanks brought up the rear. Scouts reported a barricade at the junction of I-8 and 98.

"Blow it," Ben ordered. "Blow any that you find. We're coming through."

The column rumbled on through the night.

"Scouts asking if you want them to check out Calexico, General," Corrie said.

"Ten-fifty. Get us through to our immediate objective."

"General Ike is on the horn, sir. He wants to know what the hell you think you're doing."

"Tell him to worry about his own sector. If I need a nursemaid I'll pick my own."

"Yes, sir." She relayed the message. Waited. "There is no way I'm going to tell General Raines that, sir," she said. "Fine," she said hotly. "The same to you! Eagle out!"

Ben chuckled. He could just imagine what Ike had said. "Ike get a little profane, Corrie?"

Corrie muttered something under her breath

251

and Jersey burst out laughing.

The column rolled on through the night. "Right along here is where Hollywood used to film a lot of desert scenes for movies," Ben told his team. "Hollywood," he murmured. "Gone forever."

"Hold it up," Corrie said. "Scouts reporting an overpass is blown just west of El Centro. They advise take a county road to Brawley. It's not numbered but they'll mark it for us."

Cooper nodded his head.

The county road slowed them down to an infuriating crawl.

"Brawley is occupied by thugs, General," Corrie told him.

"Tell the Scouts to hold up and wait for us. We have no choice in the matter. We'll have to blow our way through. All tanks up front."

The convoy pulled over to the side of the road, allowing those tanks in the rear to join the spearheading armor.

"Close it up, Coop," Ben said. "Stay with them."

Brawley had been a town of about fifteen thousand when the Great War enveloped the earth more than a decade past. Since it was full dark, and the age of street lamps had come and gone except in towns controlled by the Rebels, there was no telling what condition the town was in now, but Ben knew what condition it was going to be in when the Rebels left it behind: in ruins.

Ben got out of the wagon and walked to a group of Scouts, helping position the tanks. "Any guesses as to the number of crud in the town?"

"I'd guess a couple of hundred, General. They've got some big .50's in there too. They opened up on us too soon, though, and we were

252

able to hit the ditch banks. We told them who we were and they told us to kiss their ass."

"Commence shelling whenever you people are ready," Ben told a tank commander. "HE and incendiary. We don't have time for politeness. Punch us through."

The armor opened up with cannon fire and the Gatlings and Vulcans began howling. Mortar crews had set up and began dropping rounds in. Very soon, the entire eastern end of the town was burning.

"Advance," Ben ordered just as Buddy called out.

"They're bugging out, Father."

"Take some people, son. Find us a way through."

"Yes, sir."

Ben returned to his vehicle and rummaged around until he found a candy bar. He was munching on that when he noticed Smoot's ears perk up and the puppy's eyes shift to the darkness to Ben's right. "Stay, Smoot," Ben said softly, closing the door and dropping to the dewy grass beside the road.

His M-14 was propped up against the wagon and Ben didn't want to risk exposing an arm reaching for it. Belly down on the grass, he pulled his .45, carried cocked and locked, from leather and eased the autoloader off safety.

Ben slowly wormed his way deeper into the dry ditch. He had one hostile spotted, and figured there was at least one more, possibly two.

He heard the very faint snick of a pin being pulled from a grenade, and put three .45-caliber hollow-nosed rounds in the direction of the sound.

A scream reached his ears just a couple of seconds before the grenade blew. Ben saw two human shapes lift off the ground and a third shape come charging toward the muzzle blasts.

Still on his belly, Ben triggered off two fast shots, both rounds catching the man in the chest. He stopped abruptly and sat down hard in the grass. He cussed once and then toppled over and was still. Ben ejected the nearly empty clip and slipped in a full one, jacking in a round.

His team was running toward him. "Get down!" Ben yelled. "Flood this field with light."

Trucks and Jeeps and Hummers backed up and illuminated the old field just in time to see fifty or sixty men running toward them.

It was a slaughter. The Rebels cut them down to a man, then swept the bodies with more fire to insure there would be no more surprises from that bunch of outlaws.

Buddy pulled up in a Jeep. "The town is clear, Father."

"Fine. Good work, son."

"What do we do with these people?" Ben was asked, the Rebel pointing toward the body-littered field.

"All living things have to eat," Ben said, and got into his vehicle. "Let's go, people."

If there were any more towns along the route occupied by outlaws, their radio network telling each other of the Rebel's brutal treatment, soon cleared them out. The Rebels encountered no more hostiles on their push westward.

"West took some demolition teams with him

when he pulled out," Corrie told Ben. "He's blowing and burning everything behind him."

"What's his twenty?"

"Just south of Riverside."

"We'll have time for a couple of hours' sleep before the punks reach us. If the punks do what I suspect they'll do."

The old highway was in surprisingly good shape for having gone over a decade with no maintenance, and the Rebels made good time. They rolled into their sector just after two in the morning, and Ben ordered Scouts forward into the edge of Santa Ysabel, sentries out, and the rest of them to get some sleep.

"Tired, Ben?" Linda asked.

"No. Too keyed up, I guess. I'll probably grab a catnap just before dawn. You?"

"Not a bit. I dozed off and on in the wagon. Ben?"

"Umm?"

"Estimates of dead now stand at just over twenty thousand, right?"

"That's right."

"And you estimated approximately fifty thousand in the city initially."

"That's correct."

"If just twenty-five percent of those left alive manage to escape and head for Alaska, that will still be quite a formidable force we'll be facing."

"Alaska might well prove to be the toughest fight we've ever had. Much of the terrain is rugged. No telling what kind of shape the roads will be in, or how many hostiles we'll be facing."

"General Ike just radioed in," Corrie called. "The street punks finally figured out we were

255

spread real thin all around them in the city. A lot of them are trying bug-outs and Ike estimates about half of them are breaking free."

Ben nodded his understanding, then realized that Corrie could not see the minute shake of his head in the darkness. "Thank you, Corrie. Hell of a time to run out of artillery rounds, wasn't it?"

"Yes, sir," she replied. "Any reply, sir?"

"Just tell the commanders we did the best we could with what we had."

"Yes, sir."

"Damnit!" Ben muttered. "I thought we had enough equipment all the way around. I'll not make that mistake again."

"You can't predict the future, Ben," Linda said. "You did the best you could."

"It wasn't good enough. And that will be of small consolation to the Rebels who die in Alaska at the hands of punks whose bones, by that time, should have been picked clean in Los Angeles."

"It'll be ten times worse in Europe."

"If I let it be. And I have no intention of doing that. Corrie?"

"Sir?"

"Bump Base Camp One. Tell the munitions people they're going to have to keep on working around the clock, seven days a week. Start stockpiling rounds. We'll not be caught short again."

"Yes, sir."

"How long can they keep that up, Ben?"

"For as long as it takes, Linda. They won't complain. Most of those people in the factories are ex-combat people who suffered wounds that disabled them, kept them from returning to the field. They understand what it's like out here."

"You'd better get some rest, Ben."

"Later."

She left his side and Ben catnapped, sitting on the ground, his back to a tree. He opened his eyes and came fully awake a few minutes before dawn. Moving only his eyes, Ben took in his surroundings.

The Rebels had dug in and were carefully camouflaged, stretched out a thousand meters north and south of the intersection. The tanks and other armor had pulled back into the timber and brush; Ben could not see them. But he knew the machines of war were ready to start growling and biting at a second's notice.

"West is in position," Corrie said, slipping out of the darkness and squatting by his side. "No signs of the street punks yet."

"Everybody catch a few minutes' sleep?"

"Yes, sir." She handed him a mug of coffee. "They're ready for the dance to start."

Ben stood up and stretched the cold kinks from his muscles and joints. "Where are we set up?"

"Right over here."

Ben followed her across the road and into the timber. To his immediate right, Buddy sat behind a .50-caliber machine gun. To his left, Cooper lay behind a bi-podded M-60. Ben nodded his approval of the site; it offered an excellent field of fire.

Ben watched as Corrie slipped into a headset. He did not have to issue orders about noise discipline and no smoking or unnecessary movement. These people were solid professional fighting men and women. He listened as Corrie spoke softly into the headset, then turned to him.

"West reports the first few punks are straggling through his sector, General. They're following the road that will lead right past us."

"Has West shifted a team over to that road leading to Warner Springs?"

"Yes, sir."

"Tell him to hold his fire. Let's get as many in this box as we can. We'll wait all day if we have to."

"Right, sir."

An hour ticked by. The Rebels took turns catnapping and watching and waiting. Corrie sat with her headset on, waiting for some word as to the progress of the street punks.

"General!" she called in a stage whisper. "Forward recon reports punks are on 78 and heading right for us. They have them in visual. Forward speed is about thirty miles an hour."

Ben smiled. "Bingo! That means they've passed the only road that would take them north or south. They're committed now. They have to pass right by us. Tell the recon teams to get the hell back here."

"Yes, sir."

When she had done that, Ben said, "Fifteen minutes max, Corrie. Everybody heads up."

The word was passed up and down the line. Rebels clicked weapons off safety and laid out rows of clips and grenades. The tanks lowered the elevation of the cannon and waited. The forward recon people came racing back into camp, hid their vehicles, and threw themselves into position. One of them close to Ben.

"How many?" Ben asked.

"Four or five hundred in the first bunch. About

the same in a bunch about a mile behind them."

"Buddy. Take a team and cut through the timber. Get behind that second bunch. Take all the ammo you can stagger with. Get going."

"Right." The young man was gone.

"Get behind that .50," Ben told the recon. "Things are about to get interesting around here."

Grinning, the recon slipped behind the big .50 and waited.

Stan of the Flat Rocks and Carmine of the Women stopped their vehicles and got out to stand on the winding, hilly road.

"What are you thinkin?'" Stan asked.

"That's it's awful quiet. The city ain't never quiet. But this is scary. Maybe it's always like this. I don't know. I ain't never been out of the city."

"You gonna go straight, Carmine?"

She sneered at him. "Straight? Me? Hell, no! There ain't no percentages in goin' straight. Scratchin' out a garden and cannin' shit. Not me, Stan. Me and my girls'll hit the first town we come to, grab us some long-dicked ol' boys to keep around when we need them, some broads for cookin' and cleanin' and such, and set up somewheres. You goin' straight?"

"Naw. Stealin' is too easy a life for me to give up. I'll get clear of Ben Raines and his Rebels, and find me a little settlement and take it over. Kill all the old fuckers that can't work, use the fat ugly women for cleanin' and such, and the younger one for fuckin'. Then it'll be business as usual, Carmine."

"Now you're talkin.'" She looked at him. "You an' me, Stan, we always got along pretty good. You wanna link up?"

"Why not? Let's do it."

She reached down and squeezed his crotch, grinning at him. "We'll seal the bargain tonight."

They got back in their vehicles and headed out. A few miles ahead, the Rebels silently waited.

A few miles back, Ruth of the Macys and Hal of the Fifth Street Lords were making a similar pact, as were several other gang leaders. Their confidence was growing with each passing mile. The countryside was not as bad as they had thought it would be—no huge grizzly bears or mountain lions had attacked them—and they had not seen a sign of the Rebels. However, they all felt, to a person, that they would much rather see a grizzly than come in contact with Ben Raines and his Rebels.

"Let's go," Ruth yelled to those behind her.

In the city, the bug-out of the street punks had halted at first light. And getting through the Rebel lines had been very easy. Bull had put it all together and guessed accurately that the Rebels were out of artillery rounds. About twenty-five hundred punks had slipped through during the night, making their way north, on foot. But to a street punk, finding a vehicle once clear of L.A. was a very minor problem. They'd all been stealing cars for years before the Great War, and getting a stern lecture and a slap on the wrist from a judge when they were caught.

But the Rebels caught on quickly, and at first light went to work laying out mines and booby-trapping possible escape routes. But they were too late to catch Bull and Rich and Junkyard and Ishmal and their gangs. They had jumped the gun on the other gangs and cleared the city and were rolling toward the rendezvous point in Nevada.

There were still thousands of punks and creepies hiding within the battered city and in the suburbs. And they would be trying to escape come the darkness.

East of the city, Ben pulled out a battered map of the region and looked at it.

"Planning a trip?" Linda whispered.

"Yeah. Just as soon as we finish here. I want to go over to Mount Palomar and see if the telescope is still there; see if anything is left of the museum."

Linda shook her head and wiped her sweaty palms on her fatigue pants and got a fresh grip on her shotgun.

"Here they are," Corrie said, after receiving the report from a Scout hidden on high ground above the highway.

"Buddy in place?" Ben asked.

"Just got there, sir."

"We'll hold our fire until we see what they're going to do. Pass it along, Corrie."

The street punks paused at the intersection, and they all got out of their cars and trucks and off their motorcycles to stand in the middle of the road and argue about what to do next.

Ben settled it for them. "Fire!" he yelled, and held back the trigger on the Thunder Lizard.

"Ambush!" Jimmy of the Indios screamed. It was his last scream. Fire from a Gatling gun cut him to bloody ribbons and flung him in chunks out of the road and into a ditch.

Dee Dee of the Pocos and several dozen of her gang were caught in a cross fire and died in the middle of the road.

The tanks of the Rebels opened up and the high-explosive shells exploded the gas tanks of the punks' vehicles, setting dozens of punks on fire. They ran screaming in agony, running blindly in circles until Rebel bullets cut them down and silenced them forever.

Josh of the Angels, dressed all in white, very dirty white, charged Ben's position, cursing insanely. Linda sighted him in and cut him down, doubling him over with a three-inch-magnum round of double-ought buckshot.

Carmine of the Women and Stan of the Flat Rocks made it to cover. It didn't do them much good. A main battle tank swiveled its turret and blew them both to Hell with one round of high explosive. What was left of Stan was flung high into the air, in pieces, and fell back to earth with a bloody plopping sound.

Manuel of the Mayas and most of his gang ran for their lives, running back down the road. The Scouts on the high ground chopped them up with M-60 fire.

Several miles back, those punks in the rear heard the gunfire and the booming of cannon and stopped, backing up and heading in the direction they'd come from. They ran right into Buddy and his Rat Team.

The Rat Team blocked the road as two rounds from their rocket launchers turned two cars into burning, smoking piles of junk, cooking those inside.

Ruth and her Macys and Hal and his Fifth Street Lords were about to run out of time. They jumped off the road and into the timber, right into the guns of the Rat Team on the other side of the road. Ruth and Hal and most of their gang members died cursing Ben Raines and his Rebels.

In West's section, the mercenary and his men were chopping up the street punks like so much liver. They had waited until the long convoy of cars and trucks and motorcycles had stretched out on the highway, and opened up with mortar and heavy machinegun fire. Since West had a full battalion, unlike Ben's short section, the fight was just as brutal, but not nearly so time-consuming.

The Dykes were gone, wiped out to the last person. The Discos were still and silent, sprawled in death. The Rappers had been among the first to be cut down. A few of the Santees escaped, wild-eyed and running in fear into the brush and timber of the hills. The Temple Street Gang was wiped out to the last punk. And so on. The highway was slick with blood, and moaning drifted to the men behind the guns on the ridges.

"Spray them," West ordered. "No prisoners. That's what the man said."

The gunfire resumed, briefly. The moaning stopped.

"Do we pursue them into the brush?" one of his men asked.

"No," the mercenary said. "They're all washed up. The L.A. street gangs, this bunch of them anyway, are history."

Ben rose up on one knee and looked out at the carnage.

After a moment, Cooper said, "Prisoners, General?"

Ben looked at him. "No," he said softly. "They had their chance. They blew it. Let's go visit a museum."

Chapter Three

For reasons known only to God and to the pack of ignorant jerk-offs who did it, the telescope at Mount Palomar—the world's largest—and the museum on the ground had been vandalized. The telescope was pocked with hundreds of bullet holes. The museum had been destroyed.

"Ignorant bastards!" Ben said.

"Do the Rebels find this to be common?" Linda asked.

"Vandalism?" Ben looked at her. "Yes. The libraries are almost always vandalized and destroyed. As are the museums and art galleries."

"I don't understand that. But then, I've been secluded for a good many years." She smiled. "From reality, I'm sure you would say."

"That's correct. The why of the destruction? Stupid, petty, ignorant people are afraid of knowledge. Most certainly have the mental capabilities to absorb knowledge—they're just too damn lazy to make the effort."

"And few of those people are part of the Rebel

movement, right, Ben?"

"Correct."

"It seems I'm always playing devil's advocate with you. So here I go again. You and the majority of Rebels obviously don't care what happens to those people, Ben, even though they probably number in the hundreds of thousands. What happens to them?"

"Oh, some Rebel patrol will eventually roll into their sectors. We'll appraise the situation, and if they don't have schools, libraries, clinics, proper health facilities, we'll take the children and raise them ourselves."

She looked at him, disbelief in her eyes. "Goddamn, Ben. You don't mean that!"

"Oh, but I do. If we're going to pull this country out of the ashes, Linda, we can't have a nation of superstitious, shortsighted, small-minded illiterates. The kids are the hope, Linda. They're the future. They've got to be schooled, taught, and guided. We're not doing anything that child-welfare people didn't do back before the Great War. We're just not as subtle about it, that's all."

Ben winked at her and walked off, to see if anything salvageable could be found among the rubble.

Linda looked around her, saw Jersey and Beth and Corrie and Cooper smiling at her. Coop said, "Close your mouth, Linda, before you swallow a bug."

She walked over to the team. "Sorry, gang. But what he just said came as a shock."

"The taking of children to raise and educate?" Beth asked. "Why? Kids have been taken away from unsuitable parents for years, for one reason or another. We just enlarged the reasons, that's all."

"We've got over seventy-five outposts around the

266

nation, Linda," Jersey said. "Seventy-nine, I think. Ranging in size from a few hundred to a few thousand people. General Jefferys calls them literate oasis surrounded by a desert of ignorance. That's pretty fancy, but accurate. People of all colors, all religions, all living and working together. No prejudices, no hatred, no trouble. And people who have a lot of hang-ups about color, or who hate for no reason, or who like to cause trouble, are not a part of those outposts."

"Well, Jersey, what happens to those people?"

"Oh, they hang around the fringes of the outposts, for safety. But they're very careful what they say around our people. I think you're beginning to see that Rebels don't take a lot of crap from people."

"We don't claim to be one-hundred-percent right," Corrie said. "And we do try awfully hard to be as fair as we can toward anybody who will just try — just a little bit — to work with us. But we're the only game in town that's working toward restoring this nation. There are a few things that cut across our grain that we will tolerate, and a lot we won't." She smiled and patted Linda on the shoulder. "Relax, you're fitting in like a glove."

They walked away to join Ben, and Buddy strolled over to Linda. "Getting force-fed a little Rebel doctrine, Linda?"

"Oh, yes. And I find some of it appalling."

"Dad says that what we're doing certainly would be declared illegal — if the nation were as it was before the Great War. But from what I can remember and from what I read, America was falling apart back then. Lawlessness, drugs, illiteracy, misplaced values, lack of respect for the rights of law-abiding people, no faith in the elected leaders . . . it all sounds pretty dismal to me."

"But . . ." Linda started to argue. She stopped. She found she really had no argument to offer; everything Buddy had said was true.

The ruggedly handsome and muscular young man, with a bandana around his forehead and holding the old .45-caliber Thompson machine gun, stood smiling at her, waiting.

"Conditions will never be as they were before the Great War, Linda," he said. "My father will never permit that to happen. Never."

"And if, God forbid, something were to happen to him?"

"We'll all die, Linda. Eventually. Even Ben Raines. When that happens, someone will step in and take over."

"Who?"

Buddy shrugged. "Cecil, Ike, Georgi Striganov, West, me, Tina . . . who knows? Thermopolis, maybe." He smiled at her smile. "Don't laugh. It's certainly possible."

"But not very probable."

"True."

She stared at the young man for a moment, then tried another smile. "What now, Buddy?"

"We're waiting to see if any punks tried the border, and what happened. Then we're going in and take San Diego."

"But we don't have any artillery rounds!"

"That's right. We do this the old-fashioned way, house to house."

Ben left Ike, Cecil, Georgi, and Seven Battalion

in the Los Angeles area. He pulled the rest of his command down to San Diego, along with Thermopolis, Dan, and Eight Battalion. They gathered on the northern edge of the city.

"General Payon's people stacked up the punks along the border," Ben told his commanders. "Those who tried to cross over, that is. We let a lot of them slip through, heading east, and a lot of them broke past the northern perimeters. We'll meet them again some day. They're gathering somewhere, bet on that. Many of them are still in the city. We may be out of artillery rounds, but we sure as hell have plenty of rounds for our other weapons, including mortars. And Cecil and Ike and Georgi have some nasty surprises in store for them.

"Now then, let's get to our jobs down here. West, your battalion is to take I-5 down to I-8, and anything to the west of it. I-8 is the stopping point for us, for the time being. I'll take I-805 and anything to the west of that. Therm, take 163 and everything west of that to my sector. We'll link up at the crossroads, here." He pointed it out on the map. "Eight Battalion will take I-15 and everything west of that over to Therm's section. Take this airport here, Montgomery Field. We'll use that to be resupplied. Dan, I want you and your people roaming around out here between Mission Gorge Road and the Alvarado Freeway. Before we do anything, Buddy and his Rat Team are roaming around now, grabbing some prisoners. We'll see what we'll be facing in a few hours."

"Everything that could make it in from the zone," Buddy reported. "Ten thousand or so, the dregs of the earth."

"Dregs they may be," Ben said. "But are they hostile?"

Linda looked at him, dreading what she had to say, but knowing it had to be said. She had personally seen to the blood work of the prisoners Buddy had brought in. "They're carriers," she said softly.

Ben sat down on the edge of a table in a farmhouse that he was using as a CP. "We've taken some of those prisoner in the L.A. area," he reminded her.

"We don't have them anymore, Ben," Dan stated.

"What do you mean, Dan?"

"The Woods Children solved that problem."

They were all surprised when Ben walked to a small suitcase and took out a bottle of whiskey. He poured two fingers into a glass and drank it neat. He cleared his throat, gently placed the glass on a bureau, and faced the group.

"Do you mean to tell me that Ike and Cecil allowed the Woods Children to take those prisoners out and kill them?"

"They were a plague upon the land," Thermopolis said, his words soft. "A plague that if not checked would have eventually killed us all."

"Well now," Ben said, sitting back down. "Let me digest those words from the world's oldest hippie." They waited while Ben rolled a cigarette and fired it off. "I thought life was oh-so-precious to you, Therm?"

"Goddamnit, Ben!" Therm flared. "Life *is* precious to me. Rosebud's life, my life, my friends' lives, even your life, you hardheaded son of a bitch! There is no vaccine for what they carry. Chase had discovered that a certain virus that some of them

270

are carrying might—*might*—be airborne. He's sent that back to Base Camp One for further testing. This goes against everything I believe in, Ben, so just get off my ass about it, will you?"

Ben smiled. "Uneasy lies the head that wears a crown."

"Yeah! Very goddamn funny."

"Corrie," Ben said. "Contact General Payon. Advise him of this . . . disease. Tell him that he has my permission to cross over the border and sweep the zone. Advise him to be very careful."

"Yes, sir."

"Buddy, bring in a prisoner, please."

The man was a burly specimen, but his color was bad, and he had a racking cough. The normally white of his eyes was a muddy color. He stared defiantly at Ben.

"My name is Ben Raines. What's yours?"

"I'm known as Eightball."

"Do you have a proper name?"

"Why? You gonna carve it on my headstone?"

"Probably not, since we usually shoot the prisoners and burn the bodies."

That shook Eightball, right down to his shoes. "Ah . . . well, I might be able to help you, General. What is it you want to know?"

"What are we going to find in San Diego?"

Eightball chuckled, but it held no humor. "Pimps, whores, dopers, warlords, outlaws, street gangs, cannibals. You name it, and you'll find it in the city."

"You must like that kind of life."

Eightball shrugged. "Beats the hell outta joinin' up with you people and havin' to work."

"That's all there is in the city?" Ben asked.

"That's it. You done run everybody outta the zone and the no-man's-land. I 'spect them goddamn greasers south of the border will be comin' up to join you 'fore long."

"You're a very sick man, Eightball. Are you aware of that?"

"I knew somethin' was wrong with me. Cain't find no medicine to help me neither. Lots of sickness in the city. Folks dyin' ever' time you turn around."

"How do you dispose of the bodies?"

"Haul 'em out to the dump. Rats eat them. I seen rats out there big as dogs."

Ben closed his eyes and silently cursed. He opened his eyes and pointed to the wall map. "Where is this dump?"

"South of Spring Valley. Just north of the old reservoir."

"Do you still get water from that reservoir?"

"Sure."

"Get the planes up," Ben ordered. "Napalm that entire area. Blanket it with fire. Advise General Payon of this."

Ben was silent for a moment. "When you've done that, Corrie, advise Doctor Chase of this development." He turned his attentions to Eightball. "How well are the people armed, Eightball?"

The man sighed. What the hell, he thought, making up his mind. I ain't got nothin' to lose now no ways, and I sure don't owe nobody nothin' in the city. "Rifles, pistols, shotguns, grenades. Machine guns. No artillery of any kind. They's some there, but don't nobody know how to work the damn things. Got plenty of rounds for them on all the old military bases, though."

272

They all smiled at that news.

"Slaves?" Ben asked. "Prisoners?"

"Not many. Most of them was turned loose out in the zone as the folks was comin' into the city. They just was more trouble than they was worth."

"You're a middle-aged man, Eightball. What did you do before the Great War?"

Eightball shrugged. "Whatever I wanted to. Spent about half my life in prison." He lifted his eyes to stare at Ben. "And I don't need no goddamn sermon. I wouldn't change much."

"What *would* you change?"

The man grinned, exposing blackened and yellowing stumps of rotting teeth. "I'd kill them people I robbed so's they couldn't testify agin me in court and put me in the bucket."

"Get him out of here," Ben ordered.

The street punks in the rubble of Los Angeles tried to break through just after dark. The Rebels had placed sound-sensors in those areas that seemed the most likely escape routes and when the alarm was triggered, flares went up, catching the punks trying to bust out.

Heavy machine-gun fire raked the harshly lighted night and mortar crews pounded the smoking ashes with HE rounds. Booby traps ripped the night, the Claymores turning flesh and bone into bloody rags. The punks hit dark trip-wires and had about two seconds to contemplate where they had gone wrong and perhaps say a silent prayer for forgiveness. Then their world went dark. About a third of the punks make it past Rebel-held territory and headed north. About ten percent of those who broke free silently vowed to change their ways and go straight. They did not want to ever again incur the wrath of the Rebels.

The slithering shapes of the Believers were the easier for the Rebels to spot, and they were the most hated. Rebel snipers, their high-powered rifles equipped with night scopes, relentlessly and savagely picked them off as the cannibals tried to break free of their smoking prison that had once been known as the City of the Angels.

"He's a-comin' right up alongside 405," a very scared punk told Cecil. "Leroy knows you and him is brothers, so he's countin' on you to let him pass."

Cecil looked startled. *"Brothers!"* he said. "That misbegotten, ignorant bag of shit actually thinks that because we are of the same race I would let him go?"

"Yes, sir. I reckon he made a mistake, din he?"

"Yes," Cecil replied. "I reckon he did." He turned to his XO. "Let him come on. I'll be down by 405."

"Sir," the XO said. "That's . . ."

". . . all," Cecil finished with a frosty look. "Take command here."

"Yes, sir!"

Cecil picked up his M-16 and walked out of the room and to a waiting vehicle. He could not help but notice as a full company of Rebels, in deuce-and-a-halfs and armor, fell in behind him. Like Ben, he had grown used to it.

"A convoy of cars and trucks coming up north on La Brea, General," his radio operator told him. "Headlights on like they know they're not going to be stopped."

"They're in for a very large surprise," Cecil said. "Is that them up ahead?"

"Yes, sir."

"Pull over." Cecil got out and waved his troops into position in the rubble of the area. Cecil moved over into the shadows. "Give that lead vehicle some .50-caliber juice in the radiator," he ordered.

A hastily set up machine gun yammered for a couple of seconds. Both headlights were knocked out of the truck and steam hissed from a shattered radiator. Men piled out of the cab and out of the bed of the truck. Those in the vehicles behind the crippled truck bailed out and sought cover.

"Hey!" Leroy called out, crouching behind a pile of bricks. "Is y'all troops of the African-American's command?"

"African-American?" A young sergeant looked at Cecil. "Is he talking about you, sir?"

"Yes, Smith. So if we all followed that ancestral nonsense, you would be English-American. Swenson would be, probably, Swedish-American. Mac would be Irish-American, and so on and so forth until it became mind-boggling with its complications. Can you imagine writing a book with a dozen nationalities involved? The writer would spend half his or her time typing words that had nothing at all to do with the plot. Not to mention having to read the dreary mess."

"Hey, Bro!" Leroy called. "Brother General! Is you there?"

"Brother General," Cecil mused. "Now there is one for the record." He cleared his throat and yelled, "This is General Jefferys. And I am not your brother, thank God."

"Course you is, man. We brothers. We got a lot

in common," Leroy yelled.

Cecil, total disgust in his voice, lifted the bullhorn a Rebel handed him. "You and I, idiot, have absolutely nothing at all in common."

"Huh! Shore we do, man—we brothers. Let me pass on through, brother."

"Just the thought of that biological impossibility makes me nauseous, Leroy."

"You an uppity motherfucker, ain't you, General?"

Cecil smiled. "No, I don't think so. But I know what you are."

"Why don't you tell me then, Uncle Tom."

"I shall. Right before I kill you."

Leroy started hollering and cussing. Cecil turned to an aide. "Mortar crews in place and grenade launchers ready?"

"Yes, sir."

"Cream them."

The early evening was shattered by the howling of rockets and the exploding of mortar rounds. Machine guns yammered and snarled. The vehicles of the street punks exploded and the flames lit up the ruined buildings on either side of the battleground. Street punks tried to run, but Rebels with flares were ready for them. The flares were shot into the air, the brilliant harshness illuminating the punks. The Rebels cut them down.

Cecil called for a cease-fire. The sounds of moaning filled the smoky air.

"This is the way we're going to finish it," Cecil said. "Order all units forward. Search and destroy. All units into the city. Now!"

Cecil walked out onto the bloody battleground, searching for Leroy. He found him lying on his back, both hands holding his bullet-punctured belly.

Leroy cursed him. "You a traitor to your kind, Tom!" he spat at Cecil.

"One of us is, that's for sure, and I think we both know who that person is."

"You jive motherfucker!"

Cecil was not by nature a mean or cruel person. The son of a psychiatrist and a college professor, he'd spent his formative years listening to Brahms and Mozart at home, and soul music in the streets. He was highly educated, and had never run into much prejudice from educated people of any race. He was an ex-Green Beret officer who'd joined the army to see some action and, as he put it, "got shot in the ass in Laos."

He tried very hard to understand people like Leroy, but he was the first to admit that he could not. "I never cared much for jive, Leroy. I preferred Beethoven."

"That ain't what I mean, white-ass-licker!"

"I've never kissed the ass of any white, Leroy. But I have sure kicked some white ass in my time."

"Huh?"

"You wouldn't understand, Leroy. All you know is hate. And maybe you have a right to hate—or think you do, as Thermopolis says. But it's all moot, now, isn't it, Leroy. You're dying. What'd you do with your slaves?"

"Killed 'em."

Cecil shook his head. "Did you really think that because I am a black person, I would let you go free?"

"African-American!"

"No, Leroy, I was born in America. So that makes me an American first, and a black man second. I have no ties with Africa. I've never been

277

there. Wouldn't you much rather be talking about something else in the time you have left before you meet the Devil?"

Leroy spat at him and cursed him. "You said you knew what I was. What am I?"

Cecil smiled and told him.

Chapter Four

The Rebel planes began napalming the area around the dump on the outskirts of San Diego just as Cecil committed all his forces into the center of Los Angeles. The move caught the punks and the creepies by surprise and many died with shock written on their dirty faces.

The Rebels pushed forward a dozen blocks that night, before Cecil called a halt to the drive. He would resume it at first light.

At first light, Ben ordered his people across the Soledad Freeway and forward into San Diego. Black smoke was still spiraling into the sky from the burning dump as the Rebels charged across the Freeway.

Those now inhabiting the San Diego area were at first stunned by the ferocity of the attack, then began running in fear as the Rebels charged into the outskirts of the city, burning and destroying everything they came in contact with. Like those punks who had once controlled Los Angeles, these dregs of humanity had no central leader, and no plans for any type of counterattack. They found they had but two choices: stand and die or run.

For the first day, they ran.

The Rebels, with armor spearheading, smashed more than two miles into punk territory that first day, from two directions: the north and the east.

From the south, General Payon's army had pushed up nearly four miles and was holding.

In Los Angeles, the Rebels were on a roll that could not be contained by the punks and creepies remaining in the city. The Rebels were fighting night and day, crushing any who dared face them. All logical avenues of escape had been cut off by the Rebels. Snipers were posted all around the territory still in punk hands, and the sharpshooters were deadly.

In the City of the Angels, all that remained was mopping up.

"We estimate thirty-five thousand dead," Cecil reported to Ben. "Fifteen thousand broke free. Of those, probably five thousand are wounded, half of them wounded so badly they won't survive their wounds."

"Our casualties?" Ben asked.

"Extremely light considering the amount of territory we've taken. It's all but over here in Los Angeles, Ben. I'm sending Georgi and his people down to assist you."

"That's ten-four, Cec. We're facing no organized resistance here. With another battalion to help us, we can wrap this up in a few days."

"Maybe not, Ben," Cecil cautioned. "Doctor Chase just got word back from Base Camp One. Many of those people down there are infected with a virus that is airborne. It's deadly, Ben. And our lab people don't have a vaccine for it."

"All right, Cec. I'm halting all advances now and sealing off the city."

"I'll wrap it up here and be down to join you just as quickly as possible, Ben."

"That's ten-four, Cec. Eagle out."

Ben turned to Corrie. "Order all advances halted, Corrie. Advise General Payon to hold what he's got. Tell him I advise taking no prisoners. He won't like it anymore than we do, but he'll see the reasoning behind it. Order all Rebels to burn out a buffer zone and stay to the north and to the east of it. Shoot anyone who tries to cross it. Fires every one hundred yards at night. Lord knows we've got enough material on hand to keep them going."

Those in the city knew why the Rebel advance had been halted, or could guess why. Most knew they were walking disease factories. And most had sense enough to understand that if the Rebels would not get close to them, they must be contagious.

"So what have we got to lose?" many said. "Let's take some of those Rebel bastards and bitches with us. If they try to take us, we'll bite them and spit on them."

The Rebels stood behind their buffer zones and waited.

In Nevada, those punks who had broken free of Los Angeles were slowly reaching the rendezvous point.

"Leroy's dead," Ishmal said. "He told me no brother would kill him. He must have gone nuts. Word I got is that General Jefferys called him a disgrace to his race and a piece of worthless shit and then shot him right between the eyes."

"General Jefferys sounds like my kind of spade," Rich said with a smile.

Bull stepped between the two men before another killing could go down. "Just cool it, boys! We got enough problems without you two havin' at each other."

"Chang stepped on a pressure mine," Fang said, once Ishmal and Rich were separated. "I seen it. Blew both his legs off. It was horrible. Most of his gang was cut down by machine-gun fire."

"There ain't gonna be no stoppin' the Rebels. Us goin' to Alaska is only prolongin' the end."

"You got a better idea?" Bull challenged.

"No," Fang said with a sigh. "Not unless we go straight."

"That's what I'm gonna do," a woman said. "The percentages was with us in the city. Not no more. Ben Raines ain't gonna allow it. We're either gonna obey the law—right down to the last letter of it—or he's gonna shoot us. Or hang us." She shuddered at that thought. She had personally witnessed what happened to those street punks the Rebel courts had convicted on the testimony of the freed prisoners and slaves. The Rebels had left them hanging from tree limbs. It was the ugliest sight she had ever seen. "Back in the olden days we could run to a lawyer or the ACLU or something. Not no more. I think that even if the ACLU was still around, if they was to try to step in on our behalf, Ben Raines would shoot them as fast as he would us."

"What are you gonna do, Betty?" Sally asked.

"I'm gonna find me a man and then we'll find us a piece of ground. Raise chickens and hogs and stuff. Plant a garden. I don't know none of you people. I ain't never seen any of you before in my life. I never heard of none of you. I don't know where you're goin.' I don't care. Good-bye."

282

Bull looked around him at the hundreds of punks who had gathered. He reflected sourly that it looked like a bunch of bums at a hobo convention. And, he surmised, that was not an unfair comparison. Sorriest-looking bunch of no-goods he had ever seen. Beaten down, whipped, and ragged.

Every new bunch that came in from the city had a different horror story to tell, but with the same ending: Ben Raines was kicking ass.

Betty was right; going to Alaska wasn't really going to solve anything. Ben Raines would come after them, and he would eventually destroy them all.

"What are you thinkin' about, Bull?" Chico asked.

"Our future."

"We ain't got much of one," the gang leader said. "I lost more than half of my people. And of the ones that's left, more than half of them want to quit. Six walked off last night. I ain't seen them since and probably won't never see them again."

"We got to look at it this way. The ones that stays are the tough ones. And we got to get organized. If we're gonna survive, Chico, we've got to get organized. That's how Ben Raines does it. Organization."

Bobby of the Ponys said, "But that alone ain't gonna do it. We got to find artillery and tanks and shit like that. And then we've got to study on how to use them. Have classes and all that crap. Hell, we may as well go straight."

Brute said, "Please! Must you use that word? It's very depressing."

Ben had sent troops back to scour the old military bases for artillery rounds. Until they returned, there was little the Rebels surrounding San Diego could do . . . *surrounding* not being quite the right word.

"Hell, they could break through practically any damn place they wanted to," Ben said. "No telling how many thousands and thousands of people in there." He waved a hand toward the city. "And we've got five ballations of troops pretending they're containing them. Jesus!"

The situation wasn't quite as dismal as Ben painted it, but he was right. Those inside the three-sided box could bust out by sheer numbers in any one of dozens of places. The Rebels were stretched very thin. Only the burned-out three-block buffer zone all around the city gave them any kind of an edge.

"That, and the fact that those inside probably think we're much larger in numbers than we really are," Dan said. He studied Ben's face. "What's troubling you, General?"

"Waging war on the sick and dying. Oh, I know, Dan. They're thugs and murderers and punks and slavers and no-goods, but they're still sick and dying and many of them probably don't have the strength to lift a weapon or the strength to bust out if they had a chance. My God, Dan, we all smell the stench of the dead in that city every day. And every day it gets worse. Oh, hell, Dan! I don't know what's wrong with me. I've never had fifteen cents worth of compassion for the lawless in my life. And I don't think compassion is the right word for what I'm presently feeling. Maybe what I'm experiencing is . . . well, that it's morally wrong to wage war against those who don't have the strength to fight back."

284

"Well, well," Doctor Chase said from the open door of the command post—a former gas station on the edge of town. "Ben Raines is human after all."

"Come on in, you old goat," Ben said with a smile. "Where is the rest of the crew?"

"Right behind me a few miles. Cecil and his people are staying behind to mop up and to see what they can salvage." He jerked his thumb south, toward the city under siege. "You'd be doing them a favor by gassing them, Ben."

"If I had the gas, I'd do it, Lamar. Especially after reading the reports you sent down a few days ago."

"It's got to be contained here, Ben. Right here! And then we've got to chase after those who break free and destroy them. Before they spread the sickness. The ones in L.A. are not nearly so communicable or deadly. Wherever they are."

"In Nevada. About a hundred and fifty miles east of Reno. The Woods Children are tracking them, but staying well back."

"Ike on the horn, General," Corrie called. "He's bringing in several thousand artillery rounds."

"General Striganov brought in some two thousand rounds," Buddy said.

"I know, son. I know!"

"And I found more than a thousand rounds," Dan added.

Ben sighed.

Lamar Chase could move very swiftly for a man of his years. He strode across the room, grabbed Ben by the arm, and spun him around. "Goddamnit, Ben, listen to me! There is no vaccine. There is no magic bullet for this. We don't have a serum. This isn't AIDS. This isn't TB, or VD, or anything we can treat. We don't know what it is, we don't know what to use to treat it—nothing that we've got in our medical labs over at Base Camp One. It's a goddamn plague, Ben. It's everything . . . oh, hell, *evil!* And if you don't give the orders to destroy that city and everyone in it, we're all going to *die!* Do you understand me?"

Ben looked all around the large room. Thermopolis stood with Emil, staring at him. Ben shifted his gaze to the Russian. Georgi met his eyes without flinching. Dan and Buddy and Tina and West stared at him. The commander of Eight Battalion leaned against a wall, smoking his pipe and waiting.

Ben walked to the open door—it was always open, the door was gone—and stared out. It was a beautiful fall day in southern California. Temperatures very mild, a bright sun, the blue of the Pacific Ocean glimmering a few miles to the west. Perfect. If one could somehow forget the stench coming from the dying city.

He turned around and walked to his desk, taking out a map of Nevada and studying it.

"Did you hear me?" Lamar shouted at him.

"I heard you. Now hush up for a minute. How do you expect me to think with you screaming like a banshee?"

After a moment, he said, "Georgi, West, Ike, and Seven and Eight Battalions will prepare for a pull-out tomorrow morning. Cecil, Therm, and Dan, Tina, and Buddy will stay with me. Advise your XOs now. Corrie, find Ike and tell him to hold up. I have orders for him."

"Yes, sir."

"Gather around, ladies and gentlemen. I have circled where the punks from L.A. have gathered.

Georgi, you and your people will set up positions here, at the junctions of Highways 51 and 361, just to the west of the Desatoya Mountains in Nevada. Seven Battalion will set up in Tonopah, with Eight Battalion on Highway 6, blocking these two county roads. Ike will set up here, blocking highway 50 just west of Eureka. West, your people will block Highway 305 north of Austin. I want you all to roll day and night, and get in place. When you are in place, half of our planes will start napalming the area, while the other half napalms my objective." He met the eyes of everyone gathered around. "No prisoners. Get going. Good luck."

Thirty-six hours after Ben had split his forces, he walked out of his CP and he and his team drove down to where artillery was in place on the northern edge of the city. It was an hour before dawn and chilly.

"Commence firing," he said. "And may God have mercy on my soul."

Chapter Five

Several patrols had gone out from the punk gathering. They returned in a sweat. The gang leaders listening, sour expressions on their faces.

Brute was the first to break the stunned silence following the reports. "Cannon to the right of them, cannon to the left of them, cannon in front of them, volley'd and thunder'd."

Brute then stood with astonishment on his face as Cash said, "Someone had blundered: theirs not to make reply, theirs not to reason why, theirs but to do and die." He smiled at Brute. "Why not, Brute? I taught school for ten years before the Great War."

"What is this?" Bull thundered. "A goddamned fraternity meeting? You guys gonna kiss each other? Hell, people, we got to get gone from here!"

"There is no place to go, Bull," Brute told him. "All avenues of escape are blocked. It's been raining, as if you didn't know. These county roads are impassable. We'd have to stick to hard surfaces. And they're blocked. This means the city of Los Angeles has fallen, and probably San Diego as well—or it will soon be obliterated from the face of the earth."

"Will you goddamnit speak English!" Junkyard yelled at him. "What the hell does all that mean?"

Brute looked at him. "It means, you ignorant oaf, that we are dead!"

"They ain't attackin, queer-boy!" Junkyard shouted at him. "So how come you figure we dead?"

Brute had seen the dots in the sky long before anyone could hear the drone of engines. Ben had ordered up anything that could fly. Brute drew himself up to attention and snapped a salute to the south. "I salute you, Ben Raines, we who are about to die! You won, you . . . son of a bitch!"

"Planes!" a punk shouted.

The old fighters came in first, machine guns yammering as they strafed the valley. The bombers dropped their payloads of napalm, the fiery liquid spreading for hundreds of yards when the bombs blew. Ike had found several old Forest Service planes, tankers that were once used for water drops. He had ordered the tanks filled with kerosene. The misery spread as the kerosene ignited. The flames seared the valley and cooked the punks as plane after plane roared in and dropped their loads of napalm.

The old fighter planes were circling as the bombers did their work, then they returned, making pass after pass, machine guns howling and spitting. The vehicles of the punks exploded as the flames reached them. The ammunition belted around the waists and shoulders of the punks began popping as the fire touched them.

Cash of the Surfers stood on a boulder and

screamed curses at the fighters, firing a pistol at the planes. The .50-caliber guns of a fighter stitched him, knocking him off the huge rock and separating his head from his shoulders.

Ishmal of the Boogies ran screaming from the inferno, his eyes wide with fear. A napalm bomb exploded directly in from of him and the flames dissolved the gang leader.

Chico of the Swords had been thrown to the ground by an explosion, and had just staggered to his feet when a fighter plane came roaring in on a low pass. The .50-caliber machine guns tore him apart.

Junkyard made it out of the inferno and got to his car — an old Cadillac painted pink — and was trying to get the aged engine to turn over. Rich appeared at the window, a pistol in each hand.

"I never did like you, so I'd rather do this myself," Rich said. He shot Junkyard in the head just as a fighter roared in, machine guns howling. The slugs sent Rich on a wild dance into death.

Bobby lay on the ground, both legs gone, and watched as his blood poured out. He died calling for his mother.

The long narrow valley had been turned into a blazing, screaming crematorium. Charred bodies lay in every grotesque shape imaginable. Punks staggered through the carnage, blind from the intense heat, and called out for help. They begged for mercy just as their many victims over the years had begged for mercy. And just like their victims, the punks received only pain and the dark laughter of the grim reaper.

Bull and part of his gang made it clear, as did Sally, Fang, and Brute and a few of their followers.

"Dear God in Heaven!" Sally panted, as she lay on the ground a mile from the smoking valley. "I'll change my ways if You'll just give a chance. Please, God, I don't want to die!"

Bull laughed at her. "How many times have you heard that last bit from the people you ordered tortured to death, you stupid cunt?"

"Screw you!" Sally spat at him.

"Not now, bitch. We ain't got time. We got to hunt us a hole and stay put."

"We have no food, no water, and we can't build a fire to get warm," Brute said with finality. "We've had it."

"I can't believe we're the only ones who made it out," Fang said, looking at the small band of survivors. "There's less than a hundred of us."

"A bunch made it out," Bull said. "Several thousand, I'd guess. But we don't want to hook up with them. We're better off in small groups. We hole up during the day and move only at night. They's a river to the northwest of us. We can go a couple of days without water. If we can make the river, we're home free. Let's get in that little bit of timber over yonder and keep out of sight."

For the first time in years, Sally put her head to the ground and began weeping at the sheer hopelessness of it all.

Ben watched the destruction of the city through binoculars. He watched until the smoke became so thick he could no longer see what was taking place. But then he didn't have to see—he knew.

The few planes he had kept for himself were making pass after pass, first dropping napalm into

291

the heart of the city, and then working out in three directions. Those attempting to flee the flames were cut down by the troops positioned outside the buffer zone.

General Payon had moved his men forward, sealing off the south end and swinging some troops around to help the Rebels more effectively cover the southeast corner of the territory. General Payon and Ben Raines met for the first time.

The men shook hands and sat down for a cup of coffee.

"It's a terrible, terrible thing we are forced to do, General Raines," Payon said. "But when is war ever nice? But this business"—he nodded toward the burning city—"is especially repugnant."

"Yes. I investigated every other avenue. My medical people said it had to be this way. But that doesn't mean I have to like it."

"I put thugs up against the wall in my country," Payon said, his words soft. "They were killers, thieves, rapists, every kind of lowlife. They begged me not to shoot them, promised to God they would chance their ways. At first, when my army was small and the good people were still very disorganized, I listened to them beg and my heart was so heavy. I turned them loose, took them at their word. The next day they were back stealing and raping and killing." He shook his head. "I had to become hard—as you did. I had to think of the . . . larger picture, of the future. The leopard does not change its spots, as the saying goes."

"Were you always a soldier?" Ben asked.

Payon smiled. "Oh, no. I was a TV broadcaster. A reporter of news. I served my time in the armed forces years ago, as a paratrooper. I was with my family on a vacation when the Great War came. Thugs killed my small son, and then raped and killed my wife and daughter, while they were torturing me. They left me for dead. They made a very bad mistake in not killing me."

"Have you found them all?"

"All but two. I will find them. Eventually. Were you always a soldier, Ben Raines?"

"No. I was a writer. I . . . sort of got elected, unwillingly, to this job."

Payon chuckled softly. "Ah . . . as did I. The people came to me, said they needed a leader. I told them to go find one. Leave me alone. Go find a general or a colonel or something. A sergeant even. I went into the jungles for a year, to get away. The people found me. Hounded me. I started out with a hundred people. Then a thousand, then ten thousand. I was suddenly, and without my permission, named El Presidente. For life. I told them I did not want the job. The people said I had it anyway. You're smiling—our lives parallel?"

"Very much so. General, what do you hear from Europe?"

"Very little. Scattered radio broadcasts from ham operators. It is very bad over there. Very, very bad. All social order has broken down. I hear talk that you are going overseas. Is it true?"

"Yes."

"It will be dangerous."

"Very."

"I wish I could go with you. But my country is still very shaky."

"It's enough that you would even want to go, General. I know that you have committed a large portion of your army up here assisting me. It's very much appreciated."

"It's the least I could do. In my country, schools and proper medical facilities are a large concern. I have people working on proper irrigation for any land suitable for farming." He sighed. "There is so much to do. So much to do, and so little time. And I am but one man."

"The people respect you, General. That counts for a great deal. You and I, we'll get people back working, in time. Those who want to work."

"And those that don't?"

"Will inherit the earth."

"I beg your pardon?"

"Six feet of it."

"You can forget about busting out of here," Brute said, after a day-long patrol to the west of their hiding place. "Rebels are everywhere. Rolling patrols every time one looks up. Rebel lookouts are on the high ground with binoculars."

"Where's Bo?" Sally asked.

"Sniper got him. The Rebels are using those big-caliber rifles that can shoot a mile. One nailed Bo right in the center of his chest. We never did figure out where the sniper was hiding."

"I'm cold!" a punk bitched.

"I'm hungry!" another complained.

"I'm wet!" yet another whined.

"Oh, shut up!" Bull told them.

"What are we gonna do?" Sally asked.

"I don't know," Bull admitted. "We can't go much longer without water." He let his eyes drift back over the miles, to the valley where they had previously camped. Yesterday they had all seen the buzzards circling, and they knew the carrion birds were now feasting, many of them so bloated with human flesh they could not take off. They just waddled heavily along on the ground, flapping their wings and stuffing their beaks.

"Here come the planes again," a punk called. He started crying in fear.

"How in the hell do they know where we are?" another yelled, his voice breaking from his fear.

"Heat-seekers," Brute said. "We may as well say good-bye now. Because in five minutes a lot of us won't be alive."

Fang of the Hill Street Avengers began trembling as he watched the bombs start falling off the wings and out of the bellies of the planes.

After five days, Ben ordered the gunners to stand down. A strange silence settled over the land. South of his position, the city of San Diego was burning unchecked. From Imperial Beach north to the Soledad Freeway, from the blue waters of the Pacific east to the Sweetwater River, nothing could be seen but leaping flames and spiraling smoke.

The Rebels had pumped more than five thousand rounds—most of them incendiary rounds—into the city.

Even though the men and women of the Rebels bathed daily, sometimes two or three times, in cold water, they all still felt grimy from the smoke that poured out of the huge area of fire.

"Corrie, what is the latest report from the units in Nevada?"

"Ike says there couldn't be more than a couple of hundred left alive, and they've got to be a pretty miserable bunch. No food and not much water, and it's turning cold up there."

"Keep after them."

"Yes, sir."

Chase entered the CP and poured a glass of water. He drank it and grimaced. Ben knew what he was thinking. Even the water tasted like smoke.

"Do you want us to enter the city, Lamar?" Ben asked.

The doctor shook his head. "Not unless you think it's necessary. Any left alive in that inferno won't live long enough to do much damage. The trucks just rolled in from Base Camp One with the rat pellets. I've never seen so many rat pellets in my life. Must be a hundred million of the damned things."

"That's what you wanted, Lamar. I'll have the planes start dropping them tomorrow. But there is no way we're going to kill *all* the rats."

"We'll kill enough of them. I talked with research down at Base. They think they've got a handle on it. It was pure blind luck, an accident. That's very often the way it is. It looks good. If it proves out, we'll have enough vaccine for all of us in about a month. I bet the former bureaucrats in the FDA are twisting in their graves at this hurry-up job. See you, Ben."

Ben didn't like to use the rat-killing pellets because of the other wildlife they would directly and indirectly affect. But in this case he felt it was justified.

Cecil was mopping up in Los Angeles, and finding pockets of fairly stiff resistance. As soon as the pellets were dropped, Ben planned to pull out and take his time working up the coast to L.A. Once there, he would start mopping up from the south, with him and Cecil linking up in the center of the city.

"Tell the boys and girls to start packing up, Corrie," Ben said. "We'll be pulling out of this stinkhole by mid-morning tomorrow."

"Nobody will be unhappy about that," she said.

"Especially me," Ben said, smiling at her.

Therm and his forces went north on I-15, carefully checking out every town along the way, while Ben and his people took I-5 north to Los Angeles. They were all glad to leave the stink of the dead city behind them.

General Payon had visited Ben once more, and then pulled his troops back across the border. They did not lift a glass in a victory toast, for this battle had left an unpleasant taste in the mouths of all.

In Central Nevada, the Rebels continued their waiting game against those punks who had busted out of L.A. Everyone concerned — especially the punks — knew the standoff could not last much longer. In the high country, early fall had turned into early winter, and the nights were bitter with cold.

One gray morning, with a light dusting of snow on the ground, Brute crawled stiffly out of his ragged blankets and walked away from the camp without saying a word to anyone. No one was surprised when a single pistol shot cut the stillness of morning.

Bull walked over to a small gathering of brush

and scrub timber and looked at Brute. He had stuck the barrel of his pistol in his mouth and pulled the trigger. Bull left him where he lay and walked back to the cold camp.

He looked around him. Someone else was missing.

"Lennie," a punk told him. "Died in his sleep. Pneumonia, I guess. He's been awful sick. What about Brute?"

"Shot himself in the head." He picked up his AK-47 and jacked in a round.

"What are you gonna do, Bull?" Sally asked.

"End it. You all heard the shortwave last night. Nobody made it out of San Diego. Less than ten percent of the people who ran L.A. are still alive. That's a guess on somebody's part, but I'd say it's fairly accurate."

"What are you gettin' at?" Fang asked.

"We die quick, or we die slow from the cold." He was reflective for a moment. "Somebody once said that Ben Raines wasn't human. Maybe that's true. I laughed when I first heard it. But I ain't laughin' no more. A few years ago, Ben Raines said he'd clear the earth of punks and thugs and lawless types. I got a good laugh outta that too. At the time. At the time there was nearabouts sixty thousand of us in L.A. Ben Raines had about five thousand Rebels. Well, look who won. Ben Raines has got seven or eight thousand Rebels now, and we're reduced to about seventy-five. Can any of you really grasp the enormity, the awesomeness of that?"

Sally could. Before anyone could stop her, she stuck the barrel of her M-16 in her mouth and pulled the trigger, blowing the back of her head off.

Fang jumped up, staring at the bloody mess, horror in his eyes and on his face. "That's it!" he said in a hushed tone. "That's all for me. The Rebels may shoot me, they may put me up against a wall or they may hang me, but goddamnit, I'm gonna have me a good meal and be warm for a while before they do it." He let his pistol belt fall to the cold ground and let his rifle stay propped against a rock. He pulled a dirty white hankerchief from a pocket of his jeans and walked out of the camp, holding the signal of surrender high.

"You don't mean it," Bull yelled.

"The hell I don't," Fang yelled over his shoulder and kept on walking.

Bull leveled his pistol and shot the man in the back. Fang twisted and pitched face forward, falling to his knees. "You sorry bastard!" he gasped, then died, his blood staining the white dusted ground.

One of Bull's own men said, "I can't take no more of this." He pulled the trigger on a shotgun, blowing a hole in Bull's back. Bull cursed and screamed and tried to lift his pistol. "Sorry, Bull," the punk said. The shotgun roared again. Bull slumped forward and died on his knees. He stayed that way for a few seconds, then toppled over.

"Jesus Christ!" A woman had breathed the words.

"That's it," the street punk said, laying the shotgun on the ground. "It's over."

"They won't let us surrender," a thug said.

"I think they will," the punk who killed Bull said. "Leastways I'm gonna find out. Anybody goin' with me?"

They all stood up and dropped their weapons.

A punk lifted his walkie-talkie. "We're quittin'. Anybody who wants to join us, just drop your weapons and start walkin', hands in the air." He threw the walkie-talkie to the ground and lifted his hands.

The siege of southern California was nearly over. Or so Ben thought. He could not know that the gods of war were laughing hysterically.

Chapter Six

"About a thousand of the street punks surrendered, General," Corrie said, relaying the message to Ben. "They walked out with their hands in the air. A badly beaten bunch. According to the prisoners, there isn't a leader of a major Los Angeles street gang left alive."

"Tell the commanders to accept their surrender, Corrie. Transport them to that old Naval Air Station the pilots have been using. Have medical personnel check them over carefully and then hold them under guard until I get there. Get some transport planes ready for us. Tell Cecil where we're going." He looked at Therm and smiled. "You're in command here. Start the push north. Take your time, check it all carefully . . . Colonel."

"Thank you," Therm said dryly.

Emil bounced into the CP, his turban cocked sideways, down over one eye. "I'm ready, Colonel Therm," the little man said.

"Have fun," Ben said.

"To be sure," Therm replied.

* * *

Ben looked at the punks, sitting on a runway at the old Naval Air Station. There was no bluster left in any of them. He'd seen some beaten-down POWs in his time, but this bunch took the prize.

"I ought to shoot every damn one of you," he said through a bullhorn.

The arid odor of urine filled the air as many of the prisoners peed their underwear.

"But . . ." He paused. "For the first time in years, I'm going to go against my own rules. You people are going to make the town of Fallon a Rebel outpost. It's going to be a model for all others. It's going to have schools and churches and clinics and lights and running water and proper sewage. And above all, it's going to have law and order. And you people are going to do it all. All by yourselves. Prove me wrong, people. Make it work. Do that, and I'll admit I was wrong. You're going to elect a leader, and a town council, and you're going to make this outpost work. I don't think you can do it. But you'd better do it. Because if you don't, I'm going to come back here and hang every goddamn one of you!

"Dan, get some people ready to start fingerprinting and photoing these new model citizens." He turned back to the stunned but highly relieved crowd. "Notice I didn't say mug shots. See, I'm already giving you the benefit of the doubt. You're on a honor system, people. In a manner of speaking. There won't be anyone here to prevent you all from running away. But your prints will be on file and so will your pictures. And if you run away, we'll find you eventually, and we'll kill you.

"In all fairness to you, I don't know if this area can support this many people. If it can't, half of

302

you move down the road to the next town. Let me give you some advice. Have a meeting and see what group will be planting potatoes, who will raise beef and sheep, sweet corn and feed corn, and so forth. Whatever you need to get started, we'll supply you.

"I don't know if this is going to work or not. The Rebels have never done anything like this before. Usually, with people like you, we just shoot you and have done with it. Maybe I'm mellowing in my middle age. And it could be that I'm running a slight fever and not responsible for my actions. Whatever my reasons, I'm handing you a new life. You're free of all your past crimes. I'm going to stick around here for a few days. I want to talk to as many of you as possible. Take over, Dan." He handed the Englishman the bullhorn.

"It might work, General," Dan said softly.

"I hope so, Dan. I hope so."

During the next several days Ben met with former nurses, former store owners, ex-cops, people from nearly all walks of civilian life. And a lot of hard-core, lifelong punks.

He set the tone of the meetings first thing, and bluntly. "I don't want to hear about your childhood. I don't give a damn if your parents didn't have time to play games with you, or even if you had parents. I don't care if you didn't like school; that's your problem if you thought you were so smart you didn't need an education. Ninety percent of your problems is that you grew up in one of the most permissive periods that ever dawned on the face of the earth. And that's not all your fault."

At that, puzzled looks would pass over the faces

303

of those in whatever group Ben was speaking to. Then he called for questions.

And it surprised Ben that many of the questions they asked him were intelligent ones, dealing with values, morals, and the work ethic. He found many of them to be highly intelligent, and a few to be borderline-stupid. And he pulled no punches with them. He wanted them scared of him, and they were. He knew that all forms of government are, in part, based on fear. Governments cannot and will not work without that element.

He told them that if they stayed on in the town, the work would be hard and the life would sometimes be lonely. And that others would try to take what they had built from them. And that always got the same response.

"Ain't no way, General."

And the shocker from Ben was, "And of course you will be armed when we leave."

After the numbing silence had abated, Ben said, "You're part of this movement now. For every Rebel, there are five hundred others out there who want to destroy us. You are part of us now, and the word will spread. And spread quickly. If we were to leave you here unarmed, you'd be overwhelmed in a month. And bear this in mind, once you fire that first shot against outlaws, you're forever branded as a Rebel. If you need help, get on that radio and holler. There are Rebel patrols working all over America. We can have troops here by plane in a few hours. Good luck, people."

Ben landed back in southern California at the old Camp Pendleton Marine Corps base and rejoined

Thermopolis, who had worked his way up to just south of the base.

"It'll work out with a little bit of luck," Ben told him. "I actually have a good feeling about those people. Oh, some of them will cut and run. I'd guess ten to fifteen percent of them. But I think the majority of them will stay. Let's hope. Only time will tell."

If the usually optimistic Therm had any doubts about the new outpost, he did not voice them. "We're finding a few people as we go," he said. "But not many. This area was really stripped of human life by the outlaws and the creepies."

Ben nodded his agreement. "We'll probably never know how many people lost their lives to the scum and the creepies. But I'll wager it was in the hundreds of thousands. How about Camp Pendleton?"

"Looted and stripped and destroyed. If the punks felt they couldn't use a piece of armor, they dropped some type of explosives down the hatch."

"Like all vandalism, senseless. Are you meeting any resistance?"

"Very little. A few random shots fired occasionally. But other than that, our forward progress has been fast and boring."

"You get the feeling it's going too easy?"

"Very definitely. I'm getting an itchy feeling in the middle of my back."

"Others have said the same thing. What are the Scouts reporting?"

"Nothing. Absolutely nothing. And unless I'm getting paranoid, that tells me something is up."

"I agree. And with seventy-five percent of our people a couple of hundred miles away, we're vulnerable."

Dan walked up, an odd expression on his face. "I hate to be an alarmist, General. But I feel eyes on me."

"That's just what we were discussing, Dan. Go to middle alert and double the guards. I think we've got trouble coming at us."

"Punks?" Therm asked.

Ben shook his head. "Creepies. We've destroyed their last major bastion, and they've got nowhere to go and nothing to lose now. They just might be preparing for a suicide attack. I think they've dug deep holes—literally—and have been waiting us out. They know we don't have the people to search every house and building, every basement and every drainage system. I think we are going to be in for a rough time of it, very soon."

"If they stay true to form," Tina said, "they'll attack at night."

"But why wait?" Linda asked. She paused, looked at Ben, and then answered her own question. "They want you."

"That's right." He glanced at his watch. "I've got all the other battalions moving around Nevada, chasing down outlaws and searching for equipment. Cecil still has his hands full in Los Angeles. It's up to us, people. Let's batten down the hatches and get ready for a blow."

"We stay here?" Buddy asked. "On the old base?"

"It's as good a place as any to fight from." Ben smiled. "A lot of tradition here, a lot of fighting spirit still clinging to these grounds. We could sure do worse."

Ben found Lamar and briefed him. "I'll set up in the middle of the perimeter, Ben," Lamar said. "Those old concrete block buildings over there will be the best. We can tuck the generator trucks in close for protection. It would take too long to clean out the main hospital. See you around, Raines."

"Lamar." Ben's voice turned him around. "Get armed. This just might be a bad one."

Chase nodded his head, gave Ben a sloppy mock salute, and walked on, yelling for his people.

Ben chose to set up in an old office building. "Start sandbagging, gang," he ordered. "It'll be dark in about two hours. We don't have much time."

Ben found a good defensive position and began filling clips for his M-14. That done, he went outside and helped fill sandbags. He was the commanding general of all Rebel forces, but no Rebel sat on his or her ass and watched others work. Civilian or soldier, general or private, owner or employee, that didn't cut it in the Rebel system.

"General Jefferys on the horn," Corrie called from the office building.

"Go, Cec."

"You got troubles down there, Ben?"

"We all seem to think so, Cec. We all have itchy feelings. I think the creeps are going to try for a suicide charge. It's probably going to be a long night."

Linda watched the sure but unhurried movement of the Rebels as they prepared for battle. And as before, she was both impressed and a little puzzled by their movements.

"They act . . . well, I don't know whether complacent is the right word," she said to Ben.

"Smug?" Ben replied, cutting his eyes. "No, we're not smug, Linda. But we are very sure of ourselves. We've been doing this for a long time. Many of those people out there have been with me for years."

The tanks and light armor had disappeared into buildings, usually by driving right through the front or rear. They lowered the muzzles of their cannon and readied their machine guns.

Ben said, "Where is your shotgun?"

Linda smiled and lifted an Uzi machine pistol, .380 caliber.

"Lord have mercy on us all," Ben said with a smile. "Where'd you get that?"

"Buddy found it for me and helped teach me how to shoot it. I love it!"

"You can sure spray some lead around with it, that's for sure. You have lots of clips?"

"A dozen filled."

"Use it for close-in work."

"You think they'll get that close tonight, Ben?"

"I have a hunch they're going to be right on top of us before this night is over."

Ben told Corrie to pass the orders to eat now, go to the bathroom, and then get into position and stay there.

"About forty-five minutes until dark," Ben said. "They might hit us then, or they might make us sweat for half the night. No way of telling."

"It's the waiting that gets to me."

"It gets to us all. That's something you never get used to. At least I've never talked to anyone who has."

Conversation waned as dusk settled in. At full dark, all talk had ceased.

"Forward posts reporting the creepies are in sight and coming on strong," Corrie said. "No pun intended."

Ben chuckled at her reference to the creepies' hideous body odor. "Tell the forward people to fall back

308

now and join the main group."

"Yes, sir. Recon says the ground is covered with them. Like ants. Says they've never seen so many creepies."

"They got out of the city somehow," Ben said. "Probably used the sewer system."

"What now?" Linda asked nervously.

"As soon as they hit the outer perimeter bangers, flares will go up. We'll kill several hundred right off the bat. By that time, they'll be in this compound area and it'll get tough." He pointed to a windowless frame. "Take that spot and keep your cool. They're going to be crawling all over us in about two minutes. Literally so."

"The thought of that makes me nauseous."

"Puke now, then. 'Cause you won't have time in a couple of minutes."

The perimeter bangers went off with sharp, cracking pops. The flares went up, lighting the night sky.

"Jesus Christ!" Ben said, looking at the mass of inhumanity coming at them.

There appeared to be thousands of them.

Chapter Seven

The heavy machine guns of the Rebels opened up. The creepies crawled over the dead and dying carcasses of their fellow creeps and came on in a wild screaming suicide charge. No Rebel was outside on this night. Every man and woman was in a building, all working as teams, using both first and second stories when they were available.

There was really no need to aim during the first few minutes of the charge, for the Night People were massed everywhere one looked. Ben held back the trigger on his Thunder Lizard and let it bang, taking some small satisfaction in watching a line of creepies slam to the earth, the .308 slugs tearing the life from them.

A creepie leaped through the windowless frame to Ben's left. Linda fired over Ben's prone position, the little Uzi rattling and spitting. The creepie was stitched from shoulder to face and fell back outside, dead.

Ben had taken his eyes off his perimeter for only two heartbeats, but during that time a creep had grabbed the barrel of Ben's M-14 and was trying to wrest it from Ben's hands. Ben pulled the trigger and the slam of .308 slugs literally tore the creep's hands loose and knocked the slime backward, his chest mangled and his clothing burning from the muzzle blasts.

A flamethrower-equipped tank unleased a long spray of burning liquid, the thickened gas catching a group of Believers and igniting them. They ran screaming in all directions, balls of stumbling, howling fire in the night. They ran for a few seconds, then pitched forward to the ground, dying as the intense heat bubbled their brains.

Jersey was calmly picking her targets, and her aim was deadly accurate. Everytime she squeezed off a round, a creepie hit the dirt, dead, dying, or badly wounded.

Cooper was behind an M-60 machine gun, Beth helping to feed the belt. Corrie had left her radio and was using her M-16, laying down a killing field of fire.

Several creepies managed to get on top of the building directly across from Ben's position. Ben lifted his walkie-talkie. "501," he radioed to a tank commander. "Blow the top off that building directly across from my position."

Cannon roared and the old wooden building began disintegrating from the top down. An incendiary round was fired, setting the wooden structure on fire, adding more light to the night. Creepies began jumping from the building. Rebel fire cut them down before they could run for cover.

Buddy heard a choking cry from behind him. Two creeps had leaped into the building and were on Corrie, riding her down to the floor. He ran to her, grabbing one creep by the head and savagely twisting it. He heard the man's neck break and hurled the cannibal across the floor. Corrie had managed to work her weapon around and triggered off half a clip into the second creep's belly. He screamed as the lead tore into his guts. Buddy grabbed him and flung him outside.

"You all right?" Buddy asked.

"I am now," she replied.

The two of them turned their attention to the battle raging inches away from them.

Ben left his Thunder Lizard and began throwing grenades. "Get some Big Thumpers going!" he yelled.

Within seconds, half a dozen 40mm grenade-launching machine guns began hammering, hurling their deadly little anti-personnel grenades into the night. With a kill-radius of ten yards, the Big Thumpers were awesome in any kind of fight.

Ben heard scraping sounds on the roof of the building his team was operating out of. He glanced at his son. Buddy nodded his head. Father and son lifted M-14 and Thompson and held back the triggers. Within seconds, fast-fading starlight was struggling past a thickening cloud cover and through the roof; the creepies' blood was staining the ground where they'd fallen in death.

"I think it's beginning to rain," Linda said.

Ben grinned at her. "We all need a good shower. Did you bring any soap?"

"Very funny, Ben. Hysterical."

Then there was no more time for talk as the creepies regrouped and launched another attack against the Rebels. They came screaming and cursing their rage, throwing themselves against and into the buildings in a wild suicide attack. The Judges had worked them up into a fury, all of them knowing they had no future with Ben Raines alive. All they had was now, and all they had on their minds was killing Ben Raines.

The inside of Ben's CP was beginning to stink, the floor littered with the bodies of dead creepies. The battle was so intense they could not take the time to throw the bodies out into the rain.

The air around the besieged area was choking thick with gunsmoke, the night filled with the rattle of gunfire, the booming of cannon, the thundering of Big Thumpers, and the screaming of the badly wounded.

A creepie hurled himself onto Ben's back. Ben twisted and threw the man to the floor. Buddy smashed his head in with the butt of his Thompson just as another Believer knocked Ben to the floor. Ben kicked the man in the groin with the toe of his boot and clawed out his .45. He shot the creep in the face and jumped to his feet.

The building was filled with Night People; they were pouring in through the shattered back door. The Rebels backed up, formed a defensive line, and leveled automatic weapons. The roaring of a dozen weapons on full rock and roll was deafening. But the attack inside the building was broken as the creeps died in stinking piles.

"They're breaking it off," a Rebel yelled.

"No pursuit," Ben shouted. "Let them go. Finish off the wounded and regroup. Plug up the holes."

The wounded cannibals were shot in the head and dumped outside. It was suggested that bags of sand be opened and the contents poured on the slick floor, to soak up the blood.

"No good," Ben finally said. "We've got too many wounded to risk standing around in the blood of

313

those creeps. All units reposition."

One squad at a time, the Rebels left their bullet-pocked and bloody positions and ran for new cover.

"Torch the buildings we leave," Ben ordered. "It'll give us a better field of fire."

While Rebel snipers stood watch, the others shifted locations, into buildings with whole roofs and walls that had not been torn apart by automatic-weapons fire.

"Cecil on the horn, General!" Corrie called, once they had shifted locations and had set up. "He's coming under heavy attack from creepies."

"Goddamnit!" Ben cursed, taking the headset. "Eagle here, Cec."

"They must have been hiding in the sewers and the subway system, Ben. Just waiting us out. They poured out about an hour ago. We've been too busy to bump you."

"They pulled the same thing on us down here, Cec. We're holed up at the old Camp Pendleton Marine Corps base. I think they threw everything they had at us in the first round. We held and inflicted heavy casualties on them. But we're pretty well pinned down. How's your situation?"

"Just about the same. They've got us pinned down at the airport. Hell, we thought L.A. was clear and had moved over here to clear a runway for traffic. We're in good shape, we just can't get out — yet."

"What can I say, Cec. I fucked up."

"We both fucked up. Take it easy, Ben."

"Take it easy, brother. See you." He turned to his team. "Cecil and his bunch are in the same shape we are. They're pinned down at the airport and holding."

"We need some air support in here," Jersey said.

"In this weather?" Ben responded. "All we could use if the weather cleared would be the fighters. No bombs for the bombers." He shook his head and had to chuckle. "I'll say it again. All in all, it's a hell of a way to run a war!"

The Rebels waited, guns at the ready, but no more attacks came at them. At midnight, Ben stepped outside and lifted his face to the skies. The rain was still coming down and from all indications, it was going to continue for some time. Days, maybe. He wasn't sure if this was the rainy season for southern California or not. If it wasn't, it was sure doing a hell of an imitation.

"It'll rain for days," Santo said.

Ben looked at the aging hippie, one of Therm's group. "You have an inside track on the weather, Santo?"

"Yep. My big toe. Right foot. I broke it when I was kid. If it tingles that means it's gonna rain a little bit. If it hurts, it's gonna be a system that stays around for days. Never fails."

"It might be a blessing or a curse if the rain continues."

"It'll wash those stinking bastards anyway."

Ben laughed. He sure couldn't argue the merits of that. "Did you people take any hits?"

"No, sir. One of the bikers caught one in the arm. He's out of it. One of Emil's people took one in the leg, and Dan's Scouts took some wounded, no dead, and not real serious. Those flak jackets and helmets are lifesavers, for a fact."

The helmets they wore were of the type that

315

would stop many of the calibers used. They would not stop a .50-caliber slug, nor many of the big-bore magnum rounds, rifle or pistol. And the Rebels who had experienced a slug impacting and stopping against their helmets all said it was not a pleasant sensation. They all reported having head-aches that lasted for several days. But they were alive.

"Get back inside, General," Dan said from the rainy darkness.

Ben didn't argue with him. He knew he had no business being so exposed. He stepped back inside the building and the Englishman followed him.

"We were lucky the first time, General. Very lucky. They could have easily overrun us if they'd kept up the assault. Only God, or the Devil, knows why they broke it off. But they'll not make that mistake again. I have taken the liberty of repositioning many of the machine guns and the armor. I think when they come at us again, it will be all-out and no back-down on their part."

"I think you're right, Dan. Cec is pinned down at the old L.A. airport. The creeps were probably sitting out the barrages in the sewers and subways."

"They weren't such great friends of the punks after all, were they?"

"No. They never let on to the street punks that they had contingency plans or what those plans entailed. The punks were the creepies' sacrificial lambs."

"Here they come again!" Corrie informed the group.

The Rebels got into position. But the creepies did not launch an all-out offensive this rainy night. They chose instead to lay back and harass the

Rebels with sniper fire and light mortars. But the Rebels had much heavier mortars, with a much larger killing-radius, and manned by much more experienced people. As a result, as soon as the creepie mortar crews were pinpointed, they were knocked out of action.

The rain lessened in intensity and steadied down to a constant soft fall.

"Order half the people to stand down and get some rest," Ben told Corrie. "Sleep for a couple of hours and then switch with the others. It won't be enough rest, but it will help."

Ben looked around at his team. "And that order applies here, as well. Every other person lay down and get some rest."

"Fine," Dan said. "I will take over here while *you* get some rest, General."

Ben didn't argue. To refuse would have been pointless; the Englishman would argue with a stump for hours.

Ben stretched out on the floor with the others, a bedroll for a pillow, and went to sleep, seemingly oblivious of the sniper fire going on around him.

Ben opened his eyes, checked his watch, and found he had been asleep for two and a half hours. He felt refreshed. He got to his boots and walked over to Dan.

"Now, you hit the floor and get some rest, Dan. Right now."

It was a quarter till three in the morning.

Linda came to him and lay down behind the sandbagged window. "Corrie got through to the other battalions. Ike is on the Oregon border. Seven and Eight are inspecting the state of Nevada, and Georgi is over in Utah. You don't appear to be terribly worried about this situation, Ben."

"I'm not. It's a damn nuisance, that's all. They missed any chance they might have had to overrun us. Now it's too late. We're too well dug in and have far superior firepower and armor. They could keep us pinned down here for several days, and probably will, but eventually we'll drive them back. If worse comes to worst, we'll use smoke to bust out. But I don't think it will come to that."

She looked at him. "What are you smiling about?"

"You noticed that Buddy is gone?"

"Yes. Where is he?"

"He and his Rat Team are out on the edges of our perimeters, laying out Claymores and other nasty little surprises for the creepies. The next time they hit us, they're going to be terribly upset by what they find waiting for them."

An hour slipped away. Linda dozed for a time, then awakened, and she and Ben quietly talked.

"I see now why the Rebels travel with so much ammunition. I couldn't understand it at first. It just seemed like so much to carry around."

"Here they come, General," Corrie said. "They're belly-crawling to us this time. Forward people say it looks like the entire ground, all the way around us, is covered with huge worms."

"That's a pretty good way of putting it. Ready flares."

"Flares ready."

"As soon as they hit the booby traps, light up the night."

"Yes, sir."

"Wake everybody up."

Buddy and a few of his Rat Team slipped into

318

the building. Buddy came to his father's side.

"The creepies are going to be very unhappy with us in a couple of minutes, Father."

"I hate that," Ben said with a straight face. "We try so hard be loved."

Buddy choked back a laugh and slipped to his position.

Thunderous roars slammed the rainy night as creepies touched off Claymores and pressure mines. Mangled bodies were flung in all directions and wild screaming echoed through the rain. Creepies leaped to their feet, jumped over the bloody chunks of body parts, and charged the Rebels, cursing the name of Ben Raines.

Hundreds of weapons, all set on full auto, turned the night into a muzzle-blasting and sparking shooting gallery. Flares cast their artificial brilliance on the land, turning the raindrops a metallic silver that was tinged with red from the splattering blood.

The Rebels stopped the advance cold. This time not one creepie made it into any building. The Rebels suffered one wounded, and no dead. The area around the perimeter was littered with dead and dying creepies.

The creepies fell back and began their harassing tactics against the Rebels. Their sniper fire inflicted no casualties.

"You reckon they'll try again?" Cooper asked.

"Oh, yes," Ben said. "The Judges will spend all day whipping the troops up into a murderous frenzy, and tonight they'll throw everything they've got at us. Stand down and get something to eat and some sleep. Tonight is going to be the big one."

The day crawled by slowly, the Rebels eating and resting as the hours passed. They cleaned weapons and filled clips and got ready. Tank crews swabbed out their cannon and mortar crews made ready their tubes. The Rebels behind the heavy machine guns checked their guns and belts.

The rain did not let up. It was not a heavy downpour, more a gentle, consistent falling. Everyone waited for the night.

"General," Corrie called softly. "I need to see you."

Ben walked over to her. "What is it, Corrie?"

"The communications van took a hit last night. It's out until we can get in there and really take the radios down and see what the matter is. Now this one is down." She patted the small tabletop model. "Panel is out and I don't have a spare. I think I can reach Cecil with my backpack, but I'm going to have to stretch an antenna. And even then, it's going to be chancy."

Ben motioned his son over to him and quickly explained the situation.

"How high an antenna, Corrie?" Buddy asked.

"I don't know. It's going to have to be really high, and even then I don't even know if it will work. We'll be able to receive from greater distances, but transmitting?" She shrugged her shoulders. "I don't know."

Ben nixed the idea. "Anybody who went up any distance would get picked off by creepie snipers. So that's out. I'm not going to risk sending anyone out to break through to the outside. Pull the communications van in tight and go to work on that radio. Tell them to rebuild it if they have to. I know damn well we carry the spare parts."

"We don't have them anymore," a communications

320

man said from the doorway. "The van took a lot of hits last night. The radio is out. And the spare parts and extra panels were shot all to hell."

Ben grunted. "Cut off. Well, people, let's kick the creepie asses tonight and get the hell gone from here in the morning."

Chapter Eight

The long afternoon dragged on, the silence and stillness broken only by occasional long bursts of cursing from those working on the radio in the communications van, which was pulled up close to Ben's location.

Ben inspected the huge ragged circle which his people held, darting from building to building, with Dan at his heels bitching about what a ridiculous and totally unsafe idea this was.

"Hanging in there, Therm?" Ben asked.

"Oh, yeah. I'm just glad it's raining. If it was hot and sunny, those bodies out there would be hard to take."

"There must be five or six hundred of them," Emil said. Ben noticed he had put aside his turban for a helmet. "We gonna wrap this up tonight, aren't we, General?"

"We're going to do our best, Emil."

"Right on!" the little man said.

Ben moved over to the bikers' position. "I have seen and done and been a lot of things in my life," Frank said. "But I have never seen anything so disgusting as these damn Believers."

Ben agreed with him, turned, and almost collided

322

with Doctor Chase. "What the hell are you doing out here, Lamar?"

"We've got to conclude this before the weather breaks, Ben. When the sun hits those bodies, the health hazard for us goes right off the scale."

"I hadn't thought of that, Lamar. You're right. Corrie, have all cannon and mortars capable of tossing tear gas to make ready. Everybody check their masks. We've got to blind them, and we've got to punch through and get the hell out of here, tonight. Start lobbing some shells in their direction now and while that's going on, have the drivers check their engines. Check all rolling equipment and get ready to bug out."

"Toward the Interstate?" Buddy asked.

"No," Ben said with a smile. "They'll be expecting us to do that. We're going to bust out the rear of this base, heading east on this old secondary road that leads to I-15. Start laying out explosives now. When the last vehicle is clear of this area, this place is going to go up like a roman candle."

"You're a wicked, wicked man, Ben," Chase said with a satisfied grin.

"Yeah." Ben returned the grin. "Ain't I, though."

Those creepies watching the embattled perimeters of the Rebels through long lenses saw nothing that would indicate a Rebel bust-out. And they were not surprised when Rebel artillery began crashing down on their heads. To their way of thinking, the Rebels were savages, and nothing they did came as any surprise.

"All rolling equipment checked out and ready to go," Corrie told Ben.

"Tell the gunners to cease fire in one minute."

A dozen more rounds were lobbed in and the guns fell silent.

"Gas canisters?" Ben asked.

"Enough to do the job," Dan told him. "But we've got to do it quickly. We're going to be cutting it fine."

"What Rebel unit was last reported to be the closest to Los Angeles?" Ben turned to Corrie, hoping against hope.

She shook her head. "None of them," she told him. "They're all at least four or five hundred miles away."

"All right. That's it. We have no way of knowing whether or not Cecil has put out the call for help, and we can't transmit. So we're going to have to operate under the assumption that we are all alone with no help coming. And so far as I know that is our situation. Make sure that every unit knows what to do and where to go before we start our bust-out. Any screwups mean capture and torture for stragglers. Let's get packed up. We bust out at full dark."

Buddy and the Rat Team and Dan and his Scouts were busy booby-trapping the area. When the creepies pursued the Rebels following the bust-out, they were going to hit some nasty reminders of how the Rebels viewed warfare.

Ben checked his watch. Three o'clock. The rain showed no signs of abating. That was good. The moisture and high humidity would keep the tear gas close to the ground and prevent rapid dissipation. Lord knows the Rebels needed every break they could get.

At four o'clock, Buddy slipped into the building.

"That's it," he told his father. "We've used as many Claymores as we dare. We've got to keep some in reserve. We set some with trip-wires and others to be electronically detonated by us. We've laid out the pressure mines around the eastern edge of our perimeters. Any vehicle that leaves this one road"—he pointed out the route on a map—"won't make it. Tear gas is ready to bang. Big Thumpers have been set up on selected trucks. Heavy machine-gun crews are moving their guns to trucks now. Everyone is packed up. We've done all we can do except pray."

"And that wouldn't be a bad idea," Ben said.

Ben checked his watch, then checked the sky. "Fifteen minutes to bug-out," he told Corrie. "Tell the people to start loading up. We're getting the hell out of here."

"How do we know this old road is still serviceable?" Linda asked.

Ben grinned at her. "We don't. We might be driving smack into a dead end."

"And if that's the case?"

"We dismount and fight."

She shook her head and walked away, muttering about her peaceful little valley.

Ben whistled softly at her and she laughed and kept on walking.

"Creepies on the move," Corrie called.

"Tell the forward teams to get back here and load up." Ben checked his watch. Thirteen minutes.

"Start engines?"

"No. I'll give the signal."

"Creepies have stopped forward advance."

"They're puzzled as to why we have not opened

325

fire. Hold all fire. How does it look to the east?"

"Grim."

"I love your succinct reports, Corrie."

"Thank you," she said dryly.

Twelve minutes to bug-out.

"Therm and his people?"

"Loaded up and ready to go, sir. Dan is bitching about you pulling out last."

"He'll get over it. Have the creepies resumed advance?"

"Negative. Bikers have loaded their motorcycles onto trucks and are on board."

"Lamar and his people?"

"Loading now, sir."

Eleven minutes.

"All units load up except for us, Corrie."

The minutes seemed to tick by at a crawl. "Let's go, people," Ben finally ordered. "Time to wave bye-bye to the creepies."

Full dark outside. Ben held the door for Jersey. "Ladies first," he said.

"Move, General," she told him.

Ben stepped out into the rain and staying low, ran to the wagon. He opened the door. "This time, Jersey," he said with a grin, "you have to go first."

Two minutes to bust-out.

"Masks on and start engines," Ben ordered.

Dozens of engines burst into life, filling the air with roaring.

"Here they come," Corrie told Ben, listening through her headset. "From all sides."

"Fire gas."

One minute.

"They're in the perimeter!" Corrie said.

Zero.

"Go!" Ben said, his voice muffled through the gas mask.

Dozens of tanks, trucks, vans, Jeeps, Hummers, and APCs rammed their way out of concealment as the gas canisters exploded, filling the rainy air with choking tear gas.

"Hit the smoke!" Ben gave the orders.

Smoke canisters were exploded and everybody who could began throwing smoke grenades. The smoke only added to the confusion caused by the swirling tear gas.

"Just follow the lights of the truck in front of you, Cooper," Jersey said. "Don't get too close, but don't get us lost either."

"I hate backseat drivers," Cooper said. Then he slammed on the brakes to keep from plowing into the rear of the Jeep.

"Wonderful," Jersey muttered. "The man is a real whiz behind the wheel."

The creepies were shooting wildly, but hitting nothing. Tears were streaming down their eyes and they were staggering around blind.

"The last vehicle is clear of the compound," Corrie said.

"One skooby-doo, two skooby-doo," Ben started counting, as Linda stared at the commanding general.

"Skooby-doo?" she said.

Ben reached ten and said, "Let 'em bang, Beth!"

She twisted the handle on a small box and the entire compound erupted into sea of flames and explosions as the Claymores were electronically detonated. Barrels of gasoline had been left behind, and the buildings had been soaked with gas just seconds before the bug-out.

The entire area the Rebels had occupied was turned into a blazing, raging inferno. What the Claymores didn't kill, the flames engulfed and destroyed.

Clear of the blinding, choking gas, Ben pulled off his mask and said, "You can relax now. We're clear."

"Relax?" Jersey said. "We're not a mile away and there must be two or three thousand of those creeps back there."

"Yeah," Ben agreed. "But they don't have vehicles close by. By the time they get to their cars and trucks—if they have any at all—we'll be on the Interstate heading north."

"We'll have to deal with them someday," Cooper said.

"As soon as we're hooked up with Cecil, I'll have Seven and Eight Battalions head south to deal with what's left of the creepies. It'll be good experience for them."

"The Interstate is clear," Corrie said, after acknowledging the report from Scouts. "And we apparently have no pursuit."

"How soon will you be able to talk to Cecil, Corrie?"

"I'll be in range in about an hour."

Ben leaned back in the seat and closed his eyes. "Wake me as soon as you're in contact."

He was asleep in two minutes.

The convoy rolled on through the night.

"Getting to you is going to be a bitch," Ben said to Cecil. "I think our best bet is to cut off at the Riverside Freeway and just bust through from the south."

"That's affirmative, Ben. The rest of the routes are pretty well torn up. Seven and Eight Battalions are on the way down. They'll head straight for your previous location and start cleaning up."

"Tell them to stay clear of our old compound area, Cecil. There will be a number of unexploded pressure mines still operative."

"That's ten-four, Ben."

"See you when we get there, Cec." Ben changed frequencies. "Buddy, spearhead us to the Los Angeles International Airport, please. We mustn't keep the creepies waiting."

The column turned west on Riverside and soon began picking its way through the rubble. This part of the Rebels' TO had been burned, but it had been hastily done. The real devastation would not begin until they were about ten miles into Orange County. There, the destruction would be almost total.

"This time," Ben said, "we're going to search the rubble and be damn sure."

"The tunnels and subways, if any?" Beth asked.

"We're going to blow them and seal them. I will not send troops down there when there is an easier way. Future generations are going to curse my name, but future generations, I hope, will not have to deal with situations like this one."

"I'll say a prayer to that," Jersey said.

The Rebels started hitting roadblocks—of their own past making—when they took a little dogleg that crossed over 57. From that point on they were lucky to make ten miles an hour.

"General," Corrie said. "Cecil says to stop breaking our necks getting to him, but to keep a sharp eye out for ambushes. The creepies are falling back from the airport and slipping back into the rubble."

"Ten-four that, Corrie. That means there are more creepies alive than we thought. Tell Cecil to bump all units and order them back into the city. Let's do it right this time." He lifted another mike. "Buddy, backtrack and find us a fairly decent spot to hole up. I got a hunch we're going to get hit and hit hard pretty soon."

"We're going to need to be resupplied very soon, General," Dan interjected.

"Backtrack to Corona," Ben ordered. "Tell the planes to get loaded and head for that airport. We'll have something cleared for them. Beth, how do we stand?"

"Plenty of small-arms ammo, General. Practically nil on anything else."

"Then let's get up there and secure that airport — what's left of it — and clear a runway."

"The creepies, sir," Dan said, "are not leaving Los Angeles International because they fear Cecil."

"No. This may have been their plan all along."

"What do you mean, Ben?" Linda asked.

"They made us believe they were defeated, they got us separated, and now they've got us in a box. They're coming after us. To kill me."

Chapter Nine

"Cecil got in touch with General Payon," Corrie told him. "The general is moving his people up to the creepie stronghold we just left. He says for us not to worry, his people will be more than happy to rid the land of those scum."

"It took a global war for our two countries to start working fully together," Ben said. "Pray that nothing happens to General Payon."

His team looked at one another, each with the same thought: And pray that nothing happens to Ben Raines.

"Corrie, do you have a location of Seven and Eight?"

"They're not even to the Nevada line yet. They're a good three hundred miles away."

"A day and a half if everything goes right. Two and a half days would probably be more accurate. As soon as a runway is clear, have Cecil advise the pilots that if they have to make a night landing, we will light the runway with vehicle headlights and they'll go off as soon as the planes touch down. That will give the creepies less of a target. And you can bet they're all around us. Dan, lay out a perimeter and get everybody moving some dirt and bricks and concrete blocks. We've got to hold out for at least two days."

"What about Cecil?" Therm asked.

"He can't move. The creepies are waiting for him to try something like that and he knows it. At least we took some of the pressure off him. Buddy, take your Rat Team, pick some other people, and start blowing buildings for a couple of blocks around this place. Blow us out a buffer zone. No point in trying to burn anything in this damn rain. Let's go, people. We've got a lot to do and damn little time to get it done."

And once again, the Rebels went to work, digging and building and moving material, constructing bunkers and earthen walls and fortifying the existing buildings on the small airport grounds.

"General?" Corrie called. "Cecil on the horn."

"Go, Cec."

"My God, Ben, we must have vastly underestimated the number of creepies. My spotters around here say it appears there are several thousand creepies moving toward your position. And that's just from this point."

"It's as we discussed, Cec. We were overconfident. Are the planes airborne?"

"That's ten-four. They've been up for an hour. It's approximately four hundred and fifty air miles to your location. The pilots don't like to push those old crates too hard. Every engine we're using is long overdue for an overhaul. Call it four hours to touchdown. That will put them down just about one hour before dark."

"Couldn't be better, Cec. Hang tough. We'll see you."

Buddy and his Rat Team were flushing out creepies as they blew the buildings around the old airport. They took one alive, dunked him in a huge old fountain—which was now filled with fresh rainwater—and took him to Ben.

"Well, he smells some better, at least," Ben said, after the creepie was handcuffed to a radiator pipe in the old office building. "Talk to me, mister."

"I will tell you nothing!"

"Oh . . . yeah, you'll tell us. One way or the other. It's your choice."

"I'll tell you nothing!"

"Drugs can produce some amazing results," Dan said. "Obviously Buddy captured some sort of officer in the Believer movement. He knew quite a lot, actually. Very informative fellow."

"Where is he?"

"Lamar drew some blood for study. Must have scared him quite badly. Poor fellow died. Lamar is having an autopsy done on the remains."

"I can see you're all broken up about it."

"Oh, quite. The creepies really suckered us this time, General. Us, and the street punks. Obviously the street punks never had a clue that the majority of the creepies were living below the city. They had quite an elaborate system worked out. But once we're free of this little upcoming altercation here at the airport, it will be a very simple matter to seal off any underground tube systems and the sewer systems."

"How many are we facing, Dan?"

"About fifteen thousand, Ben."

Ben whistled softly. "Damn. Were we ever suck-

333

ered! Now tell me the rest of it, Dan."

"They've got Cecil pinned down. There is no way he can move to help us. They've split their forces. They are anticipating help from the north and they'll be waiting. As far as we are concerned, they'll be throwing about five thousand people at us tonight."

"Corrie, how many planes are bringing us supplies?"

"Everything that can fly, General."

Ben turned to Therm. "You heard it. Let's get ready for it."

Therm nodded and left the office building.

"Is everything and everybody positioned, Dan?"

"Ready and waiting, sir."

"I want teams standing by to off-load supplies as quickly as possible so those planes can get the hell out of here. I want them back in the air to start ferrying West's people in to the airport at Santa Monica. Corrie, do we still have a strip open there?"

"As far as I know, sir."

"All right. That will take some more pressure off Cecil. We can't use the runways up here at Ontario because they were destroyed. Corrie, bump Cecil and tell him to radio Seven and Eight. Tell them to come down behind us, through Barstow and San Bernardino. We know that's reasonably clear. Fighters are escorting the transports so we can use them to strafe any mortar emplacements past the buffer zone. They've been advised of that, Corrie?"

"Yes, sir."

"All right, Dan. Let's you and me make an inspection tour and see just how good a shape we're in."

* * *

The planes began coming in right on schedule, about an hour before dark.

Almost immediately, sniper fire began coming from the ruins surrounding the airport. And just as quickly, Rebel gunners began shelling the ruins with mortar and cannon fire, while the fighter plane escorts straffed the ruins.

The pilots did not cut their engines. They taxied out of the way of incoming planes, the cargo was off-loaded, and within minutes they were taking off, heading back to base, while other planes were landing.

Mortar rounds and artillery shells were off-loaded and rushed to waiting crews. Medical supplies were taken to Doctor Chase. Rounds for Big Thumpers and Vulcans and Gatling guns were rushed to waiting crews. Claymores and pressure mines were off-loaded and Buddy and his Rat Team began laying them out on the perimeters. Flares were brought in, as were tear gas rounds and canisters, clean socks and underwear, and food.

Beth checked off the contents of each plane, and then relayed that information to Ben. "It won't be a picnic," Ben said to Linda. "But I believe we can withstand anything the creepies throw at us." He smiled grimly and added, "We'll probably know in about an hour."

She was pushing .380 rounds into clips and slipping the clips into an ammo pouch. "It's bad, isn't it, Ben?"

He nodded his head. The movement was barely noticeable in the waning light. "Yes, it is. Very bad. And they're going to start lobbing mortar rounds in

335

here before long. The reason they haven't done so before now is because they haven't had time to move the mortars into position. The streets are in such bad shape, getting cars and trucks through them takes hours. They're having to hand-carry the tubes and rounds in for long distances."

Dan walked in. "We've got your bunker dug, General. It's about a hundred yards behind and to the east of this building."

"Thank you, Dan. Let's go, people. We're moving."

The bunker was about twenty by twenty and seven feet deep. It was damp and it was cold, but it was a hell of a lot safer than what Ben and his team had just left. The roof was beamed with heavy timbers, corrugated metal placed on that, and earth on top of that. Boards had been placed on the floor as walkways to keep from churning up the mud.

"The last plane has left, General," Corrie told him. "Everyone got in and got out safely. Cecil is now coming under small-arms and mortar fire."

"We're next, then. Everybody in flak jackets and helmets. Check gas masks."

"Done," Corrie told him after a moment.

Linda looked up. "Sounds like a covey of quails overheard."

"Mortars," Ben told her, just as the first rounds began exploding, knocking chunks of earth and mud from the walls of the bunkers. "Tell the artillery to return the fire, Corrie. Let's get this dance going."

For a few moments, it was a battle of cannon and mortar, a deafening, nerve-wracking cacophony of ground-trembling thunder.

During a few seconds' lull, Ben said, "Corrie, advise the troops the creepies will be moving into place while this is going on. Ready flares."

"Flares ready, sir."

Creepie mortar fire stopped. "Flares up."

Flares were fired and the harsh brilliance caught the creepies as they were advancing across the buffer zone.

"Fire!"

The Rebels opened up with every weapon that could make the range. Creepies went down like pins in a bowling alley. The Believers called their people back. The first attack had been beaten back without a single Rebel dead or wounded.

Ben waited in silence for a couple of minutes. Then he smiled. "They're short of mortar rounds," he said. "I believe they gave us all they had during the last barrage."

"That won't disappoint me," Jersey said.

"Get Cecil, Corrie."

She handed him the mike. "Cec. Are you still coming under mortar attack?"

"That's ten-fifty, Ben. Small-arms fire only."

"That's ten-four, Cec. They've shot their wad, then. I'd guess they're out of rounds."

"They've still got us pinned down tight."

"Same here. But if small arms is all they have, we've got the fight won. It'll just take a little time. We'll wear them down with artillery and then bust out as soon as Seven and Eight show up. As soon as West shows up with enough people north of you, he'll push to your location."

"I damn sure won't complain about that."

"See you in a couple of days, Cec."

* * *

After twenty-four hours of exchanging fire, the Rebels could tell the creepies were losing steam. By noon of the second day, spotters reported the creepies falling back into the ruins.

"Keep up the artillery fire," Ben ordered. "Don't give them a chance to catch their breath."

"Seven and Eight are a few miles out, sir," Corrie said. "They want orders."

"Tell them to come on in and share supplies with us. Eight will occupy this airport and Seven will accompany us into the city."

The next day's dawning brought an end to the rain. "Saddle up," Ben ordered. "We're moving. Scouts out along the Interstate to the junction with 55."

Eight Battalion moved into the airport, and Ben took his people and Seven Battalion in pursuit of the creepies holed up inside the ruins of the city.

They advanced twelve miles the first day, moving over to within a few miles of what was left of Anaheim. Ike was barreling in with Georgi paralleling him. The rest of West's troops were coming in with the rolling equipment. Cecil had cleared LAX and planes were landing every hour, bringing in explosives from Base Camp One.

Dan's Scouts had found maps of the sewer system and the tunnels under the city. "Blow them," Ben ordered. "Blow every entrance and exit you can find. Seal it off—block it. The bastards like the tunnels and the darkness. Let's give it to them. Let it become their tombs."

The Rebels advanced, working block by block, blowing and burning everything that stood in their way. This time the devastation was total. They left nothing standing behind them. Early fall melted

338

into late fall, and more rains came. The Rebels worked on, destroying the city and flushing out creepies.

It was the most massive undertaking the Rebels had ever tackled. House-to-house and building-to-building searching and destroying and fighting.

Cecil was working from LAX east, West and Ike working from the north down, and Georgi and Ben from the west toward the ocean. Seven and Eight were working from the south northward. They left nothing behind them except devastation.

On a blustery cool day in mid-November, a man came staggering out of the smoking, battle-ravaged ashes of what remained of Los Angeles, carrying a white flag.

"You hold it right there, asshole!" a Rebel yelled.

The creepie stopped.

"What do you want?"

"To speak with General Raines."

"About what?"

"Surrender," the Believer said bitterly.

"When hell freezes over!" Ben said.

"Anybody else, I'd say give them a chance," Ike said. "But not these people. No way."

"I will not accept the surrender of those creatures," Dan said emphatically.

"*Nyet!*" Georgi Striganov said.

"No," Cecil said.

"No," West said.

Thermopolis shook his head. "No."

The commanders of Seven and Eight Battalions shook their heads.

Buddy and Tina appeared in the doorway of the

339

CP. Both of them wore odd expressions on their faces.

"What's the matter with you two?" Ben asked.

"It appears that we all misunderstood what the creepie meant by surrender," Buddy said.

"What are you talking about?" Ike asked.

"There are no more of them," Tina said. "At least not in this city. He's the last one left."

Chapter Ten

"What the hell am I going to do with you?" Ben asked the Believer.

"What difference does it make?" the ragged man asked. "The mighty General Ben Raines and his army of Rebels have won—at least here in the remnants of America. Europe, my good general, will be quite another matter, I assure you."

"I don't suppose you'd like to tell me what you know about it?"

"Ah . . . no."

"Why did you surrender?"

"To receive proper medical treatment. I am sick."

"Yes. We know. You're probably dying."

"I suspected as much. I contracted the disease while visiting friends down in San Diego."

"San Diego no longer exists."

"I know. You're a vicious man, General." He reached around and scratched his butt for the umpteenth time, and Ben's eyes followed the movement.

Lamar grunted his astonishment at that remark and Ben laughed at the man. "*You* call *me* vicious?"

"We were exercising our right to practice our religion. What gives you the right to wage war against us?"

"I don't think our Founding Fathers had cannibal-

341

ism in mind when they wrote the First Amendment."

"No matter. Are you going to kill me, General Raines?"

"I don't know what I'm going to do with you."

He reached around to scratch his butt. With a smile on his face he said, "Good-bye General Raines."

The booming of Ben's .45 was very loud in the closed room. The slug took the creep in the center of his forehead and when it exited, made a big mess on the wall behind where the creep had been sitting.

"What the hell, Ben!" Lamar shouted.

"Ten bucks says he had a grenade wedged in the crack of his ass," Ben said, easing the hammer back down on his .45.

Ike and Dan turned the creep over and jerked up his ragged robes. "How did you know?" Dan asked softly.

"He scratched his butt one time too many."

"I can't believe it's over here," Linda said. "It just doesn't seem possible."

"He may or may not have been the last creepie," Ben replied. "I think he was sent here on a suicide mission. But I also believe there are damn few of them left."

"General," Corrie said, walking up behind him. "Five and Six Battalions report everything is clean all the way up to the Canadian border. Their recon people have found where large numbers of men have bivouacked. They followed their trail straight to the border. They want to know if you want them

342

to cross over and engage."

"Tell them to stand down and go on back to Base Camp One. They've earned the break. They've been on the road for two months." He paused. "What month is it, anyway?"

"November," Jersey said. "It's almost Thanksgiving, I think."

"One week from today," Beth, the unofficial record-keeper said.

"Thank you, Beth," Ben said. "We'll pull out six days from today. We'll have Thanksgiving dinner on the road. For the next six days we'll break up into platoon-sized units and sweep the city. It looks dead, it feels dead, but let's make sure. I don't want any more surprises sprung on me."

The Rebels fanned out all over the smoking and rubbled ruins of the City of the Angels. If any building they came to was still intact, they either blew it or burned it. When the Rebels left the city this time, there would be precious little left. They found very small pockets of creepies, and the creepies had anything but surrender on their minds.

It wouldn't have done them any good if they had chosen to surrender.

Ben and his team, accompanied by a platoon of Rebels, roamed the city, inspecting what used to be called—by the tourist board—points of interest. The tall buildings of downtown Los Angeles still stood, but they were shattered and torn from artillery and mortar rounds, huge gaping holes knocked in them from 105 and 155 artillery rounds.

"Bring them down," Ben told his demolition people.

The destruction of the city was in its final stages. Ben personally inspected the city's museums and waves of disgust swept him at what he found. Price-less and precious works of art had been wantonly destroyed by the punks. Paintings had been slashed for no apparent reason — other than ignorance. They lay on the littered floors, amid the other rat-chewed objects.

"Can they be restored?" Jersey asked.

"We'll try," Ben told her.

The Los Angeles Zoo had lain in ruins for years. "They let the animals starve," Beth said, looking at the skeletal remains of the long dead captives.

"You maybe expected compassion from punks?" Coop asked her.

"What is all this?" Jersey asked, as they stood amid the ruins of the Chinese Theatre's Forecourt.

"Bob Hope's nose, Betty Grable's legs, and John Wayne's fist," Ben told her, looking down at the impressions in the cement. "It was a gentler time."

"Must have been nice," Beth lamented softly. "I can just remember when there wasn't war. I remember sitting in front of the TV set on Saturday mornings, watching the cartoons." She shook her head and said, "A long time ago and never to return."

The team drove on.

At the Hollywood Wax Museum, little was left of the hundreds of mannequins that had once stood still and silent, watching the viewers as they passed by.

Jersey picked up a head and looked at it. "A movie star," Ben said. "I can't even remember her name."

The team inspected the fossil pits and walked through what was left of Dodger Stadium. Little To-kyo lay in ruins, still smoking from the fires that had ravaged it.

At Union Station, they hit trouble.

"I smell them," Ben said softly. "Hit the deck."

The rattle of gunfire echoed around the huge terminal, the lead whistling and whining in ricochet. The battle was brief, bloody, and deadly.

Ben stood over a dying creepie, his belly bullet-shattered, glaring up at him through eyes that shone with hate. "You've killed me!" he gasped.

"That's the general idea," Ben told him.

Ben took his people and prowled carefully through what was left of the University of Southern California. Huge piles were all that was left after the punks and the creepies had burned all the books.

"Disgusting," Ben said. "Ignorant assholes."

"The buildings?" Buddy asked.

"Bring them down."

The top floors were gone from what was once the twenty-eight-story City Hall. The Rebels inspected what floors remained and were considered to be structurally safe. Here, a mass suicide had taken place, with more than a hundred bodies of creepies stinking in self-imposed death.

With a bandanna covering his mouth and nose, Ben said, "Bring it down."

Back on the street, Jersey said, "I don't like cities. They're too cold, too impersonal."

"This one won't be much longer," Coop declared.

On the fourth day, the commanders began calling in. "There are no signs of life in my sector," was each one's report.

"Corrie," Ben said. "Order all Rebels out of the city. When that is done, I want planes equipped with heat-seekers to make flybys. Do it systematically and do it right."

The Rebels pulled back to the edges of the city, north and east, and waited.

Ben studied the reports as they came in. The heat-seekers showed very small concentrations of warm, breathing bodies in a few locations. He handed the reports to West.

"Flush them out and destroy them."

On Thanksgiving Day, the mercenary reported back. "Done," he said.

"Corrie, order the pilots up again and sweep it."

When those reports came in, Ben read the graphs, folded them, and put them in a briefcase. "It's a dead city."

Chapter Eleven

To a person, the Rebels experienced a let-down feeling. A depression that was hard to explain and even harder to shake. Many stood on the high ground, miles from the ruined city, and stared at the smoke that still rose in narrow plumes. And many thought the same thought: When future generations read about this, how will they view us?

"Many will condemn us for it," Ben said. "But they will know only that we did it. They won't be able to understand why we did it, because they were not of this time. Some will view us as heroes, some will write that we were thugs and villains. Others will say that we were tyrants and twenty-first-century pirates. And a few will defend what we did. But I want you all to remember this: We did what we had to do, with what we had to do it with. And if future historians don't understand that, then they can all kiss my ass."

"Right on!" Emil shouted from out of the crowd which had gathered around. "Those who will write about us in the years to come aren't here to bury

347

the dead or smell the stink of battle. So what the hell do they know about it?"

Ben smiled at the small man. "That's right, Emil. You're absolutely right. Everybody ready to get the hell gone from this place?"

A chorus of cheers went up at that.

"Pack it up, then. Let's go see some country!"

It took the Rebels several days to get everything road-ready. It was the first week in December when they were all ready to go. Ben stood on a rise and looked toward the long columns of Rebel freedom fighters. All faiths, all nationalities, all coming together to fight for the most precious thing on earth. Freedom.

The column stretched out on the Interstate for miles. And Ben could easily see why the sight of the Rebels struck fear in some hearts and hope in others. The Rebels not only looked awesome, they *were* awesome.

He lifted his eyes toward the ruins of Los Angeles. A low haze of smoke hung over the rubble of the city. What had once been the two largest cities in America, New York City and Los Angeles, were now destroyed, and with their passing had come the end of the cannibalistic cult called the Believers. Ben knew there were a few Believers left, hiding in holes in the ground and in dank, evil-smelling basements. But the backs and the spirits of those remaining had been broken. They would never again rise to such prominence as they had once enjoyed.

"Scouts out?" Ben asked Corrie.

"Ranging five miles in front, sir."

348

The Rebels were planning on wintering in central California. Ben felt there was no point in heading to a warmer clime when they were probably going to spend at least a year in Alaska. Might as well get used to it, although winters in central California—out of the mountains—in no way matched the winters in the interior of Alaska.

"We'll find us a town somewhere between Sacramento and Redding to winter."

"Yes, sir."

"Or we may split up and occupy several towns."

"Yes, sir."

"Advise the Scouts of that, Corrie."

"Yes, sir." Advise the Scouts of what? That the general couldn't make up his mind? The general was stalling for some reason, and his personal team knew it. Why was what they did not know.

"Tell the main column to go on," Ben ordered. "We'll catch up along the way."

Corrie relayed the orders and Ben squatted down on the rise and watched the tanks and trucks and other rolling equipment pass by. He received a lot of salutes from the Rebels, and he returned them all.

Then Little Jersey knew why Ben was stalling. They were heading back north, each day bringing them closer and closer to where Jerre was buried.

"She ain't there, General," Jersey said, her voice low so only Ben could hear. "She's gone. She won't be back. Never. You've got to bury the dead and go on living. It's stupid to let a dead woman screw up your life."

Ben looked up at her.

Jersey continued, "We got a lot of things to do. We've got places to go and battles to fight. Years

349

and years of battles. There's gonna be a lot more dead before it's over. That's all I got to say."

Ben stood up, smiled, and then hugged her. "You're right, Jersey. Let's go kick some ass!"

WILLIAM W. JOHNSTONE
THE ASHES SERIES